WARRIOR AND PRIEST

KATIE HOWE

DREAMSPINNER PRESS

Published by

DREAMSPINNER PRESS

5032 Capital Circle SW, Suite 2, PMB# 279, Tallahassee, FL 32305-7886 USA
www.dreamspinnerpress.com

This is a work of fiction. Names, characters, places, and incidents either are the product of Katie Howe imagination or are used fictitiously, and any resemblance to actual persons, living or dead, business establishments, events, or locales is entirely coincidental.

ISBN: 978-1-63476-529-9
Digital ISBN: 978-1-63476-530-5
Library of Congress Control Number: 2015948189
First Edition October 2015

Printed in the United States of America
(∞)
This paper meets the requirements of
ANSI/NISO Z39.48-1992 (Permanence of Paper).

For my mother, who taught me the importance and value of equality.
Miss you, Mum. xxx

Acknowledgments

A huge thank-you to Georgina Ford, who cheered me on throughout the writing process. Your support and your love mean so much. It's a privilege to know you, Georgie. xxx

PART ONE

IGNORING THE sniggering behind him, Nico Stamford hurried toward the dormitories so he could change for the afternoon walk. He had always hated Eros class, but today he'd made even more of a fool of himself than usual. Why had he choked on the banana? It could only happen to him. He'd been tempted to use magick, but had managed to overcome the urge. Magick was too dangerous to play about with. It was only to be used as a last resort. Nico took a deep breath and squared his shoulders. He made a determined effort to slow his pace. He wouldn't give in to the petty bullying of Perfect Pants Percy. Not now and not ever. He had more important things to do. Percy might clearly be the number one athlete, diplomatist, and top in a whole host of other classes, but he was also vain, arrogant, and snobbish. Not to mention mean. And vain, definitely vain. Percy was the pinnacle of his own little social clique, but Nico had noticed there were other candidates who weren't impressed by him. A couple of them had sent sympathetic looks Nico's way during class. Needless to say, Percy had never noticed that he was disliked. His vanity wouldn't allow for it. Nico shook his head as he entered the main dorm. Why was he wasting thoughts on Perfect Pants when he could be planning his future?

Nico went straight to his room. At this stage of the competition, the candidates all had their own rooms and he was glad of it. Sometimes he craved solitude and needed to withdraw. Alone he could sort out all the thoughts rushing through his head. He could calm his spirit. He achieved balance, and balance was important.

It was unfortunate, then, that at that precise thought, Nico tripped over a discarded shoe and fell, arms flailing, forward onto his knees. He groaned. Why was there a shoe in the middle of the room? Surely he'd put them both away. Had someone put the shoe there on purpose? Why would they do that? Nico rubbed his knees and determined he was being paranoid. He'd probably forgotten to put the shoe away.

He pondered playing truant from the afternoon walk but decided against it. He'd be too easily missed. There were only ten boys going on the walk, with just two of the ten from the graduating class. Missing the walk would almost certainly raise questions about his health. Nico couldn't stand the fussing, coaxing, and general palpitations that would take place. Until he gave in to whatever the Grand Seers wanted, that is. It might be a smothering of love, but it was still a suffocating experience.

Strange to think that in just a few days the Grand Seers wouldn't be governing his life. He'd miss them. How could he not? They'd been a major influence in his life for eight years, ever since he was twelve. Even earlier than that. He'd been training for priesthood since his abilities were discovered when he was small. He just hadn't known that at the time. Not that you could truly be "trained" into priesthood. There had to be instinct. After that it was just natural learning. As much as he loved his tutors, he wouldn't miss them as much as he would welcome his freedom. Well, potential freedom, he admitted to himself; prison could well be going on for another year and a day. But he could cope with that. If it happened, which he seriously doubted. Either way, life was about to change.

He changed into his walking outfit, frowning as he pulled the sailor top over his head. The number of uniforms was ridiculous, and of all of them, this was the one he disliked most. He acknowledged that it was the oldest of the uniform designs, going back to Old Earth times. He even admitted to himself that tradition was important, but really… a sailor suit? At his age? It was just another reason that he would be glad to escape Academia Hall. He was tired of uniforms and rules and classes. He was ready to move on. Straightening his linen trousers, Nico reached for the hat that accompanied the outfit and made his way out of the dormitory. It was going to take at least five minutes to reach the laundry gate, and he'd have to hurry or be late.

SPRING HAD brought the gift of a sunny day, so Nico was pleased to be on the afternoon walk. It gave him time to think. The problem, of course, was the cooking. Nico liked to cook. More than that, he positively needed to cook. Unfortunately it was getting harder and harder to find time in the kitchen. The Grand Seers seemed to thwart him at every turn despite his attempts to explain how important food was. They would pat him on the shoulder and say, "Plenty of time for that, dear son," and basically ignore him. He didn't understand it. Life had been much easier when he was younger. Everyone had encouraged his interests, even the Grand Seers. They'd found it charming that he liked making cupcakes. They were impressed when he went on to learn more. The chef had been his biggest fan and had no problem passing on his secret recipes and cooking methods. In fact, it had all been going extremely well and his plans were progressing nicely until a couple of months ago. Suddenly, there had been extra classes, or rather, extra basic classes. Nico had always been given different classes, usually because he was so abominable at the usual classes. It hadn't bothered him. He'd quite welcomed it, especially the priest and ritual classes. The healing classes had been an opportunity to put all his knowledge of herbs and plants into use. His affinity with plants and, more importantly, his ability to listen to them, had given him a huge advantage in that class. It hadn't taken long to qualify as a healer. None of those classes had been usual for the Gleaning candidates. Other boys had graduated as priests and healers but it was rare. Art and Home Decor had been interesting, and he had developed a good sense of design. Other classes had given him excellent administrative skills, including time management. He was now very good at managing his time. Now it seemed as though every second of the day was accounted for. He was required at all his classes, including the ones he regularly failed. Then there were the endless costume fittings. A total waste of time if ever he had seen one. Photographs, too, more photographs than had ever been needed before. It used to be a once-a-year thing; now it was almost every day. And that was just the "official" photos. He wasn't even counting the number of photographs taken outside Academia Hall. Nico shook his head. He didn't want to think about that. It was more important that he concentrate on the need to get into the kitchen. All of his plans….

No. Now wasn't the time to go over his plans again. Long-term plans could wait. Now was the time for dealing with the kitchen situation. He was determined to find time in the kitchen. He was just on the verge of creating a new dessert, had only one or two more flavors to blend into it and, he pondered, maybe some extra crunch. He knew he was a couple of bakes from perfection. If only the Grand Seers would let him into the kitchen. He'd tried everything, reasoning and demanding and cajoling and all the other "ings." It wasn't working. He wanted to kick something in his frustration, but it was hardly the place or the time. That sort of behavior was heavily frowned upon anyway. Out in public, they were supposed to be demure or something. He couldn't remember the proper wording, as it was something of a list. Perhaps he shouldn't be surprised that he wasn't allowed to cook. They were a week away from the Gleaning, and he was in the graduating class, even if he really didn't belong there. The week would be one full of demonstrations and events. Whether he liked it or not, he had to take part and he had to get through the ceremony. He just prayed he wasn't picked.

He took a deep breath and had a look around. It was busy on the street and there was no end of people taking photos and films as he walked in crocodile with the other prospects. Out in public, there was no chance of any privacy, and all he could do was ignore the stares and pointed fingers. He'd always loved the area around Academia Hall. It was stately, majestic. He'd enjoyed studying architecture, and best of all, it had gotten him out of learning the tea ceremony. Dropping the delicate teapot on top of the equally delicate cups and demolishing the lot had been the last straw for Grand Seer Mabel, and he'd been hurried off to the library to take up his new class.

The streets were wide, and it seemed no piece of litter would dare to linger. No traffic was allowed on the inner roads, so there was plenty of room to walk. The area was largely populated with houses instead of businesses. Commerce still thrived, and there were all sorts of stalls selling vegetables and fruits as well as handmade crafts. He caught the scent of lemons from a nearby stand and a hundred recipes came to mind. He didn't make the mistake of listening to them. He'd heard lemons before and couldn't imagine a more discordant set of fruit. Nico smiled. It was a beautiful day to be out. The crocodile made its way back to the hall, and Nico looked over to his favorite house on the street. Like the other houses, it was based on a period of architecture from Old Earth. Europe in the Renaissance period. That period especially pleased him. The houses opened straight onto the street with no gardens to separate them either at the front or the side. Both sides of the street were long rows of uniformly beautiful homes. The homes promised huge interiors, and Nico knew that most of them had internal courtyards. His favorite house was built out of old red stone and the exposed quartz glinted in the afternoon sun. Nico approved of the simplicity of the Tuscan columns gracing either side of the front door. His eye followed the line of the building, and he was surprised to see a tall, muscular man standing there. He'd never seen anyone there before. He'd thought the house empty. Now that he did see him, Nico happily acknowledged that this was a prime example of masculinity. From the loftiness of his stature to the abundance of muscles, he was a giant chimney stack of a man. Nico could make out the black gloss of his hair, the trace of stubble on his jaw, the breadth of his shoulders. He fitted the house perfectly; he, too, was stately and majestic. Nico took a breath. Now that man would be worth trying marriage for. A wedding night with him? Not that Nico had any thought of marriage, he reminded himself, despite being forced into the Gleaning. He had different plans. Still, if he was forced into marriage, it wouldn't be so bad with a man like that. At least the sex would be good. Or would it? He shook his head again. That was the problem with his brain. It went round and round for ages unless he made a concentrated effort to stop. Nico couldn't take his eyes away from the man, though. He was just so beautiful.

Suddenly, the man turned his gaze to Nico and their eyes met. Nico stopped, stunned by the slow smile the man gave him. It felt like his muscles couldn't move. His breath caught in his throat. He wanted to smile back, but he'd lost the ability. Unfortunately, the boy behind him didn't stop and promptly ran into Nico. Nico floundered and reached forward, trying to grab hold of the boy in front of him, only to take him down too. Nico's cheeks burned. As he scrambled to his feet, he took a furtive look around. Had anyone seen it? Of course they had. There were lots of pointed fingers, even more giggling, and some outright laughter from the crowd. He couldn't say whether he was embarrassed or angry, but some sort of emotion was definitely on the surge. His frown deepened as he waited for his colleagues to gather themselves and once again stand in formation. The crowd was seriously getting on his nerves. So what if they'd witnessed a few boys fall over? It wasn't that funny, and someone could have been hurt. The giggles and laughter were just rude. Who decided that they should walk in formation anyway? What sort of stupid rule was that? Forcing them to walk in a crocodile was asking for trouble. Anyone of them could have tripped. Well, perhaps not everyone. Not someone like Percy, the golden boy, the one who should be studied and emulated. Percy was graceful and beautiful. So light on his feet that he moved like a ballet dancer even when he walked. Never in a million years would he do something as clumsy as trip up, let alone take other boys with him. No, Nico admitted that out of the ten boys walking in formation, he was the only one who would screw up walking. His shoulders slumped. Holy Mother of Everything, he couldn't even walk from A to B without getting it wrong. For the umpteenth time, he wondered why he was still in competition for the Gleaning.

He scanned the buildings again, and once again his eyes came to the handsome man on the balcony. The man was smiling, as though amused, and Nico quickly averted his eyes. Why wouldn't his cheeks stop blushing? Bad enough to fall over, but to do so in front of this man? A man so tall he towered over the balustrade, with shoulders so wide.... Nico checked himself. Like he'd ever see the man again. He made a show of checking the angle of his hat and the well-being of his walking companion. Luckily, the class master indicated that they should start walking again, and Nico fell into step with the other boys. Concentrating on putting one foot in front of the other, Nico forced the handsome stranger out of his thoughts.

"ALL HAIL the conquering hero!"

Alexander DeVrie rose up from where he was leaning over the balustrade and turned toward the voice claiming his attention.

"Your Highness." He bowed low.

"Your Grace," mocked his companion, bowing equally low. They laughed as they straightened to clench each other like the old friends they were. Prince Jael, third son of the king, stood back, taking a moment to observe.

"It's been years, Alex, but I see the years have treated you well."

"Hardly years, Jael. It's been eighteen months at the most. But thank you. I have no complaints."

"No indeed. A dukedom and estates worth billions, you are the man of the century, a true hero. Not to mention one of only two men in our history ever to be promoted to field marshal on the battlefield. It's no surprise that Father made you a duke."

"I was lucky a dukedom became vacant," replied Alex dryly.

"Not at all. You've earned this, Alex, I've seen no man work harder than you. Nor any man be so accomplished in his actions. If anyone deserves a dukedom, it's you. The way you handled the Battle of the Long Flats alone would have won you the dukedom, but when we add the rest of the war...."

"The Goddess is Good."

Jael laughed. "Humility doesn't suit you, Alex. We all know that you're the master of strategy. I wouldn't be surprised if you hadn't planned the whole thing when you were a child. You've always achieved what you set out to do. As I've found out to my cost on more than one occasion."

"The good old days, eh?" Alex grinned back at his friend, then sighed. "We had no knowledge of what we'd be facing in those days. No idea of the sacrifices that would have to be made."

"We will always remember the Fallen," agreed Jael solemnly. "It's because of their sacrifice that we can now enjoy peace. Ten years fighting across three different planets. There were times we didn't think we'd make it." He paused. "It was your brilliance that won the war, Alex. Your knowledge and understanding of military terrain. This was a war won on the ground."

"I hardly succeeded on my own. How far would an army get without the Flying Space Corps to transport us there? And without pilots like yourself to support us once we got there? You took on your own share of dangerous missions, Jael. You also know that I had help on the ground."

"Ah, but that's classified, isn't it, my friend?" Jael grinned. "Have you fought your last skirmish? Or are there more in the not-too-distant future? By all accounts, you'll have your work cut out for you when you get to the Sixth Land. The stories coming from there are not encouraging."

"I've faced bigger battles."

"How true, and my father can think of no better man to send." Jael started suddenly. "Tell me, is it true that you agreed to take part in the Gleaning?"

Alex shrugged, thinking of the cute blond he'd seen fall over in the street. "It's time I found a spouse," he said offhandedly. "Now I'm retired from battle, I've a yen to start a nursery."

"No doubt, and no man deserves it better, but the Gleaning?"

A grunt came from the shadows of the room. Alex ignored it and gave a shrug.

"Why not? It's as good a way as anything else. My parents were matched through the ceremonies. They had a long and happy marriage. I can think of no better example."

Another grunt from the shadows. Jael grinned.

"The ceremonies certainly grant many blessings," Jael conceded with a smirk, "but are you really sure that you want a pretty boy as a mate?"

"Yes!" emphasized the voice from the shadows. An older man came forward into the light, his finger pointing straight at Alex. "A pretty boy!" he spat. Alex frowned at Sergeant Major Watkins. Watkins frowned right back.

"Well, I don't want a soldier, if that's what the pair of you are implying. I've had years of dealing with soldiers, enough to know that there's only room for one in any relationship."

"Maybe so, maybe not," Jael mused, tipping his head to one side. "Soldiers understand rank when all is said and done, as well as the chain of command. Yours will be a military household. Another soldier may fit into that more easily."

"My spouse will fit into it easily enough. And I find that I crave softness, not regimen."

Watkins gave a final grunt and threw his hands in the air. He turned and bowed to the prince, ignoring Alex. "You'll have to excuse me, Your Highness, *I find* I cannot suffer a fool gladly." With an angry glare in Alex's direction, the man left the room.

Jael failed to hide his grin. He turned to Alex. "Well if it's softness you crave, you'll certainly acquire it in the Geisha class. A softer group of boys would be hard to find."

"They have their merits," Alex replied mildly. "They're highly trained in household skills, biddable, and eager to please. Diplomacy is taught from an early age, and if I'm to take over the dukedom, then I'll need a diplomat. I'll need someone who can run a house, and I need someone who will follow every order I give them. Plus I have first choice at the Gleaning, which is both an honor and a privilege. I don't look upon those things lightly. I think I shall do very well at the Gleaning, and if I don't? What's a year and a day? I'll pay the boy off and look elsewhere for my mate. But I'm hopeful. The Gleaning is a powerful religious rite, and, as you say, it brings many blessings. As a soldier, I've learned to trust the Goddess. If she protects me on the battlefield, perhaps she will protect me at the Marriage Mart. Enough of such talk, though. I would hear your news. How goes the world of the pilot?"

"That I cannot tell you. I resigned my commission yesterday."

"Resigned?" Alex repeated. "Why would you resign? You love flying."

Jael nodded in agreement. "I love my family more, and now that Father is ill, I'm required at home."

"I believe Prince Alphonse is taking over more of your father's duties?"

"And therein lies the problem," said Jael. "I love my brother dearly, but…."

Alex nodded. He knew what Jael meant. Prince Alphonse, whilst intending to do good, more often than not made a situation worse. He made poor decisions, kept the wrong company, and rarely listened to advice from his brothers. There had been several unfortunate stories in the press with more than one journalist asking, "Is this man fit to be king?"

He beckoned to Jael. "Come. Let's sit down and order some wine. We can talk this out." Jael relaxed and moved toward the velvet sofa. He grinned at Alex. "Is your cellar as good as they say?"

Alex grinned back. "Better."

Eased by the wine, the conversation soon returned to Alphonse.

"I love my brother," Jael said quietly. "I just don't believe that he should be king, and you don't need to tell me that that is a treasonous statement." He paused. "You're the only person I can discuss this with. I can't even talk to Elias. He refuses to discuss it, and when I push he says 'The King is True to the People' as if that's the be-all and end-all of everything. Of course the king should be true to the people. That's the only way a society like ours can work. Limited monarchy where the king is the servant of the people. Everyone Equal before the Goddess, and the Blessing of Being Made Paramount. The king must protect those beliefs. They are the foundation stones of everything that we are. Alphy is taking no notice of them. He's being less and less true to the people. He's so surrounded by fawning cronies that he's forgotten that his title is a duty as well as a privilege. He isn't doing his duty and he's taking advantage of the privilege. He'll be a disaster as king, may the Goddess forgive my soul." He sat back in disgust.

Alex leaned forward. "Elias refuses to discuss it? He must see what's happening."

"Of course he sees what's happening. Everyone can see what's happening. It's in the bloody papers, for Goddess's sake. Every time you turn on a screen, it's there. You can't avoid the stuff. Elias does everything he can to rescue Alphy. He gives as much support as he possibly can. He can see every single thing that Alphonse has done, but Elias believes in the monarchy. He firmly believes that when Alphy is king, he will be true. You know how religious Elias can be. But I don't see it, Alex. Alphy isn't made to be king. Elias is. Elias is the one with the brains. Out of the three of us, he's the only one who is suited to be king."

"Elias is a good man."

"Not just a good man, he's the best of men. He understands the people, and he understands their needs. He also knows that the king only has the power that the people give him. There's nobody better for the role of king." Jael's frustration was discernible as he poured himself another glass of wine.

"He has the humility," Alex agreed. "Of the three of you, Elias is the most like your father. I've always felt that he is a man with many hidden depths. He keeps something of himself withdrawn, I feel. As for Alphonse, I understand your concerns, Jael, I do. But the fact is, Alphonse is the next in line to the throne. He's been preparing for the role his entire life, and the Goddess is Good. Elias may well be right and Alphonse will be true to the people. He will always have Elias as his advisor and he listens to Elias. You know he does, Jael."

"Not enough," Jael said scornfully. He sighed, anxiety creeping into his eyes. "You know I don't want the throne."

"Of course I know that," laughed Alex. "I can just imagine what sort of king you'd be," he teased before returning to seriousness. "Jael, don't borrow trouble. As it stands, your father is king, and there's time yet for Alphonse to see the error of his ways. He has you to advise him now as well as Elias. Between the two of you, he'll be fine."

"Do you think so? I worry about the company Alphy keeps. They seem to be getting more and more influential. In fact, that's one of the reasons I'm here. I need to get out in society for a few days and see just how big an influence they are. Plus, it shuts up the staff. You wouldn't believe how much they go on about it. I swear, Alex, do you know how hard it is to argue with staff when they've known you since you were a tiny tot?"

"I have Watkins," retorted Alex. "So, you need to be seen in society?"

"I do, and if you're taking part in the Gleaning, then you'll be taking part in all the rubbish that accompanies it. I thought I'd tag along."

"Not scared that a boy may catch your attention?"

"No! I have no intention of taking part. I like my men more than pretty, thank you very much. No. Alphy will be representing my father at the ceremonies. He'll be at every occasion and so will all his cronies. You know how the Elite love that stuff. They lap it up. No offense."

"None taken, I'd welcome your company. I'm no fan of society myself, but sadly it can't be avoided if I'm to take part in the Gleaning."

"Are you sure you...."

"Enough!" Alex laughed. "I'm getting enough bother from Watkins. I've made the decision, Jael, I'm not going to change my mind. I think I'll be very happy with whoever the Goddess supplies." His thoughts turned to the cute blond. Why did he keep thinking about that boy? He returned to the topic at hand. "Who are the cronies?"

"The Elites, of course. I swear I've never met such a bunch of greedy, self-involved, indolent wastrels in my life. And I'd also swear that they're getting worse. Do you know they think they should have all the money? As if they didn't have enough, they now want to make the people poorer so they get richer. It goes completely against the Blessing of Being. Every child of the Goddess has the same basic rights, and the Elites should know that. And Alphy is listening to this nonsense. He believes the idea has economic merit. As if Alphy has ever studied economics. He doesn't know the first thing about them."

"I believe Lord Lunette is leading that particular theory." Alex thought for a moment. "Can't say I like the man, although I've only met him once or twice. Come to think of it, on both occasions he was in the company of Prince Alphonse. I didn't think anything of it at the time. Alphonse is usually surrounded by a gaggle of geese."

"Lunette is the loudest of the geese, believe me. He's the one I'm most interested in observing too. I don't trust the man. There's something off about him."

"I agree. In fact, I have my own interest in Lunette. He's one of my new tenants, and I suspect one of the main agitators in the Sixth Land. I have no doubt that our paths will cross in the near future."

"You intend to leave for the Sixth Land soon?"

"As soon as the Gleaning is over. I intend to fly down to Tane. We'll travel by road from there until we reach the capital of the Sixth Land. Or at least the castle. I believe it's something of a sight."

"So I've heard," Jael said. "Do I get an invite?"

"You're always welcome in my home, Jael. You know that. It would be good to see you, though, once I'm in place. Give it a couple of months and you'll be glad to leave the capital."

"A couple of months?" Jael looked at him in horror. "I'm thinking a couple of weeks. No way can I handle society any longer than that, and I'll deserve a medal if I manage to get to the fortnight."

The sound of boots stomping up the staircase disturbed them, and they both looked to the doorway. Watkins arrived within seconds, his demeanor as glum as when he'd left them.

"Hitting the wine?" he asked. "What's wrong with beer, lad? That's what I want to know. What's wrong with beer?"

"There's nothing wrong with beer, old man, and you should help yourself to a bottle and come and sit down," retorted Alex whilst Jael tried to hide his smile.

"I've no time to be drinking, lad. I've jobs to do. It seems to me that you shouldn't be doing nothing either. If you must sit there and drink, the least you could do is discuss that man Lunette. Nasty character, if you ask me, and popping up in unusual places for an aristo."

Alex sat up immediately. "What do you know of Lunette?"

"Not enough," retorted Watkins. "Like I said, there's jobs to be done, lad, jobs to be done." He turned and left the room, leaving Alex and Jael staring at each other in disbelief.

"He really does know everything, doesn't he?" said Jael in wonder. "I don't understand how he can do that."

"Me neither," Alex replied. "It's like he's got a gift. I've never known him to be wrong."

"Perhaps he has foresight and just hasn't mentioned it."

"As if Watkins wouldn't announce something like foresight. I'd have had years of 'you need to work on your foresight, lad, work to be done.' No, anything Watkins knows, he's taught me, and foresight wasn't part of it. It would have been damn handy on occasion."

"Yes," agreed Jael. "It's a shame it's so rare."

"If he's interested in Lunette, though, there's definitely something to be interested in. Like I said, I've never known him to be wrong. What do you think about him saying that Lunette was turning up in unusual places? Most Elites never leave their own circle. Come. Let me get another bottle of wine. We clearly have much to discuss."

PART TWO

THE CLASS had music practice after dinner, but Nico was excused. Thank the Goddess. With no sense of time or rhythm, he hadn't lasted long with music. He couldn't carry a tune in a bucket and had been reduced to playing the triangle until one of the Grand Seers announced that he would be studying the history of music instead. It had been a relief all around when he'd handed the triangle over and left the class. The sudden insistence on his attendance was beyond him. The years hadn't changed anything. He was still tone-deaf. When he'd entered the class as instructed, the maestro had looked horrified. There had been a quick deliberation between him and another Grand Seer, and then Nico had been instructed to go and work on his presentation for music night. He was glad of the escape. Perfect Pants and his friends had been discussing the rumor that a warrior was entering the Gleaning. It had been floating around for a couple of days, but Percy seemed determined to make it the sole topic of conversation. His two closest friends had predictably jumped on board, and between the three of them there had been the usual preening and posing. Nico had tried to ignore them, but the constant giggles got on his nerves. The endless squealing that Percy would be first picked; Percy would be wed to a warrior; Percy would be having sex with a warrior. At that point they'd all collapse into giggles and whispers, and the cycle would begin again. Nico thought them fools. He'd be questioning how long it had been since the warrior had actually been a warrior. Just because he was a member of the warrior class didn't mean he wasn't an elderly, bloodsucking leech. Nico wasn't impressed at all. He'd seen his idea of the perfect man and no warrior could match up.

Ensconced in the library and left entirely to his devices, Nico relaxed. It was a win-win situation as far as he was concerned. Well, almost. A true win-win would mean that he was in the kitchen, but he could make the most of this. He'd hidden himself in the oldest part of the library. The oak table was said to have come from Old Earth with the first of the Grand Seers. The ladder-back chair wasn't quite so ancient but it was seasoned enough and worn into a comfortable shape.

The room itself was comforting with its cozy nooks and crannies. The wooden wall paneling added warmth, and the stained-glass windows allowed rays of early evening sunshine to beam through. Blues, reds, and yellows celebrated the space within, and Nico was happily settled into it and, more important, was happily researching food. The library had several very old cookbooks hidden amongst the herbals, and Nico was determined to make the most of them whilst he was still living in Academia Hall. He'd first discovered them when transferring to the capital's Academia Hall when he was seventeen. There had been only thirty boys in the competition by then, and they'd had years of training before they could enter. In turn, entering the hall was seen as a major achievement. Nico, for the life of him, couldn't understand why. He had, however, been thrilled to discover the recipe books. In fact, no pirate had ever beheld a finer hoard of treasure. He'd spent years studying them. Writing down every recipe, every recommendation. He'd spent hours discussing them with the various chefs at the hall. Learning from each one and adding more to his knowledge. Now it was like reading an old friend, a much-loved friend. One who had never let him down. Well, almost never. There had been that recipe for treacle fish, but he could forgive that.

He was happiest in the kitchen but the library came in second, or perhaps third after the garden. He quite liked the food markets too. No, the library was definitely his second-favorite place. He wasn't allowed to help in the garden anyway, except with the herbs. All of them were much better than music practice, and he was going to enjoy his stolen hours. He did have to show some understanding of the history of music, but it had only taken a couple of hours to write a paper about some long-dead Earth composers whose music was still being played today. He'd entitled the essay "Yesterday," which he thought was rather clever. At the testing time he would have to present the paper, but he doubted anyone would listen. At least he wasn't stuck with the terrible triangle.

Alone in his corner, Nico was sunk deep into an essay about fungi when Grand Seer Nelson interrupted him.

"My boy." The man signaled Nico to remain seated as he took the seat opposite him. Nico wondered what he'd done now. Surely it wasn't about him tripping up during the walk? That was hardly his fault. "Do not alarm yourself, Nico," the man said with a gentle smile. "You're not in any trouble." He raised one eyebrow. "Although I must point out that you're supposed to be studying the history of music, not…." He paused, leaning forward to see the treatise occupying Nico's attention. "Fungi, hmn."

Nico had the grace to blush. "I've finished my paper," he said hurriedly. "It's being checked over by Master Clements, and then I'll be all ready to present it."

The other man's smile widened. "I'm sure it will be excellent, Nico, but that's not what I'm here to discuss." The Grand Seer paused, seeming to weigh his words. Nico waited politely.

"The King Must be True to the People," the Grand Seer began.

Nico frowned even as he gave the correct response. "And the People Will Love the King."

"Yes!" The Grand Seer seized upon the words with some apparent relief. "It's the nature of our society, son. The king is dependent on the people and the people are dependent on the king. The king is given great power and wealth but both are limited. He has no power over the law-abiding citizen and must never forget the rights of the individual. We are all entitled to the Blessing of Being and above all else that blessing must be protected. When it comes to the wealth, the king is merely a custodian and he is required to practice benevolence. That is the role of monarchy. As you are aware, each of us has a role to play within the paradigm. We all have responsibilities in accordance with our abilities."

Nico was mystified. What on earth was Grand Seer Nelson talking about? He understood the rules of society. Goddess knew they'd been driven into him from a very early age. It was due to the stupid rules that he was stuck where he was. He knew a moment of self-disgust and promptly corrected himself. He'd been brought up surrounded by love and given access to the best education possible. Nico knew that he'd been given a specific talent. Really, he had no right to complain.

"How do you think you are doing, Nico?" the older man finally asked.

Nico shrugged, his forehead wrinkling. "Not very well? I've been thrown out of music, singing, and diplomacy. All of the physical education classes. I'm only allowed in yoga if I stay as far away as possible from my classmates. Master Young is worried I may hurt one of them. I'd have been kicked out of dance but for the presentation performance. I don't have a solo spot. I've written a paper on the History of Dance instead."

"I'm sure it will be very good," Grand Seer Nelson interrupted. "But that's not what I meant exactly. How are you in yourself? You don't seem as eager as your classmates to enter the Gleaning."

Nico wasn't sure how he should reply. It was true; he wasn't excited about the Gleaning. In all truth he couldn't have cared less about it. It was just a process for him to go through in order to be free. Free to do what he wanted, free to follow his dreams.

Of course he couldn't say any of that to the Grand Seer, or indeed to anyone. To be chosen for the Gleaning was considered a huge privilege in society. It was a major religious rite, held sacred by the priesthood. Thousands of boys were entered every year, but only ten were chosen. The final number, on the eve of the ceremonies, would be seven. Nico was hoping to be one of the three withdrawn from the contest, but that thought definitely couldn't be spoken. To be one of the seven was acknowledged to be the achievement of a lifetime. The opportunity to secure an excellent marriage, a life of wealth and privilege. To have every indulgence, to live in the very top of society's hierarchy. Shame Nico had no interest in any of those things. Not at the price that came with it. Anyway, all he really wanted to do was cook. He could hardly announce that to the Grand Seer.

"It's not that I'm not excited," he began carefully, wondering how best to state his case. "It's more that I don't expect to be one of the chosen. All the others are so much more suitable than I am, and we all know that not every boy is chosen."

"That is true, indeed." The Grand Seer nodded. "But you have no reason to fear that, Nico. You're a talented, personable young man. Certainly one of the most intelligent boys we've trained. Why shouldn't you be chosen? No other son of this house has ever achieved priesthood as early as you did. You're an expert herbalist, and even Grand Seer Stephen listens to your opinions when it comes to healing. You are naturally talented at healing. In fact, you have a great many credits before the Goddess. To not be chosen? Really, my son, your fears are groundless."

And that was the problem, thought Nico. He didn't have fears; he had hopes.

He was twelve when he had been inducted into the Geisha class, and it had never been his choice. An orphan brought up through the system, he had no parents or family to help him. The authorities had decided which training he would undergo, not him. At first it hadn't mattered. He'd been one of a class of a thousand and had fully expected to be dismissed as each milestone of the training had been achieved. That he wasn't dismissed remained a huge shock. He still didn't understand why it hadn't happened. To be in the final ten… Goddess knew how that had happened because he certainly didn't. The one thing that kept him going throughout was the certain knowledge that he would never be chosen. That he'd be free to leave the academy with his dowry and use it to start his own business. He'd already put a lot of work into his business plan, although he'd had to keep the work hidden. To have some overprivileged, self-absorbed letch of a man come along and choose him now would be the worst thing that could happen. It would be another year before he could start his business, and he didn't want to wait that long. Of course he would get to finally have sex, and that would be some consolation, but no, he wouldn't be chosen, he promised himself. He'd be dismissed before the Gleaning even started.

"We should discuss your responsibilities, Nico. You will be entering the world soon. You must take your rightful place in society."

Oh, hell no, thought Nico. How was he going to get out of this? He closed the book in resignation, accepting that no, he wouldn't get out of this. Grand Seer Nelson was clearly settling down for the long haul.

"I've mentioned your talent for healing. I also mentioned that you are the youngest person ever to be admitted to the priesthood. These are heavy responsibilities, Nico. It will be your role in life to bring both to the people. The Goddess Herself has chosen you, and I do not say that lightly. Now you will show Her Grace through your work. You must work, Nico. I know that the popular feeling is that the Gleaning leads to a life of indolence, but that isn't true. Like the king, you must be true to the people. You are being given a huge privilege, but you mustn't abuse it."

Nico kept silent. What could he say? It was true he had been given gifts, but the best gift of all was the cooking, and he didn't know how to explain that. He didn't know how to say that yes, the healing was important, and yes, the priesthood was important, but most important was the provision of food. The basic need of fuel for human beings, the creativity of meeting those needs. Grand Seer Nelson wouldn't understand that.

"You have good qualities, Nico. You do not give in to peer pressure, and you hold yourself to a high standard. You are a decent, honest young man, and we're very proud of you. You will always have a home with us should you want it. With your intelligence you would have no problem becoming a Grand Seer if you choose to take that path."

Nico looked up in shock. He was being offered a permanent place at Academia Hall? He'd never considered that. Not once.

"You've excelled in all your extra classes, although you did struggle with the usual classes," the Grand Seer hurriedly added. "But those classes aren't really necessary for a Grand Seer. Of course, it must be your choice." The man peered at Nico through the spectacles propped on his nose. "It must be a path that you wish to follow."

But it wasn't, thought Nico wistfully. His path led elsewhere.

Grand Seer Nelson sighed. "I think perhaps you know your path. Don't you, Nico?"

Nico nodded.

"I've no doubt that you will find the success you seek, but you mustn't forget your debts to the Lady. You must use your gifts. You must be true to the people."

Nico thought that was a bit much. He was well aware of his responsibilities in society. He had every intention of fulfilling them, but he was hardly the king.

"There's a reason you are here for the final Gleaning." The teacher interrupted his thoughts. "We may not know what the reason is, but She Who Weaves the Web knows what She is doing. You must place your trust in Her."

"The Goddess Knows All." Nico automatically slipped into the High Speech instigated by the Grand Seer. High Speech required talking in capitals and was generally reserved for discussing the deities. It was popular amongst the Elites since speaking in High Speech required the other conversant to do the same. Sliding into High Speech was an excellent way to avoid sticky topics.

"Precisely." The Grand Seer looked relieved. "You must have faith, my boy. Everything will turn out well."

Here's hoping. Nico kept the thought to himself as he stood politely and bowed to his teacher. He was going to miss his tutors, he realized. They'd been so patient with him over the years, and he had learned a lot from them. And not just from his classes. He'd learned compassion and a strong sense of justice. He'd learned the difference between right and wrong. Then there was all the stuff they didn't mean to teach him. Nico had learned the benefit of self-examination. Learned not to get so totally lost in one theory as to be unaware of the material world around him.

"The first of the presentations begins on Monday. You should spend some time in reflection before then."

Nico bowed again, acknowledging the instruction. He was rather hoping that he would be one of the three boys leaving the competition. He knew, even if the Grand Seer didn't, that he wasn't the only boy hoping for that. And he didn't have time for reflection; he needed to get back in the kitchen. He paused. Perhaps he could argue that he reflected best when he was cooking. That might get him some time. Especially if he went to Grand Seer Esme. She was a total sucker if ever there was one. And a wonderful, kind, and generous woman, he reminded himself guiltily. It might just work. Then if his luck held, he'd be dismissed from the competition on Sunday evening. If the worst happened and he was presented at the Gleaning itself, then he'd have just five days before, Goddess willing, he was free.

ALEX LEANED over the glass counter and looked at the jewelry displayed. Watkins had taken up a post by the shop door, his arms folded and a look of disgust on his face.

"So you're going to dress the pretty boy up like a Yule tree?"

Alex ignored the disdain and continued to peruse the gems. Jael turned from where he was inspecting a row of diamonds and said, "Not the cheapest shop in the district."

"I'm not buying cheap," Alex retorted and cast a glance in Watkins's direction. "It's also tradition that jewels are presented before the promise. You're a big believer in tradition, old man."

Watkins grunted and turned away. He could be heard muttering under his breath, but Alex knew from experience not to inquire further. The man really didn't need any encouragement.

The shop assistants were in an excited huddle at the back of the room whilst their manager waited on Alex.

"If I may make a suggestion, Your Grace," the man offered, bowing so many times that he reminded Alex of a nodding-dog toy he'd had as a child. "We have a private room for customers such as yourself. If you'd like to come with me, I can bring the gems to you and send for refreshments whilst you make your choices. I'm sure we'll be able to help you, Your Grace."

Alex signaled that the man should lead the way and nodded to Watkins that he was to follow them.

"Oh don't you worry, lad," he snorted. "I've no problem with accepting a little refreshment. As long as they're not offering tea." He looked alarmed at the thought.

"Oh, we have all sorts of refreshments, sir," the manager said. "I'm sure we'll be able to meet your needs. This way Your Grace, Your Highness, and, er, sir."

Within seconds they were whisked into a comfortable lounge. There was heavy leather furniture in the chesterfield style. Pale blue silk papered the walls. Lush drapes curtained the windows, though they were pulled back to let in the sun. Alex and Jael chose to sit on two sofas facing each other. There was a comfortable coffee table ideal for inspecting the jewelry. A large magnifying glass stood to one side, ready to be brought into use. They were offered every refreshment, and Alex and Jael chose champagne. Watkins went for the beer. Settled into place, they watched as a stream of shop assistants brought in tray after tray of gold and platinum, diamonds and rubies, and every other sort of jewel known to man. Every gem sparkled against the black velvet and soon the table was full. Alex leaned forward to pick up a bracelet. Watkins turned his attention to the staff. "His Grace will be wanting some privacy now." The words were stern and the staff jumped to attention. The manager began bowing again as he hurried the staff from the room. He bowed three times just before shutting the door behind him, and Alex wondered whether he was still bowing to the closed door. He glanced down at the bracelet. It was a simple design, two ropes of pearls with every third pearl separated by a gold embossed bauble. The whole thing was attached to a gold clasp consisting of a circle and a bar. He liked it. It was understated, quiet, and elegant. He rubbed one pearl against his thumb.

"You'll be casting pearls before swine, lad, if you insist on going down this path. I never took you for a fool, lad."

"Then perhaps you should trust my judgment," countered Alex smoothly. He reached for another bangle, this one rich in emeralds. He wondered how they would look on a certain cute boy who wouldn't leave his thoughts. Was the Goddess sending him a message? Like many warriors, Alex firmly believed in the Goddess. She had saved his life on too many occasions to not believe in Her. But, again like many other warriors, he kept quiet about his faith. He paid his debts in silence.

"I'd rather hear your thoughts on Lunette, Watkins, if you please." It wasn't a question, and Watkins took a moment to gather his thoughts.

"He's living beyond his means and has taken out debts with some very unsavory villains. Nasty pieces of work and not a club where you'll find those of the privileged class. They say that he's very close to getting a proposal of marriage for his daughter and that proposal will come from Prince Alphonse. He's betting to clear his debts through the dowry." He took a quick drink of beer and continued. "But the do-gooders are saying even more than that."

"The do-gooders? Since when did you ever talk to do-gooders?" asked Alex.

"I'm a child of the Goddess just like any other man," responded Watkins curtly. "I know my share of good people, even if some of them have odd ideas."

"What sort of odd ideas?" demanded Alex. "Have you been listening to conspiracy theories again, old man?"

"We've had good information out of conspiracy theories, lad. It pays to listen to everything. Haven't I always told you that?"

"We get 1 percent truth and the rest is rubbish. I'm not convinced the time wasted is worth it."

"Always worth it, lad, if it might save a life."

Alex rolled his hand for Watkins to continue. He rolled his eyes too.

"They say that Lunette is trying to upset the balance of society."

Alex gave a deep sigh. "Not another *upset the balance of society* theory. Really, I can't handle another one."

"No," interrupted Jael quickly. "Let him speak. I have information of my own when he is finished." Alex looked at him in disbelief but sat back and allowed Watkins to continue.

"They say Lunette treats his tenants badly, that he encourages this amongst his set. He's putting more and more land into producing exports. He believes he can make more money through exports than he can feeding his tenants."

"He's not feeding his tenants?" Alex sat up in disbelief. "How are they surviving?"

"Who knows? There's talk of riots and demonstrations. Jail sentences even. Yet no news of it here. The media are avoiding all

mention of the troubles. Though there is much in the news about you."
He nodded to Alex. "Total flummery, all of it. Never thought to see you
as a media pro, lad, never thought to see that." Alex grimaced. He was
well aware that Watkins didn't mean "professional" when he said "pro."

"You know full well that all that stuff is left to my media team. I
have nothing to do with it. I don't even read it."

"Well you should, lad. You should see the nonsense they write
about you. That's beside the point, however. The point is that Lunette
is causing problems and you need to go and get it sorted. You have
new responsibilities now. Responsibilities to the land. You shouldn't be
wasting your time picking pretty boys!" Watkins's tone rose with his
words. "You need to be out on the land—"

Alex cut him off with a curt "Enough" and turned his attention to
Jael. To his huge relief, Watkins sat back, muttering under his breath.

"What is your news, Jael?"

"Much the same as Watkins. Lunette is spreading discontent
amongst the Elites, and there are so many whispers it's hard to make
sense of them. Of all my brother's set, Lunette is the one that worries me
most. My brother is so impressed by him and constantly listens to what
Lunette is saying. It's true, too, that Lunette is pushing his daughter in
my brother's way. I have no care who my brother marries as long as he
is happy with his choice, but I must admit I don't want to see someone
like Lunette in the family."

"It will be good to find out more about Lunette, that's for sure. I
wonder, though, if I should send some men ahead to the Sixth Land, just
to see how the land lies."

"You should be going there yourself, lad. I've told you."

"Oh, hush, Watkins. I've heard your bleatings and I have no wish
to hear them anymore. Is that understood?"

"Bleatings?" Watkins repeated. "Bleatings? I'll give you bleatings,
lad. What do you think you'll be getting out of your pretty boy? You'll
soon find out what bleatings are."

"Enough," Alex roared, throwing his hands in the air and frightening
the manager who was just creeping through the door. The man squealed
in shock, clutching his hands to his heart.

He began to make his apologies, but Alex waved them aside. "Not
you, man. You come in. I've made my choices."

"Excellent, Your Grace." More bows. "If you'd like to tell me which pieces?"

"All of them." Alex stood up and made his way to the door, closely followed by his friends. "Have them sent to my house, if you'd be so kind."

PART THREE

THE FIRST day of the Gleaning proved to be cold, the sun hiding behind a gray overcast sky. Nico knew how it felt. He wanted to hide too. He couldn't believe he'd made the cut... again. Three boys had been culled the night before. Not that they were supposed to call it "culled." It wasn't as though the boys were killed, after all. But no other term worked quite as well. The Grand Seers referred to it as withdrawal, but all the boys called it the cull. Nico had seen the look of relief quickly masked on two of the boys and the look of upset, also quickly masked, on the third. Nico had fully expected that he'd be one of them, thought it was a shame that he and Wilf couldn't swap places. It was only five more days, he reminded himself. Unfortunately, it was five days of hell. Presentations, soirees, and finally at the end of the week, a grand ball. It would mean endless costume changes, constant photographs, and Goddess only knew what else. One thing would be certain—he wouldn't get to be in the kitchen.

He took a deep breath and squared his shoulders. Currently in line with the other six boys, they were getting ready to be presented to the public. In fact, presentation was on the other side of the huge black curtain in front of them.

Nico checked his costume. It was quite a nice blue color, but he wasn't so impressed by the velvet. The latest fashion called for a calf-length trouser and he wore silk stockings beneath them. His waistcoat was a pale blue silk highlighted by a white linen shirt and a silk tie. He pulled at the high collar, feeling more constricted than comfortable. All the candidates were dressed in a similar way, albeit in different colors, and most of them were dragging on the collar. The only ones standing still were Percy and his friends. They looked excited, eager, and far more comfortable than they should. They'd also worked their way to the front of the line. Percy looked almost ecstatic. He was dressed in a vivid red and black, the colors suiting his dark complexion and glossy black hair. *Five more days*, thought Nico, *and I'll never have to deal with you again.*

There was a hush from the other side of the curtain and the stage manager started waving his arm frantically to make them all line up properly. Nico felt someone grasp his arm and turned to see Grand Seer Esme. She leaned forward and kissed him on the cheek. "Don't talk about cooking," she whispered urgently in his ear and then she was gone. The stage manager gesticulated at him, and he moved forward in line, ready to take his place on the stage.

The noise and the lights were overwhelming, and Nico wanted to shrink away from the assault. He'd never really experienced being onstage. He'd withdrawn from performing at quite an early age. He just wasn't suited to it. Now he wished he'd had some experience. He forced himself to stand straight, put his shoulders back, and walk calmly to his spot. He allowed a small smile as he'd been instructed. Hopefully it didn't look like smirking. He'd hate to smirk onstage. Nico tried hard not to blink as the overhead lights rippled over the boys over and over again. A quick glance down the line showed Percy slightly more forward than the other boys. He was preening under the lights, making Nico check his own posture quickly. He didn't want to preen but working his way slightly behind the line might work to his advantage. He knew it could only be a subliminal thing, but subliminal things worked. He surreptitiously edged his way backward. The overhead lights faded out to be replaced by the stage light. Suddenly there was no shadow to hide in. He looked out at the audience and found himself faced by a sea of cameras. They seemed to be everywhere he looked, and he knew within moments there would be photographs all over the Social Web. He'd never seen the Social Web but he'd been warned about it by the Grand Seers. They made it sound like a den of iniquity. Which was odd because they also had their own Social Web page. When challenged on this apparent discrepancy, the Grand Seers replied that of course they must be open to the people—the people benefited from the knowledge they held. More important, they had complete control over their own page, and what appeared there had been carefully constructed. It was a control they kept when it came to individual pages for each of the candidates. Nico had long gotten used to the idea that there was a page somewhere with all sorts of information about him, but it was a page he wasn't allowed to see. He'd only ever been allowed access to the Academic Web. He had occasionally sneaked onto the Commercial Web. There was an access screen in the kitchen. He'd only ever used it to look at kitchen equipment, though, just so he had an idea of the cost. He wouldn't have dared access the Social Web.

He realized that someone had started talking, and he glanced to the right of the stage where a man was interviewing the head of the Grand Seers, Grand Seer William. He was commonly known as "the Grandest" by the boys. He was currently discussing the Grace of the Goddess with the compere. Nico tuned them out. He relaxed into his pose and the smile was easier to achieve. He now had a good fifteen minutes to think. Each boy would have a two-minute interview and the Grandest was bound to go on about the Goddess for at least another five minutes. Nico had heard his sermons before. So, fifteen minutes. He could review his thoughts on Yorkshire pudding.

All too soon he found himself at the top of the line with the compere urging him forward. What was the man's name again? He couldn't remember. He was some sort of famous person, but Nico wasn't sure what he was famous for. He took a breath, stepped forward, and was very glad when time went into hyperdrive and his two minutes were over and done with in two seconds…. Being interviewed had been a surreal experience, the questions bizarre. And the Grandest had been unbelievable. It was as though the man was drunk. Which was impossible; the Grandest was a confirmed teetotaler and believed everyone else should be too. Was it possible to be drunk on attention? He'd certainly claimed his share, often answering Nico's questions before Nico could. Which suited Nico down to the ground. The duller he looked, the better. Being apparently unable to answer the question "What's your favorite book?" had delighted him, although he didn't show it. The Grandest had leaned forward to say, "Oh, I can answer that. It's a Herbal, isn't it, my son?" If that didn't show him to be duller than dull, what would? Once the interview was done, he made his escape quite happily. Out of all the questions asked, he'd only answered three. And two of those had been yes/no answers. If he was honest, he only said blue was his favorite color because it was the first one to come to mind. Probably because he was wearing it. In truth he didn't have a favorite color. He liked all of them. It was a stupid question anyway. Who cared?

He made his way to the green room to join the rest of the candidates. Percy and his friends were squealing excitedly in the corner. The others occupied the central sofas and were talking quietly. They beckoned him to join them.

"How did it go?" asked Jake, who was known for his musical ability. He was sure to be chosen.

"It was okay. The Grandest answered most of the questions for me."

"He did that for all of us." Jake nodded. "I wanted to answer my own questions."

"I didn't care."

"No, you don't, do you? You don't want to be amongst the chosen." Jake looked at him with interest. "Can't say I do either."

"You?" Nico was shocked. "I thought you wanted to be part of the Gleaning."

"I do, I just don't want to be chosen. I want to go and do my music. I don't need some old letch stopping me from doing that. Why would I?"

"But you've always been so studious."

"I wanted the education. I can play ten different instruments, and that's thanks to the Grand Seers. I wouldn't have gotten that education from my family. I knew it and they knew it. That's why they entered me for the Gleaning. It was never the intention, though, that I should be chosen. My family is poor. They need me to go out and earn money, and I can do that now. The Gleaning is an excellent way to enter society. I've already gotten recording offers. I'm praying to the Goddess that there are fewer suitors than candidates."

"Well that makes two of us," said Nico. "I want to cook."

A much louder squeal came from the corner, and he turned to see Percy giggling and his friends chanting, "Percy gets a warrior, Percy gets a warrior," until they too collapsed into giggles.

"Do they even have a brain?" muttered Nico in disgust.

"Not so you'd notice," said a boy across the way. "We're trying to ignore them, but it's not always easy. How did your interview go, Nico? Did the Grandest answer all the questions?"

Nico nodded, relaxing back into his chair. He realized he wouldn't see the other boys after this week, possibly ever again. It was strange. He'd never been close to anyone. It was hard to be close when they might disappear at the end of the year. He knew some had kept up correspondence with some of the excluded ones, but he'd never been one to write letters. There had been far too many other things to do, and every minute had to be carefully hoarded so he could spend time in the kitchen. He did feel some camaraderie with the others, though. They had all shared an eight-year education together. They'd all been molded toward the same point, yet they were all so different. Jake had his music and Simon had his art. Deepak was an incredible storyteller and had often held them all spellbound with his stories. Percy swept the field in athletics and dancing. Even his friends had their talents. Nico's own cooking talent wasn't held in high regard in society, and he still couldn't understand why he was in the Gleaning. He was totally the wrong sort of person.

The doors opened and the Grandest entered, closely followed by Grand Seers Amos and Lucy. Nico stood up politely.

"Boys, boys, do sit down," began the Grandest, clearly in his element. "Well, sit down for a moment. It's actually time to return to Academia Hall and prepare for tonight. The excitement isn't stopping here." He beamed. "Tonight you meet the suitors as well as the aristocracy. I know that you're all looking forward to it very much. Now, as soon as we return, I want each of you boys to go and have a nap. A good two hours, mind. It's important that you be rested for this evening. Oh, and don't forget that it's evening wear tonight, though you may of course wear your ribbons." He clapped his hands in glee. "So exciting," he caroled. "So exciting. Now, Brother Amos, Sister Lucy? Do you have any words for the boys?"

"Yes," announced Grand Seer Amos loudly and deliberately. "I do have some words for the boys if you'd be so kind, Brother."

"As I would too," stated Grand Seer Lucy pertly. "I have quite a lot to say to the boys."

"Well, if that's the case, then perhaps we should return to Academia Hall and you can tell the boys on the trip there," said the Grandest pleasantly. "In the meantime, I do want to remind you boys of your covenant with the Goddess...."

He continued for the fifteen minutes that it took them to leave the screen studio. The place was so big that Nico was quite certain the Grandest had gotten them lost at least twice. When they finally located their vehicle, he was still in full flow and it didn't look like the other Grand Seers were going to get a word in edgewise. Once seated in the vehicle, it became clear, though, that neither of them was willing to be pushed to the side by the Grandest.

"What a lovely sentiment to the Goddess, Brother," Grand Seer Lucy said. "I'm sure the boys will carry that image with them for a long time. Now if I may...." She stood up in the aisle. "Now, boys, it is a very exciting week for you, but you mustn't lose sight of your responsibilities." Nico groaned. Another speech on responsibilities? As if they hadn't been indoctrinated enough. He tuned it out. She couldn't possibly be saying anything new. And he hadn't made a decision on the recipe for Yorkshire pudding. He stared out of the window, glad no one could stare back in. People were still filming and taking photos, and Nico just couldn't understand why. He closed his eyes and thought about batter.

He realized that Grand Seer Lucy had stopped, and Grand Seer Amos had apparently been talking for a while when they pulled up at the Hall. Hopefully he hadn't missed anything. "Oy," he whispered across the aisle to Jake. "What did I miss?"

"How the hell should I know?" Jake whispered back. "I'm working on a new song."

Inside the hall they discovered that they had missed something quite momentous. There were only five suitors, and two boys wouldn't be part of the chosen. Jake grinned at Nico, and Nico couldn't help but grin back.

ALEX ADJUSTED his cuffs. He stood back and looked at himself in the mirror. Being a warrior meant that he was more at home in uniform than formal wear and the flounces of fashion took some getting used to. His coat was cut in the military style, double-breasted with large covered buttons down each lapel. The coat was shaped so as to allow a view of the plain black waistcoat beneath and the white linen shirt that accompanied it. His linen scarf was tied in the simplest knot he could get away with. Not for him the high collars and tight knots of the Elites. He liked to keep things simple, including his personal style. Even so, the collar did feel a little higher than he was used to. But he was a warrior, so he could live with it.

He'd considered wearing his medals but decided against it. He had no need to show off who he was. Leave the ribbons to other people.

Entering the sitting room, he was pleased to see Jael and equally pleased that there was no sign of Watkins. He walked over to the side table and poured himself a drink. Jael had already helped himself.

"Need to calm your nerves?" Jael asked, one eyebrow arched. "Are you having second thoughts?"

"No, I'm not," responded Alex bluntly, taking a moment to look over his shoulder toward the door. "And you watch what you say in front of Watkins. I don't want him set off again."

"Did you get a look at the presentations today? It's been on the screen all afternoon."

"I looked."

"And did you like what you saw?"

Yes, he'd liked. He'd been delighted to discover that the cute blond had gotten through to the final Gleaning, but he hadn't expected to have a reaction that strong. It was strange. Almost as if he was being pushed. He took another sip of his drink. He had to stop thinking of him as "cute blond." He knew now that his boy had a name. Nico. Nico was the one trying to hide behind the others onstage. The one who'd happily sat dumb throughout his interview. At least the other boys had tried to answer, though it was clear that the Grand Seer had no intention of giving up the limelight. No, his boy had given three one-word answers and happily handed the whole thing over. It was as though he had nothing to talk about. Or something to hide. Alex wondered which one was the more likely. He knew what Watkins would say. Watkins had no good words for the candidates, but he did have strong opinions on their intellect and abilities. Jael was a different matter, though.

"Did you watch it?" he questioned.

"Yes, indeed. There's a really good-looking brunet who looks interesting. He was on first and was the only one who got to answer questions. Managed to get in before that teacher type could interrupt. Good at athletics, they said."

"Really?" Alex couldn't say he'd noticed that, but then all the other boys were merging together. He'd only had eyes for one.

Suddenly Alex was eager to move. He wanted to get to the reception as quickly as possible. He wanted to make the acquaintance of Nico, find out for himself if the boy was just pretty or whether he had any depths to him at all. Something told Alex there would definitely be depths, and Alex had learned to trust in his instincts. "Where's Watkins?" he asked Jael, standing up suddenly. "He should be ready by now."

"And so I am" came the gruff voice from the doorway. "No need to get yourself in a twist, lad. I'm standing right here."

Jael also stood up, drinking the last of his whiskey. "Is it time to go? Must say I'm quite looking forward to this. I've never attended a Gleaning before. Always been damned glad I was never entered either."

"I'll say," agreed Watkins. "Damn fool path to follow."

Alex threw Jael a look and turned his attention back to Watkins. "You don't have to come if you don't want to," he said, knowing it was useless.

Watkins glared back at him. "And leave you to mess it all up? If you're determined to go through with it, then I'm determined to have some say in the pretty boy you choose. You're not the only one who'll have to live with him."

"It's going to be my choice, old man," growled Alex, stomping out of the door. "My choice!"

THEY ARRIVED at Academia Hall in good time and made their way up the steps to the red carpet. Everywhere they looked there were film cameras and journalists shouting questions. Alex ignored them, although Jael stopped to confer with one or two. It wasn't long, though, before he was back at Alex's side and they waited in line for entrance to the reception hall itself. It appeared they would be "announced" into the reception.

"Sounds like Alphy is here already," said Jael as shrill laughter came from the room. "Elias said he'd be attending too. Something about an announcement being made this week."

"What sort of announcement?" Alex looked at Jael in interest.

"Who knows? He implied it was something to do with the Gleaning but changed the subject onto something else, and I didn't get a chance to ask what."

The line slowly moved forward.

"Probably some special award or something. I've heard they do that all the time."

"Oh, they do. My father usually attends and he's always handing out prizes. It will be Alphy tonight, though. I don't know why Elias feels the need to turn up."

"Perhaps he wants to see what his brother is up to. After all, that's why you're here."

Jael barely had time to reply "True" as they were swept forward into the reception hall and their titles announced so loudly that they both almost staggered from the effect. It was only a sharp hand from Watkins that kept them upright.

"Good Goddess, do they have to be so loud?" whispered Jael. "I've got Sergeant Major Watkins ringing in my ears. I need a drink." He set off straight in the direction of the bar, ignoring the bows aimed toward him from the room.

Alex and Watkins followed closely, neither man making eye contact with the guests so they didn't have to keep bowing. They might be relatively new to society, but they had no intention of getting comfortable.

The announcements kept going every bit as loudly and made a mockery of the string quartet in the corner. Acoustic instruments had no chance against the volume of the PA. The men found they had little chance of conversation even at the bar, since every possible corner held a speaker.

Alex took the whiskey Jael handed him and tossed it back in one. He was nervous and had no idea why. He hadn't been this nervous since his first battlefield, and that had been quite some years ago.

He was nursing his second drink when he realized the doors were finally being closed. The PA system shut down with an audible click, and a hush descended on the room. Even the musicians had stopped playing and were standing up, looking toward the curtains at the back.

The curtains drew back, and one by one the boys entered the room. Each boy was accompanied by a Grand Seer, and they slowly walked out into the dance area. They were followed by the Grandest, who appeared to think the audience was there for him. He bowed and waved his way to the front of the dance area and approached the microphone that stood there.

"Your Highness, Your Highness, and Your Grace," he boomed, nodding at Prince Alphonse, Prince Jael, and Alex. Thankfully, there was a smaller PA system in this part of the room and eardrums remained intact.

"Ladies and gentlemen. I'm delighted to announce the candidates for this year's Gleaning." He nodded happily whilst the audience gave a polite smattering of applause. "Yes, yes, the boys are being introduced by their tutors, and I'm sure they'll want to meet everyone. If I could just have one moment however, I feel it's important to remember the Grace of the Goddess at a time like this. Why I remember...."

Alex stopped listening. He was looking for his boy, dismissing faces one by one until he came to the last boy. The boy who was carefully trying to make his tutor step slightly back with him. Alex smiled. He wasn't getting anywhere. The tutor seemed equally determined that they should shuffle forward instead, and there was a very sedate tug-of-war going on. Suddenly the tutor tugged a little too hard, and Nico sprawled forward at her feet. A gasp ran through the crowd, and Alex heard laughter behind him. He moved forward, intending to help, but the look Nico sent him stopped him in his tracks. Nico glared at him, actually glared at him. Alex was taken aback; he didn't know of anyone who'd dare to glare at him. Except Watkins, of course. His interest piqued, he moved back toward his friends. Let the boy come to him. He'd have to before the evening was out, as all the boys were to be introduced to the suitors. He placed his elbow on the bar and bided his time.

Before long, the Grand Seer finished his speech and urged the boys forward into the crowd. Alex smiled. Now it was game time.

The first boy to approach was a pushy brunet. He was introduced as Peter or Paul or some such name. Alex wasn't really paying attention. He said everything that was polite to both the boy and the tutor but left any questions to Watkins and Jael. Watkins would know what to say, and Jael would say it more politely. Neither of them needed Alex's input. Alex spent most of the time trying to work out where his boy was. He couldn't see him anywhere. Perhaps he needed to move position. He was just about to do so when he realized that the boy, Patrick, or whatever his name was, was being moved on by his tutor but didn't seem to be in any rush. Alex sorted that out by holding his hand out and saying, "Very nice to have met you," which meant the boy had no choice but to shake his hand. He did try to hang on to Alex's hand but with no success, and Alex was soon able to step farther into the room to look for his boy. It didn't last long, however, and another boy was brought forward to meet him and then another boy and another boy. Alex wanted to yell in frustration. Why were they parading all these boys when they should have been bringing his boy to him? And just how many boys had entered this Gleaning? It seemed like dozens.

Finally. Finally after what seemed like a never-ending queue of boys, the only one who mattered appeared in front of him accompanied by his tutor. She introduced herself first, with a bow that included Watkins as well as himself and Jael. Alex was impressed. So far she was the only tutor who had treated Watkins as an equal. "If I may introduce Nico Stamford. Gentlemen, Nico is one of our most accomplished candidates."

Excellent, thought Alex. A diplomat was going to be very useful. He held out his hand. "How do you do, Mr. Stamford."

Two sapphire eyes looked up at him beneath a fringe of loose blond curls. Nico held his hand out and they shook. Alex made the most of it, feeling the softness of the hand in his. It was a firm grip, and something in those eyes made him realize Nico was angry. What was going on? He allowed Nico to step back and shake hands with Jael and Watkins. There was no animosity in Nico's eyes when he looked at Jael and Watkins. Just him, then.

"So, lad," Watkins began in his gruff voice. "What experience of the military do you have?"

"None, sir," replied Nico politely. If he was bothered about the question, he didn't show it.

"How about fighting? All you boys living together, there must have been the odd fight or two, I'll wager."

"There is no fighting at Academia Hall, sir," the Grand Seer interrupted hotly. "We are academics. We don't tolerate violence," she added with a steely glare.

"But what about self-defense?" questioned Watkins belligerently. "Surely you've taught the lads some self-defense?"

"Of course we have taught them self-defense," snapped the teacher, "but we call it '*good manners.*'"

Alex decided to step in.

"So, Mr. Stamford, have you enjoyed your time at Academia Hall?"

"Very much so, sir." The animosity was back in the eyes. Alex, for the life of him, couldn't work out why. When the boy didn't elaborate, Alex decided to push further.

"You must be looking forward to the dancing. May I have the pleasure of the first dance?"

"No, thank you. I don't dance." Nico looked away, apparently finding the opposite side of the room very interesting.

Alex didn't know what to say. If there was to be no dancing, then how could he seduce the boy? The tutor interrupted once again.

"I'm afraid that Nico isn't a dancer, but he has many excellent qualities. He's a wonderful conversationalist, for example." She looked at Nico only to discover that he was still examining the opposite side of the room. "Of course tonight is tremendously exciting for him," she added, taking Nico's arm and patting it. It had the desired effect and brought Nico back to the small group. The tutor smiled encouragingly at him. He looked at her in confusion. Alex stepped in again.

"Perhaps you'd like some refreshment, Mr. Stamford."

"No, thank you."

"Something to eat?"

"No, thank you." This time it was said with much blunter emphasis and even the tutor looked shocked. Watkins had actually perked up in interest, and Jael was studying Nico with wonder. Nico looked unrepentant. There was a gleam in his eye that challenged Alex, and Alex was more than happy to accept.

He smiled broadly. "Perhaps I can call you Nico?" he requested softly. Nico bowed his head politely but his expression was bored.

"As Your Grace wishes," he said with the tone of High Speech. "Now if you'll excuse us." He pulled on his tutor's arm and practically pulled her farther into the room.

Alex watched him leave but a smile played about his lips. Nico hadn't seen the last of him yet.

PART FOUR

RETURNING TO his room, Nico wished that he was done with the whole thing. The night had been worse than he could have imagined. Not only was he dressed in a hideous embroidered suit more suited to a baby, but some letch had felt up his backside. He felt violated. But, much worse by a long margin, Perfect Man had turned up. He'd had the nerve to turn up at the Gleaning. Nico couldn't believe it. Was he there to ogle like the rest of them? Size up the goods on the Marriage Mart? Perhaps he was secretly laughing at the pretty Geisha boys. Just what sort of man was he? Nico couldn't remember being so angry in ages. How dare Perfect Man turn out to have feet of clay. It wasn't acceptable. He should have stayed in Nico's memory where he belonged.

Well, his fantasy was ruined now. He'd never look at the man in the same way again. Now Nico would have to look elsewhere for his perfect man. He had no doubt there was one. The Goddess provided when all was said and done.

He flopped onto his bed, pulling the scarf from around his neck. Thank Goddess they hadn't embroidered that as well. He gave a deep sigh. He'd done his duty and was introduced to every suitor as well as various members of the aristocracy. He'd got out of dancing and conversation quite easily, the dull ploy working well. In fact, much better than he'd have thought. Society was glittering, and dull really didn't fit in. Grand Seer Esme had been beside herself trying to coax him into conversations and urging him to talk. Between each introduction she'd said "talk" several times only adding "but not about cooking" once, which was quite reserved of her. She needn't have bothered. He had no intention of talking about cooking, no intention of talking about anything. He fully intended to spend the week of the Gleaning as dull as he could be. It would all work out fine.

His thoughts returned to Perfect Man. Except he wasn't Perfect Man anymore. He was just another imperfect man. Also he had a name now. Alexander DeVrie, Duke of the Sixth Land. He was the warrior that

Percy had been yapping on about all weekend. Well, Percy was welcome to him. Nico was sure they'd get along fine.

He sat up and shrugged his way out of his clothes. Tomorrow would mean a new outfit. He'd quite happily throw the embroidered one in the trash, but that would earn gentle rebuke and endless lectures from the Grand Seers. Yes, Perfect Man and Percy would get along fine, and Nico had only four more days to go. He could handle four more days.

ALEX CHECKED his watch and smiled. Finally it was the last evening of the Gleaning and he'd be able to make his choice. There was no doubt in his mind who it should be.

He thought about the past week. Tuesday had been a display of athletics held on the sports field behind the main reception hall. Six boys competed together, dressed in shorts and vests despite the coldness of the day. Alex had immediately noticed that Nico wasn't one of them, and it was only looking farther afield that he spotted the boy. Dressed in a tracksuit, he was helping one of the Grand Seers with the equipment. Alex approved. He didn't want Nico to be showing off his body like the other boys were. Nico was his.

Tuesday evening he'd discovered Nico hiding behind the curtains in the staged area. It had taken him a good thirty minutes before he thought to look there and another five minutes to discover that Nico would not be coaxed out. Every time he'd tried to get the boy's attention, Nico would slip into High Speech, effectively ending the conversation. Alex could High Speak with the best of them, but there was a limit to what you could use to answer to such gems as "The Tree of Life is Full of Diversity" and "She Who Weaves the Web Tells the Story." In anyone else Alex might have seen it as a sign of pomposity, but not in Nico. He was quite obviously playing some sort of game. Alex just wasn't sure what it was. He had decided to err on the side of caution and withdrew from the conversation. No one else was going to find Nico hidden in the curtains, so he had no worries there. He'd left early that evening.

Wednesday proved to be a day of dance. The brunet, whilst irritating in person, turned out to be an excellent dancer. Alex remembered that he'd done well in athletics too, but he hadn't been taking much notice so he could be wrong. Nico, once again, was nowhere to be seen.

"Your boy isn't there," observed Watkins, unnecessarily to Alex's mind. Jael simply shrugged, his attention on the irritating brunet. Alex decided to check the backstage area and sure enough, there was Nico. He was dressed in a gray suit with braids around the cuffs and lapels. Alex couldn't see what sort of waistcoat he was wearing because Nico stood with his back to Alex and was staring through a gap in the curtains.

"Mr. Stamford.... Nico," Alex said softly.

Nico nearly jumped out of his skin. "Good Goddess," he sputtered as he turned around to look at Alex. "What are you doing here, sir?" he demanded. "This space is for the candidates and the tutors. You shouldn't be here."

"And you should?" Alex raised one eyebrow.

"Well, actually, yes. I'm waiting to give a paper on the History of Dance," Nico answered primly. "Now if you'd like to return to the audience, Your Grace, you'll be able to watch the performance."

"I think I'll wait for your presentation. I may find that more interesting."

"More interesting?" Nico sputtered again, clearly annoyed. "Do you know how hard the candidates have worked for today? Do you?"

Alex stepped back, surprised at the anger in Nico's eyes. Nico continued. "Years. Years have been spent reaching this point, and the very least you can do is have enough respect to watch the performance. I hope I'm making myself clear, Your Grace." Alex felt like a small child being reproved.

"Er, yes, I shall go and do that now." Alex limped away from that one, but even more annoying was that Nico's presentation didn't happen. No reason was given, and the Grand Seers had left before he could inquire.

Thursday had given him one more day before the choosing. He'd woken up with a determination that he hadn't felt since the war. It was like going into battle. Which he supposed it was. He was certainly going to demand a surrender before the week was out. He was intrigued by the boy. Fascinated by that haughty look, the insistence on High Speech, and the constant rejections. Even the rejections, for Goddess's sake. He'd never been rejected before. Most men were all too eager to get into his bed. His military rank was usually enough to guarantee his success. But not with Nico. Of course the candidates were sheltered, and Nico probably didn't know his military rank, but he did know about the dukedom. Not that it fazed him, thought Alex. The boy obviously didn't care a jot about the dukedom. Alex smiled at the thought. His boy had depths.

Friday was the music presentation and Alex wondered what instrument Nico would play, or perhaps he'd sing instead. Alex approved of music. It was a good skill for a spouse to have. As a duke he would be expected to entertain often, and Goddess knew he didn't have a clue how to go about it. He could entertain other warriors fine, but somehow he didn't think that sort of entertainment would go down well with the good people of the Sixth Land. No, a musical husband would suit him fine. Forget the athletics and dancing. They weren't necessary.

It was to be a full day and Alex, Jael, and Watkins made their way to the reception hall early. Being one of the suitors, Alex and his party were seated in the front row and found themselves next to Prince Elias. He looked sober and thoughtful, though he smiled as he embraced his brother. He turned toward Alex, shaking his hand. "Are you enjoying the Gleaning, Your Grace?"

"I don't know if 'enjoying' is the right word," replied Alex with a laugh. "I'll be grateful to see tonight."

"Ah, then you've made your decision?"

"I have," agreed Alex with a grin.

Watkins gave a snort of alarm. "Made your decision? Now, lad, I thought we'd agreed to discuss this…."

Jael and Elias started laughing, then Elias continued. "You've picked a good year," he said with a smile. "There's to be a very special announcement tonight."

"What about?" demanded Jael. "Is it another stupid book prize? I mean, really, why have a book as a prize? It's easy enough to go out and buy them."

"It's not a book prize, brother, though there will be a couple of them. Along with all the other prizes of course. No, this is really special, and I can't say another word about it. I'm under oath to the Goddess."

"You could at least give us a hint," objected Jael. "You can't just leave us wondering."

Elias turned toward Alex. "Jael was always the child who went looking for his yuletide presents early." He laughed. "He never could wait for the surprise."

"He'd never be described as patient now," agreed Alex, smiling at Jael. He started laughing at Jael's expression.

"Watkins, why don't you and I go and get refreshments?" Jael said, leaving Alex and Elias alone. The Hall was quite empty. It was early and those who had arrived were mainly gathered in the refreshment area. Alex and Elias had no issue with being overheard. Alex took the seat next to Elias and the two men looked at each other.

"Jael has told you of his worries," Elias said with a sigh. "I should have known he'd talk to you."

"I doubt he has mentioned it to anyone else, Your Highness, and you know that none will hear it from me."

"You're a good friend to us, Alex. We know the gift of your loyalty," the prince replied. "I know Jael fears my brother's reign, but I am convinced that the King will be True to the People. There is still time for Alphonse to grow into the person he should be." He paused. "I am concerned about other rumors that I'm hearing, though. The stories of violence in the Sixth Land, the whispers of social unrest here. I have never known such a time."

"We shall know the truth of the Sixth Land soon enough. I travel there tomorrow. Then we'll have four days across the land."

"You're not flying in?"

"No, we'll fly to Tarn and then on to the castle by land. I want to see the actual land, see if there is any truth to the rumors. There is much to learn there, I think."

"And you'll want to make an entrance," laughed the prince.

"It won't hurt," agreed Alex with a smile.

ALL TOO soon people began to fill the chairs in the auditorium and private conversation was over. Jael and Watkins returned. They all took their seats.

Alex was handed a program and skimmed the list looking for Nico. He was right at the bottom presenting a paper on the History of Music. Not a musician, then, he thought wryly. Oh well, music was overrated. At least he'd still get his diplomat. He was tempted to sneak off behind the curtains but remembered the lecture from Wednesday. Perhaps he could get one of the Grand Seers to show him round. If it was during the interval, there could hardly be censure. He glanced around the room to see who was there. Not that he knew any of the Grand Seers, but the one who'd introduced him to Nico had been nice enough. Yes, there she was, in discussion with another tutor. He'd have to nab her as soon as the interval started.

The interval couldn't come soon enough, he decided, anxious to see Nico. Not that the music was bad. It wasn't; he just didn't have an interest in it. He had much better things to do, and the sooner evening came, the better.

NICO WAITED anxiously in the wings, wanting his presentation over and done with. He was not happy with Perfect Man turning up again. Not Perfect Man, he scolded himself, the duke of wherever. Why wouldn't he go away? Nico had been less than polite to him, had forced him into High Speech, which was a low blow by anyone's standards, and had more or less told him to go away. In fact, he had outright said so on Wednesday. Yesterday he'd been a bit more polite because Grand Seer Esme had been with him and she'd kept the conversation going. When he'd finally managed to get rid of the duke, she'd taken him to one side and questioned his actions. He had pretended innocence and promised to be more gracious in the future.

EVENING CAME much too soon, and Nico was dressed in the worst outfit of the week: bright yellow coat with bright yellow pantaloons and a startlingly white embroidered waistcoat. He felt like a giant inverted daisy. He took a deep breath and reminded himself that he only had to get through this last evening and it would all be over. He could start his life. Nico was pretty sure that he'd be one of the two who weren't chosen. He'd managed to put a lot of distance between him and the suitors, hiding in the shadows whenever possible. The only one who'd made any attempt to talk to him had been Perfect—no, not perfect, the duke of somewhere. Nico had no time for him. He'd spent the week listening to Percy's cronies talking endlessly about the man. How brave he was, how many wars he'd taken part in, how so very masculine and virile. He heard masculine and virile a lot and personally thought that Percy and his set should invest in a thesaurus. On one occasion he'd actually heard the words "suck" and "pinkywinkle" in the same sentence. He wasn't the only boy to look nauseated. It wasn't that he had no interest in sex. He was interested, very interested. In fact, the only good thing from being chosen was that he would get to have sex. But then he'd also get to have sex if he wasn't chosen. Once he'd graduated from the Gleaning, he'd be able to have as much sex as he'd like. There was no denying that freedom and sex sounded much better than marriage and sex. Even if he did get to have sex with someone like Perfect Man. Well, whoever the duke chose would get to have sex with him. In truth, the other suitors didn't come anywhere near the man. They were a very motley-looking crew. Nico had found it very easy to dissuade them from getting to know him. He'd told Lord Mace that he was allergic to dogs, knowing that the man loved his animals. Lord Taylor was informed that Nico felt a priest should spend much of the year celibate and meditating. He'd dismissed both Sir Malcolm and Sir Richard simply by out-High Speaking them. Both men were wary of High Speech and not particularly fluent in it. In fact, he'd managed to place considerable distance between himself and the suitors. Except for the duke. He'd kept up with the High Speech, commiserated with the role of a priest, and hadn't even blinked when Nico announced his nonexistent allergies. And he kept turning up. It didn't matter what Nico did, the duke still appeared at his elbow every day without fail. Nico was sure that it was some sort of bet thing. He'd heard warriors were great gamblers. Presumably there was a bet going on between the duke, Prince Jael, and that very grumpy man who was with them. Well, Nico wouldn't be reduced to the level of a wager, and once he got out of Academia Hall he fully intended to show people just who he was. There was just one evening to go and he'd be free.

The Grand Seers gathered the boys together to lead in a moment of self-reflection. Nico didn't want to self-reflect. He just wanted the night to end. He wondered how many other boys felt the same. The Grandest ended the moment by raising his hands and getting the boys' attention. "Now, my sons, this is the moment that you have all been working toward all of these years. The Goddess has not ignored your effort and soon you will all move on to the next stage of your lives. I'm sure it will be a happy and fulfilling time. Now, you must not forget your debt to the Goddess…."

Nico stopped listening.

ALEX TAPPED his foot impatiently. When was the damn thing going to start? He stared around the room, taking in society around him. He didn't think he'd ever met such a group of egos. He dismissed them from his thoughts and turned his attention to the staged area. The room had been transformed into a theater. Seven chairs were spaced around the perimeter, each with a further eight chairs spaced out behind them. Most of the suitors had brought members of their family or retinue. Alex had only brought Jael and Watkins, but he knew the empty chairs would be given to the overflow of Elites who had turned up to witness the ceremonies. No doubt the individual egos would compete for the right to sit. At the eighth point of the stage stood a statue of the Goddess Juno. Known as the Goddess of Marriage but also the Goddess of the Military. Alex wasn't sure how those two things went together, but she was an old friend and he was happy to see her. It was a good sign. Alex noticed the discreet cameras that had been spaced about the theater to ensure that the whole event was captured. He'd been promised a film of the event when he entered the Gleaning. He knew that between the ceremony and the ball, all of the staging and seating would be removed. The only thing that would remain was the statue of the Goddess.

He took a swift drink of his champagne and looked at his watch. Five minutes since the last time he looked. He got his impatience under control. Losing control didn't win wars, and this particular battle was about to be won.

"Nervous?" asked Jael, glancing around the room.

"No," replied Alex. "Impatient."

Watkins grunted. "Patience is a virtue, lad, and those who marry in haste repent at leisure."

"It's a year and a day, old man, not the rest of my life."

Watkins muttered under his breath and both Alex and Jael ignored him. "Are your brothers here?" asked Alex.

"Yes, they've just arrived. They're working their way through the crowd towards us. Alphy has his usual crowd with him, and one of them is Lunette." He grinned. "Finally, we get to have a close look at the man. Hopefully he'll stay for the ball."

"Is that likely?" asked Alex.

Jael nodded enthusiastically. "Since when did Alphy miss a ball? Especially one of the balls of the year. In fact, this is the last of the triumvirate. The heterosexual and lesbian ceremonies have already taken place. We just have to hope that Lunette wants to stay too."

"Aye, lad, let's concentrate on Lunette. There's no law says you have to choose a candidate. You can come back next year when we've dealt with the important things. This is a good opportunity, lad."

Alex glared at Watkins. "Enough! There's no reason why all three of us have to concentrate on Lunette tonight. I can trust your instincts. You two do it. I fully intend to be busy." And with a boy who couldn't dance, they wouldn't be at the ball for long. He glanced at his watch again. Another five minutes. Would this evening ever begin? The arrival of Princes Alphonse and Elias distracted him. He noted how closely Elias stayed to Alphonse. Both brothers embraced Jael and shook hands with Alex and Watkins. Alphonse was clearly in a good mood.

"Wonderful, wonderful. It's so good to see you, Your Grace. I'm delighted to find you in good health. And entering the Gleaning. Marvelous, marvelous. Have you met my very good friend Lunette?" He reached around Elias to grab his friend's arm. Elias patiently moved out of the way. "Lunette has some interesting theories on society, Your Grace. You'd be very interested in hearing them, I dare say. Very clever man, Lunette. I myself have been very impressed with his insight."

Lunette came forward, bowing to the company and smiling widely. "It's an honor, Your Grace." He held his hand out. "I have heard many stories of your bravery and valor. And good to see you too, Prince Jael. I know your brother misses you all the time." He was a small man with a Vandyke beard and graying hair. Once upon a time he might have been described as good-looking, but he had aged with sourness and it showed. There was cunning in his obsequiousness and Alex took an instant dislike. The fact that he ignored Watkins spoke volumes, and Alex was about to correct him when Jael beat him to it.

"I'm sorry, Lunette, it would appear you haven't been introduced to Sergeant Major Watkins." He brought Watkins forward as he spoke.

"Yes, yes, Lunette," added Prince Alphonse, "you must meet Watkins, a very good friend of ours. Isn't that so, Elias?"

"We know his loyalty and we are proud to be counted amongst his friends," said Elias haughtily. Clearly he too had been annoyed by the snub and felt that High Speech was warranted. Alex hid his grin as Lunette gushed apologies and held out his hand to Watkins. It didn't take long for Lunette to regroup, however, and once again he turned his attention to Alex.

"Your Grace," he began smoothly, "I would enjoy discussing economics with you at some point. I have interests in the Sixth Land and much experience there to share with you."

Not a chance in hell, thought Alex. The man reminded him of a snake. Unfortunately Prince Alphonse responded before he could.

"Oh, I'm sure the duke would like that, Lunette. He's bound to be as fascinated as I am over your economical model. I've been trying to persuade Elias to join our little set. We discuss society, you know, and how we can improve it. Lunette has several theories that are of great interest. Really, we feel positively motivated. The Goddess is smiling kindly at us when we have great minds like Lunette's in society, yes indeed. Don't you agree, Jael?" Not waiting for his brother to answer, he was suddenly distracted by some noise farther down the room. "Oh look!" he exclaimed in delight. "Lord Peel is here. Oh, what fun. I didn't think he was going to make it. We must make room for him to sit with us. Elias?" He looked to his brother for agreement. "Now I must go and talk to him. Your Grace, you must excuse me but I'm sure you'll be looking to take your place too. It's such an exciting night." And with that, he was gone.

Alex watched him go. He liked Alphonse, it was hard not to, but there was no denying Elias would make a better king. Alphonse was too easily influenced, too easily distracted. He believed that if he himself had a good heart, then all the men around him did too. This naivety was proving to be his downfall.

He looked at his watch. Ten minutes. Other people were starting to take their seats and a couple of Grand Seers were already in place. The ceremony was about to commence. Sure enough, the lights around the stage began to dim. Alex nodded at Jael and Watkins, and the three men went to sit in the section marked out for Alex. The night was finally about to begin.

NICO WAITED in the wings with the other boys. There was a deathly hush amongst them as though they were weighed down with the seriousness of the occasion. Even Percy was looking a little nervous. Then again, he was first on and had to walk the whole circumference of the stage in order to get to his position. Nico was last and he was very grateful for it. He'd only have to take a couple of steps on the stage and he'd be in position. Plus, he was hoping that being last might help make him look duller as well. Or at least last in everyone's thoughts. *Let it be over soon, let it be over soon.* Then he remembered his clumsiness and the chant became *don't let me fall over* instead, which in turn became *don't let me be picked* with a quick *dear Goddess* between each sentence. His heart was speeding up and he began to take deep breaths to slow it down. The deep breathing didn't really help and he was relieved to see the Grandest ready to lead them onto the stage. Just a few more minutes and it would all be over.

The drums rolled, the lights came up, and the Grandest led them out onto the circular stage. Nico followed the boy in front of him, still breathing deep and carefully placing one foot in front of the other. He managed the steps up to the stage with no mishap and knew a moment of relief but that didn't stop him from studying his feet as he walked. He quickly got to his place on the stage and turned outward to the audience as he'd been told. And he found himself face-to-face with the duke. He quickly looked away, a blush rising on his cheeks. Of all the rotten luck. Typical. Well, at least Perfect Man wasn't picking him. Percy had gloated all week that the duke belonged to him. The two had spent a lot of time together, according to Percy, and there were even hints that a kiss had been shared. Percy was welcome to him and really, since the stage was a circle, the duke wouldn't have far to go. Nico had ended up standing next to Percy. He took another deep breath and squared his shoulders. This was the last hurdle. Eight years of education culminated in this moment.

The Grandest had stopped in front of the Goddess whilst the boys took their places and was leading the audience in the first of the ritual prayers. Nico tried to concentrate on the words, but his gaze kept going back to Perfect Man. He was so beautiful. Of course, warriors were violent, everyone knew that. Then there was the constant rumor that they gambled. Nico also believed that they probably drank. No one had ever told him that, but he was sure that they must. Violence and alcohol often went together from what he had gathered in health class. It would stand to reason that all warriors were drunks, then. Except the man didn't look drunk. Not from what Nico could tell, but admittedly he had no experience with drunks. Things like that simply didn't happen in Academia Hall. He could believe the man was violent, though. He could see the strength in his muscles, the way he was relaxed but not relaxed. All that power held tightly under control. He wondered what it would be like to touch those muscles, feel them around him…. He shook his head. No. He would not think about Perfect Man. He'd concentrate on the prayers and his own prayer of freedom.

He closed his eyes and listened to the Grandest drone on. He was getting quite into the zone when it happened. One minute there was the comforting buzz of the Grandest and the next minute there was silence and a hand on his shoulder. He opened his eyes and looked up into the greenest eyes he'd ever seen. The spotlight dazzled him, and he blinked, clearing his vision. The green eyes were still there, and there was still a hand on his shoulder. He looked at Perfect Man in confusion. The duke smiled and said, "I choose you."

PART FIVE

LEAVING THE stage hadn't registered in Nico's consciousness, although he must have done it somehow. He found himself backstage, a hand still firmly on his shoulder and the Grandest giving him hearty congratulations. "My son," he exclaimed, "I knew you would do it. You've made history tonight, history. Congratulations, my son, Your Grace, congratulations. You do realize under the circumstances we'll have to make some adjustments to Nico's commitments, but nothing too worrying I'm sure. History, Your Grace, you've made history."

Nico thought that was a bit much, but he was used to the Grandest's enthusiasm and exaggerations if he was honest. He looked up at the warrior behind him and was surprised to see the man smiling down at him. Surely he'd made a mistake? He was supposed to choose Percy; it was all planned. Typical of the man to let everyone else down, he thought with a scowl. Warriors were known for their self-centered behavior, he was sure. Obviously this was a mix-up that Nico would have to sort out. It didn't look like he'd be getting any help from the Grandest. The duke laughed and leaned down closer to Nico's ear. "Shall we go somewhere and discuss this?" he suggested with a smile.

"I'm not allowed to leave this area," Nico responded, wondering why the hot breath in his ear should feel so good.

"Trust me" was the reply. The hand on his shoulder became a hand on his elbow, and he felt himself being led to the very back of the backstage area and out into a corridor.

"Really, we're not supposed to leave." Nico tried again but was led farther down the corridor to a small room.

"Let's just go in here," said the duke, opening the door and leading him in.

It was a small lounge sometimes used by the Grand Seers as a waiting area before they were due onstage. There were two settees facing each other.

"Tell me what you're thinking," said the duke, seating Nico on one of the settees and taking the seat next to him. He held Nico's hands in his.

"You were supposed to pick Percy," said Nico, looking at their enjoined hands but not doing anything to stop it. "In fact, Percy is probably really upset. Have you thought of that? You've probably hurt Percy."

"Who's Percy?" The duke looked confused and tightened his hold on Nico's hands.

"Percy is the one you were supposed to pick. Not me. I didn't want to be picked." His hands whipped up to his mouth as he realized what he'd said. Now there was going to be trouble. No boy would ever admit that he didn't want to be picked. It just wasn't done.

"You don't want to be picked, baby? Why wouldn't you want to be picked?"

"Er, never mind. Let's not go into that now. You were supposed to pick Percy, so we should go back to the others and get the situation worked out. Just tell them you made a mistake or something."

"But I haven't made a mistake. I picked you. I don't know who Percy is, but he's not who I want. I want you."

Nico looked at him in shock. "But why?"

ALEX PAUSED and took hold of Nico's hands again. He rubbed his thumb against them and was surprised to find calluses. Calluses? What had the boy been doing to get calluses? Really, Alex thought, the boy was mystery upon mystery. How had he got through the Gleaning? He wasn't athletic, musical; he couldn't dance or sing. Or act, apparently. All things expected of a boy at the Gleaning. He appeared to be much more academic than anything else. That was good, though; a well-rounded education would serve a diplomat well. Plus, he was a priest and a healer. Alex wouldn't mind him leading the rituals on holidays and High Days. It would be an excellent thing for the spouse of a duke to do.

"I think we'll work well together," he said softly, "and I think you're hot." He laughed at the bright red blush that resulted. "I'm happy for you to pursue your interests if that's what you're worried about."

"Really?" asked Nico in disbelief. Alex grinned. The boy probably thought he wouldn't be able to pay his priesthood and healing debts. Of course Alex wouldn't stop him. Within reason, anyway.

"Of course," he replied smoothly. "You will always have my support. High Days and holidays are important to the priesthood and to the people. I'm happy that you can lead the people in this way."

Nico looked pensive for a moment and then looked up, a serious expression on his face. "A year and a day?"

"If that's what you want."

"I can follow my own pursuits?"

"Of course. I respect your gifts. We all must pay our debts to the Goddess."

"The Goddess Knows All." Nico nodded, automatically slipping into High Speech.

"Then you agree?" asked Alex, still rubbing Nico's hands.

Another long pause, but then Nico spoke. "I agree."

"Then let's go get married," Alex said with a wide smile and a feeling of triumph.

WHEN THEY returned to the backstage area, Nico was immediately mobbed by two of the Grand Seers. "Nico, where have you been?"

"We've been looking for you."

He was pulled back by the duke and felt an arm around his shoulders. Why did that feel good? He realized the duke was scowling at the Grand Seers and felt compelled to intervene.

"I'm okay, Grand Seer Amos, Grand Seer Esme. We were just talking." Nico didn't have a clue who else had been chosen. He looked around the room, which seemed packed with all the suitors, candidates, and Grand Seers. In the corner he could see Simon and Jake being consoled by Grand Seer Lucy and Grand Seer Tostig. Neither of the boys looked as though they needed consoling. They were both making an effort to look upset but even from across the room, their relief was obvious. Nico was glad for them. He wondered if the boys who were chosen were as pleased. Certainly Deepak was, happily hanging on to the arm of a well-dressed lord. Percy's friends also seemed pleased with their lot. Percy was putting a good face on it, but Nico didn't think he was really pleased. He'd wanted the warrior. They'd even kissed, which was as good a promise as anything. Nico glanced up at the duke. Did the duke know that? He'd spent his life in the military, so perhaps not. Plus, he had heard that warriors were quite wanton. Someone had told him that they were lewd. The duke didn't look lewd or wanton, but Nico had no idea what those things would look like.

"Now, line up, boys," called out Grand Seer Amos, "and er… suitors, of course. Now Nico and er… Your Grace, as the first chosen, you'll be first in line. Come here to the front, boy, and er… Your Grace. That's right. Now Percy, you're next…."

Nico realized just how upset Percy was when the other candidate gave him the evil eye. He was shocked to find there was magickal power behind it and automatically put up his defenses. Really, what was Percy playing at? It wasn't his fault he'd been chosen first, and it wasn't his fault the duke had chosen him. And if Percy didn't know that empowering the evil eye would bring back evil into his own life, then he hadn't been paying much attention in Priest class. Then again, was Percy a priest? Nico wasn't sure that he was. Nico had attained priesthood at an early age, mainly because he was such a good healer. He hadn't really paid attention to who else had attained priesthood. He did vaguely remember a ceremony, but he'd been thinking about the best way to serve vegetables at the time.

Nico decided to put it out of mind and concentrated on his breathing. He had to go back onstage and he hated being onstage. He'd have to talk, he realized to his horror. He had to say his part of the Promise. Nico decided not to think about that now. First he had to get up the steps of the stage. He'd concentrate on that and forget the Promise. Hopefully the Goddess would get him through it somehow. If the Goddess got him through the speaking, then he would deal with the stage steps, he bargained. All he had to do was get up those steps.

It seemed almost too soon that they got the signal to walk onto the stage. One of the duke's arms went around Nico's waist and the other held his hand as he was led into the staging area. He was held so securely that the heavy push he received from Percy at the stages steps didn't matter. He was simply lifted up the steps onto the stage itself. After that they were under the lights, so Percy wouldn't have another chance.

Alex led him to the statue of the Goddess where the Grandest stood, smiling benevolently. This was it. The Goddess should hopefully come up with her side of the bargain now and his voice wouldn't squeak or tremble.

The Grandest beamed at them both, and holding his hands up, began.

"The Goddess Gives Love To Us All, The Goddess Guides Love For Us All, The Goddess Grants Love To You Both Today." He lowered his hands and continued.

"Alexander DeVrie, Duke of the Sixth Land. Do you accept the Gift of the Goddess?"

"I do."

"Do you affirm, attest, and assert that you will walk the path of love?"

"I do."

Nico took a deep breath and squared his shoulders. *Goddess don't let me squeak*, he pleaded silently.

"Nico Stamford, Priest and Healer. Do you accept the Gift of the Goddess?"

"I do."

"Do you affirm, attest, and assert that you will walk the path of love?"

"I do."

Thank Goddess, he hadn't squeaked once. The Grandest raised his hands again.

"I solemnly bear witness to your vows and declare that for one year and one day you shall both walk as one under the Goddess."

And that was it, thought Nico. He was married now.

THEY LEFT the stage and sat in Alex's section, where a small stool had been placed beside Alex's chair. Did that sum them up in some way, wondered Nico. Was he always going to be seen as the smaller, the lesser, the unimportant one? No, the duke had promised he'd be able to follow his own pursuits, and Nico was determined to go as far as he could. It wasn't as though the duke could pull rank or anything. Within the sacred bond of marriage, titles didn't exist.

The other weddings passed in a haze. Nico could hardly get his thoughts in order. He was married now. He'd taken an oath, or rather, two oaths. In turn, they had become a promise, and now he was married, and he wasn't sure he knew how to handle that. It had never been part of his plans. He wasn't even sure why he'd agreed. Now he had to come up with a new plan.

On the bright side he would get to have sex. In fact, he got to have sex with Perfect Man, and he quite liked that idea. Except he wasn't Perfect Man, he was the duke. Alex. No, Nico couldn't call him Alex; it didn't feel right. He'd have to just call him the duke. That felt better. More formal. Perhaps they'd have formal sex.

The duke patted him on the arm and he came out of his reverie. The wedding promises had been made and the Grandest was about to make the concluding remarks. Nico sat up straighter so it looked like he was paying attention. From the corner of his eye, he was aware that the duke smiled, seemingly amused at something. The duke reached over and took his hand, although his eyes never left the Grandest.

"Your Highnesses." The Grandest bowed to the three princes. "Your Grace." He bowed to Alex. "Lords, ladies, gentlemen. We have a historic announcement to make this evening. Truly we have been blessed by the Goddess." The duke sat up and his grasp on Nico's hand tightened.

"Yes, dear friends, it is my privilege, my honor, and very much my pleasure to make this announcement."

"Then get on with it," muttered the duke under his breath. Nico sympathized but knew full well that the Grandest wouldn't be hurried when he had something to say.

"As you know, dear friends, this graduation class began eight years ago. Each candidate has succeeded through each withdrawal. What has never been mentioned is that one candidate succeeded by the Gift of the Goddess at each point. Now, many boys have survived by the Gift of the Goddess during past Gleanings, but most boys only do so once during their apprenticeship. However, this year, one candidate has succeeded at every single point of withdrawal. He has shown a natural talent for the priesthood and healing. Tonight he proved that he is specially chosen by the Goddess. My fellow Grand Seers have prayed and have meditated, and the only true conclusion that we can come to is that this candidate is a Royal Prince of the Goddess." The Grandest paused dramatically, and there was a rumble of hushed voices before the auditorium became quiet again. Nico noticed that his hand was being squeezed harder and it was starting to hurt. He tried to pull away and the hand relaxed but didn't let go.

"Beloved friends," said the Grandest dramatically. "Allow me to present your Prince, Nico of the Sixth Land."

Applause thundered and Nico looked at the Grandest in shock. What was he talking about? Nico wasn't a Prince. He looked to Alex, who was standing up and encouraging him to do so too. The Grandest was gesticulating wildly that Nico should join him on the stage. Alex bowed to him and smiled encouragingly, but Nico could tell he wasn't happy. Dazed and confused, he allowed Alex to help him onto the stage and went and stood by the Grandest.

The older man bowed to him, which was even more confusing. Then he began to speak again. "Those of you who are aware of the traditions will know that with every Prince of the Goddess comes the prophecies. Three prophecies as befits such an important being. These prophecies have been spoken by the highest of the Foresights. If I may, Your Highness?" He lifted a document off the altar and looked to Nico. Nico looked at Prince Alphonse and then back at the Greatest. Did the man mean him? He nodded just in case the Grandest did.

"One. The Prince of the Goddess will feed the people.

"Two. The Prince of the Goddess will heal the sick.

"Three. The Prince of the Goddess will hear the lion roar when he vanquishes the enemy."

"That's four things," objected Nico. There was a smattering of laughter quickly hushed in the audience. The Grandest ignored him.

"Prince Nico of the Sixth Land," he said, grandly waving one hand in Nico's direction.

The room went quiet as Prince Alphonse stood and bowed. "Welcome, my brother," he announced. "We Thank the Goddess for Our Gift."

Princes Elias and Jael also stood, bowed, and chorused, "We Give Thanks to the Goddess for Our Gift." Nico didn't know what to do. He bowed back purely by instinct. He had no idea what to say despite how the Grandest was looking at him. He looked back at Alex for guidance and received more of the encouraging smiling. Except he seemed to mean it this time.

Nico did the only thing he could think of. He slipped into High Speech and gave the concluding address. "The Goddess has Granted Many Gifts this Evening. We Should Go Forth and Celebrate Her Love as We Celebrate Our Own."

If the Grandest was surprised at being robbed of his role, he didn't show it. He enthusiastically joined in the applause that rang about the stage. Nico sent a desperate look to the duke and was relieved when he started to move straight to Nico on the stage. The duke took hold of his hand, and Nico felt stronger. He wanted off the stage. This information needed to be clarified. Had the Grandest just announced he was a Prince? How had that happened? And why were the princes calling him brother? They weren't related.

The applause was still loud, but the duke led him from the stage to the back area. He wasn't given a moment of respite, however, as the

Grandest immediately started to make plans. Nico ignored him. He needed to think.

The duke, however, had no such qualms. "Just what the hell is going on here?" he demanded of the Grandest. The Grandest looked taken aback both at the tone and the question.

"Well, Nico is the Gift of the Goddess, dear duke," he said. "He must now take on the Priestly duties that involves. We must make plans. He must be allowed to reach his full potential. He'll be needed here in the capital, Your Grace. I'm afraid you will have to adapt your plans accordingly."

"You can forget that. Nico and I leave for the Sixth Land tomorrow."

"Tomorrow?" Nico interrupted in horror. "Tomorrow? There's no way that I can be ready for tomorrow. I have too much to do here."

"Precisely," agreed the Grandest. "He has his duties to the Goddess."

"He can fulfill his duties to the Goddess in the Sixth Land," stated the duke coldly. "We leave tomorrow."

"But I've just told you I can't go tomorrow. I have to pack, and there are things I have to buy. I have no idea of what I'm going to need in the Sixth Land. You can't expect me to just take off," Nico protested.

"You can buy anything you need on the way there." The duke wasn't to be budged.

Grand Seers Amos, Lucy, and Esme joined the discussion. "Nico must be trained into his new position, Your Grace," said Grand Seer Lucy. "Surely you can see that?"

"No," Alex stated. "He's trained as a priest and healer already. What more does he need to know?"

"Well, he's a Prince now...," began Grand Seer Esme slowly.

"What difference does that make? He can be a Prince in the Sixth Land. In fact, you announced him as Prince of the Sixth Land. Seems to me that means he should be in the Sixth Land." The duke did not look convinced.

"I suppose that is true," said Esme thoughtfully. "In fact, there are no rules over where a Prince of the Goddess has to live. It may be that his fate does not lie here, brothers and sister."

"Fine," snapped Alex. "We're all agreed, then. Now what do we have to do so we can leave?"

"You can't leave," chorused the Grand Seers, with Amos continuing, "You have to stay for the ball. Nico must be prepared for tonight. You can't just leave. It's unheard of." He looked around and said, "And look, here are the princes to welcome their new brother. You can't take him away."

The duke did not look happy with the new arrivals.

Prince Alphonse came toward them first, holding his hands out to Nico.

"I would welcome you to the family, my dear brother," he said, grasping Nico into his arms. "You are very welcome indeed. We are honored to have a Prince of the Goddess amongst us."

He stepped back, and his brothers also hugged Nico, each with his own welcoming words. Prince Jael turned to Alex and held out his hand. "You're a member of the family now, Alex." He grinned. "Bet you weren't expecting that."

ALEX SHOOK his hand. "Do you know what's going on here, Jael?" Jael took him to one side, allowing the Grand Seers to continue clucking around Nico.

"He's a Prince of the Goddess." Jael spoke quietly. "There's only ever been one before and that was centuries ago. It means that the Goddess has chosen her royalty. Nico is now a member of our family. He's a brother to me, Alphonse, and Elias, and a son of my father. We must go to the palace immediately so that father can meet him."

"Hell no," retorted Alex strongly. "I've only just got him and everyone is trying to take him away. I won't have it." He folded his arms across his chest firmly, his stance one of determination. Nico was beginning to look stressed and it was Alex's duty to protect him. Besides, it wasn't as though the princes could demand that Nico go with them; they could only ask. Even the king could only ask. Nico's privacy was protected by the laws, and Alex was well within his rights to refuse on behalf of his husband. "But Alex, he must meet my father. I think Elias has already made the arrangements."

"No."

"But…."

"No."

They were interrupted by Prince Elias, who effectively stopped Alex's stance by hugging him and welcoming him to the family. "I can think of no one we'd want more," he said.

"You're not taking Nico," Alex responded.

Elias looked shocked. "We have to take Nico; he must meet our father."

Another interruption, this time in the form of Grand Seer Tostig. "Well, the arrangements are made. Prince Nico will go to meet the king accompanied by Their Highnesses. He'll then return to Academia Hall so that he can attend the ball. Then he'll be prepared for… well, I'm sure you know what for, and tomorrow we'll all meet in Grand Seer's office to discuss the Prince's new duties."

"Alex, be reasonable," said Jael. "This is huge. The Grand Seer wasn't lying when he said it was historic. Nico doesn't just belong to you now. He belongs to the whole of the land. He's going to need a lot of support. My brothers and I will support him, but he must go and meet our father. The people must see that the king welcomes his new son. Without the blessing of the king, Nico will find it very hard to perform his duties and pay his debts. You must see that."

Alex grunted. He supposed he could see Jael's point. Nico would need the king's blessing. He had no intention of stopping Nico from performing his duties, but he'd be doing it in the Sixth Land. Alex would need his diplomat. The trip to the palace and back would also give the boy some time to calm himself and gather his thoughts. He looked like he needed the space.

"He can meet the king," he said begrudgingly, "but there'll be no meeting tomorrow. We leave for the Sixth Land first thing."

"First thing." Grand Seer Tostig sounded horrified. "You can't take him tomorrow. That's far too soon." He gave Alex a beseeching look. "If you'll only consider, Your Grace, what tonight is…. Nico may need help tomorrow, some guidance from his Grand Seers, perhaps medical assistance."

"What the hell do you think I'm going to do to him?" roared Alex, affronted and effectively shutting the entire room up. Grand Seer Tostig went bright red, looking around himself in panic.

"No, no, Your Grace, I didn't mean to imply…. Well, it's just that when passions are roused… with the best will in the world… I… er."

"We leave tomorrow first thing," Alex repeated coldly. He looked around the room until he spotted Watkins. The man was standing close to Nico. Not too close since Nico was surrounded by Grand Seers and other candidates, but close enough. Catching Watkins's eye, Alex beckoned him over.

"The Prince will be going to the palace to meet the king. Go with him." He got a grunt in reply but knew his order would be followed.

He turned his attention back to the princes. "You've got one hour," he stated bluntly.

"And that's all we'll need," promised Jael. "Father is too ill to have guests for long."

"Then I want him at my house," he growled at Grand Seer Tostig. "Forget the ball."

"But—"

"I said forget it. Just have the boy delivered to my door."

NICO CLOSED the door on his room and leaned back against it. Alone at last. He'd thought he'd never get another minute to himself. The whole evening had been surreal and he still wasn't quite sure what had happened. The visit to the king, the welcome he received... surely that had happened to someone else. He couldn't be a Prince.

He sat on the bed shrugging out of the horrible bright yellow jacket. At least he wouldn't have to wear that again. In fact, when he thought about it, he realized he'd never have to wear anything he didn't like in future. He didn't have to do things he didn't want to do. He could garden if he wanted. He could spend all the time he wanted reading cookbooks. Freedom. Except for the husband bit of course, but hey! Sex! How much of a problem could a husband be? It was only a year and a day, after all.

He stripped out of his clothes and took a quick shower. It felt good to get under the spray, and the water relaxed him. He dried off and looked to the wardrobe where his second wedding outfit had been hung. Blue silk trousers, calf length, of course. The jacket, though... the jacket was fully buttoned with what looked like a hundred mother-of-pearl buttons. It was made of embroidered silk panels, each one taking hours to work. One of the Grand Seers had given a lengthy lecture on it. Nico had been pondering on the problem of hot water pastry so he hadn't paid much attention. He had to admit it was a very nice suit, if a bit stiff-looking. He thought the color matched his eyes. He saw a pair of silk briefs left on the bed and got the hint that he wasn't to wear anything else under the coat. That was strange. Fashion called for layers of clothing.

Undershirts, shirts, waistcoat, jacket and trousers…. Then a scarf to top it all off. It didn't feel right to wear practically nothing. It might be spring but the night was still cold. He decided to wear his best coat over the outfit. He had no intention of getting cold. He was glad that the jacket slipped over his head and on. He didn't fancy undoing all those buttons. Dressed, he looked at himself in the full-length mirror. He looked okay, he decided. He hated the curls, of course, but for some reason the Grand Seers wouldn't let him cut them off. That was something else he'd be able to change. He grinned at himself in the mirror.

He left the room and made his way down to the dressing room behind the stage. The other boys had long since joined the ball, so the room was empty of all but Grand Seer Esme.

She beamed at him and gestured that he should sit in the chair. Wrapping a protective cover over his clothes, she leaned the chair back and began to apply kohl around his eyes. Once completed, she then applied mascara to his lashes, which always made him want to blink.

"Now, Prince Nico," she began, but he interrupted her.

"Please call me Nico. I don't feel like a Prince."

She took one of his hands. "It will all be all right, you know. She Who Creates the Web Tells the Story, and You Must Never Lose Faith in the Goddess."

"The Goddess is Good," replied Nico automatically. The grip on his hand tightened.

"The Goddess is Good, Nico, and you can have no fear. You are truly blessed, son, and we are very proud of you. Now you must go out into the world and be what you are destined to be." He managed a smile for her but was starting to feel increasingly nervous. He'd be leaving Academia Hall soon, and he didn't really know what was waiting for him.

Grand Seer Esme pulled away the cover and stood back so he could stand. She pointed over to a table where a large wooden box sat. It was beautifully carved. He went over and lifted the lid.

Nico looked in disbelief at the amount of jewelry before him. Good grief, did the man think he had eight arms? No one could possibly wear that amount on two. It was a ridiculous amount of money to spend. Didn't the duke know how much kitchen equipment that would buy? He paused, turning the thought over and over in his head. The jewels wouldn't just buy a whole lot of kitchen, they would buy a whole lot of restaurant too. In fact, there was enough money there to set himself up in business and have lots left over to see him through the first few years. And the jewels belonged to him. Not the duke—Nico. They would form part of his dowry when the year and a day were over. Nico brightened, the jewels before him turning into pots and pans. Ovens and fridges and knives and forks sparkled before his very eyes. Suddenly the jewels didn't seem that bad at all.

He turned his attention to the rings. Ten in all, with one marked specifically for his wedding finger. He carefully lifted the lid on that one. A huge sapphire glittered against a background of cream satin. He lifted the ring out of the box, the light catching on the gold band supporting the sapphire.

Slowly he slid the ring onto his wedding finger. It was a perfect fit and a perfect match to his jacket. That was supposed to be lucky, he remembered. To match the stone to the jacket. How had the duke done that? Grand Seer Esme gasped when she saw it. "Oh, my goodness, could this day become more portent? Oh, Nico, you are so blessed."

Nico didn't answer, but he allowed her to choose some of the bangles and bracelets to add to his outfit. The rest of the rings were placed on his fingers. He felt like a yuletide tree and wasn't sure he liked it. The jewelry felt heavy and unnatural. He didn't think he'd be wearing much of it in the future. He looked at his wedding ring again. Would the duke insist he continue to wear it? Did he have the right to refuse? He was a Prince now, which placed him above the duke. Not wearing it might indicate that he wasn't really committed, though, and Nico had made a promise. At least one that would last a year and a day. That ring could stay, he decided. The rest of them could stay in the box once the night was over. Grand Seer Esme finished fussing and turned Nico so that he could see himself in the mirror at the end of the room. His eyes opened wide. Did a bit of kohl and mascara make that big a difference? Clearly it did. He had a more exotic look and the jewels only added to that. Of course, the lighting helped, he thought dismissively. What did it matter how he looked anyway? Look at Percy, who was considered to be incredibly beautiful. The horrible character still showed through, and as far as Nico was concerned, Percy was ugly.

The grumpy old man who generally accompanied the duke came in the door. He'd been with Nico since Nico had been separated from the duke.

The man bowed. "If you're ready, Your Highness, it's time to leave."

"But the ball...."

"The duke doesn't want you attending the ball. You're to be taken straight to the duke's home" was the gruff response. "Come along, lad. We don't keep the duke waiting."

Nico looked over at Grand Seer Esme in confusion. "But I haven't said good-bye to anyone."

"You can do that by screen, lad. It's time to be moving now," interrupted the older man. He clearly wasn't going to budge.

Nico shrugged and went over to kiss Grand Seer Esme good-bye. "You'll tell the others that I wanted to say good-bye?" he asked and she nodded. He realized by the tears forming in her eyes that she couldn't actually speak, so he hugged her. Turning toward the door, he made his way into his new life.

PART SIX

ALEX TURNED to see Nico paused on the steps leading down to the chamber. His blond curls peeped out from beneath a silken hood, and Alex slowly lowered his eyes to take in the full picture of his boy before him.

His eyes had been outlined in kohl and his lashes dyed sooty black. He looked exotic, exquisite, and... altogether far too nervous, Alex thought, noting the tremble of Nico's hands, the rise and fall of his chest as he breathed a touch too quickly, and the cautious trepidation in those beautiful blue eyes.

Alex smiled gently, encouragingly as he held out one hand. "Come here," he said softly. "Let me see you."

Nico started, his eyes momentarily widening in fear. Then it was gone, and he took a deep breath and squared his shoulders.

"Can't you see me from over there?" Nico asked, his tone one of High Speech and only a slight waver to his voice.

Alex grinned both at the tone and the content. Time for the High Speech barrier to come tumbling down.

"Ah, but if you come over here, I don't just get to see you. I get to touch you too." His smile was playful. "And I want to touch you very badly."

Nico took a step back.

"I think you're supposed to admire the gown," he said quickly. "It's been specially made and a lot of work went into it."

"It's a beautiful robe, Nico, almost worthy of the man inside it."

"Each panel took eighteen hours to complete, at least I think it was eighteen, it might have been eight, I wasn't really paying attention. I do know, however, that it was a long time. I mean I wouldn't want to spend eight hours embroidering one of these panels, would you?"

"Actually, I think they take about eighty hours," murmured Alex somewhat apologetically.

"Eighty hours?" Nico looked at him in disbelief and horror. "Eighty hours on one panel? Why on earth would they do that? Didn't they get bored?"

"Presumably they enjoy the work."

"Really?" Nico looked doubtful and then appeared to shake the thought off. He took another deep breath and once again squared his shoulders. "Well, clearly you haven't admired the robe enough. We're told that it's a really important part of the ceremony. The robe is supposed to represent…." He looked lost for a moment but quickly revived. "It's supposed to represent something, I just can't remember what it is at the moment. I know." He brightened. "You could spend some time admiring the front and then I can turn around and you can admire the back for a while."

An image of that sweet, tight ass inserted itself into Alex's mind and he groaned. Enough of this. It was time to get the boy into his arms and into his bed. Who needed a robe when there was so much perfection promised beneath it? The boy needed to stop prevaricating and…. Alex stopped. Why was the boy prevaricating? He suddenly saw the scene from Nico's eyes. His boy was scared.

"Come here," he said softly. "Let me touch you."

Nico must have realized that he wasn't going to get any more mileage out of the robe and he sighed deeply, clasping his hands together so that the heavy rings clashed. He looked down at them in annoyance and began removing one of the bigger rings, twisting it off his finger.

"I think that's my privilege," murmured Alex, crossing over to the boy and gently taking the ring from his hand. He retained hold of Nico's hand but didn't pull, merely held it, allowing Nico to take his time.

"I don't think we should rush into this," Nico said with a hint of desperation.

"We're not rushing into anything. We're just moving it along a little."

Nico shivered and Alex's smile turned into a grin. "Are you cold?" he asked. "Or are you excited?" That brought another shiver. Excited it was, then.

There was another sigh, another deep breath, and another squaring of shoulders.

"I may not be very good at this," Nico began cautiously. "I may suffer from performance anxiety."

"Performance anxiety?" Alex raised one eyebrow.

"Yes," said Nico, then acting like a man compelled to give evidence against himself, he continued. "I may not get an erection, for example."

Alex eyed the bulge beneath Nico's robe. "I don't think we have to worry about that," he murmured, moving closer to the bed.

"Or I may suffer from premature ejaculation," Nico continued, clearly warming to his subject. "That's when you orgasm too quickly. Or I may just feel so overwhelmed that I can't perform anyway. That's why they call it performance anxiety." He took a deep breath and looked straight into Alex's eyes. "Actually I'm not sure that I can perform. I've never been able to perform before: acting, singing, and dancing. I've never been able to do any of them and this is like being asked to dance without practicing the steps first. In fact, I don't really know what the steps are… I mean I know what the steps are, I just haven't been taught how to do it. In fact, it's not fair to expect me to perform if I haven't had practice first, don't you think? Perhaps we should put this off until I've had a chance to practice?"

"I'm the one you practice with, boy," Alex growled possessively. "I'm the one who teaches you the steps, and we're gonna dance just fine."

He tugged Nico toward him and Nico automatically responded, coming to a stop directly in front of Alex on the marble floor.

Alex reached out to pull Nico in closer, only to have him jump back with a start. "Oh," Nico said quickly. "You may hurt me and I may cry out."

Alex stilled. "I'm not going to hurt you, baby." The words were both a whisper and a vow.

NICO LOOKED into Alex's eyes and he shivered again. Alex moved closer, reached out to slowly trace the curve of Nico's cheekbone.

"We should make you more comfortable," Alex murmured, slowly leading Nico toward the bed. "And Nico, any crying out you do with me will be in pleasure, not pain." His smile was slow and seductive. "I have so much to teach you, baby."

"I, er, I've always wondered what it would be like," Nico confided. "The Grand Seers don't really go into detail."

"No?" Alex sat down on the bed and widened his knees, pulling Nico to stand between them.

"I'm here to teach you all the things the Grand Seers didn't," he promised. He picked up one of Nico's hands and gently began to remove each ring. He paused when he reached Nico's wedding ring finger, studying the pale perfection of the sapphire. Lifting the hand, he bowed down to kiss the knuckle above the ring.

"How did you know? How did you know what color my robe would be?"

Alex looked up to see Nico's eyes upon him. Beautiful eyes, sapphire eyes. Eyes that gleamed greater than the gem upon his finger. "What makes you think that I knew? Surely this is just another sign that the Goddess approves our match?"

"Hah!" snorted Nico. "You would never leave anything to chance. Every report ever written about you is clear on that."

"Every report?" Alex looked up in delight. "You've read every report?"

Nico blushed and sputtered before finally saying, "We're required to have some knowledge of the suitors. We're given a bio of everyone."

"Ah, but you said every report ever written," retorted Alex playfully. "That means that you read more. Did you read more about old Taylor? Did you look further into him?"

He removed the last of the rings, leaving the sapphire firmly in place. When Nico didn't reply, he laughed. "I didn't think so." He smirked, moving on to remove the bangles and bracelets decorating Nico's wrists.

"You've been very generous, Your Grace." Nico nodded toward the growing pile of treasure heaped onto the bed. "But you still haven't told me how you knew about the color of the robe."

Alex grinned. "I knew they'd match the color of your eyes. But it was the Grace of the Goddess that allowed me to find a sapphire that matched both."

The last of the jewelry gone, Alex leaned back and studied the boy in front of him. He reached up to entangle his fingers in the loose blond curls, then slowly started to massage Nico's scalp. "I love this hair," he whispered, fingers moving in gentle circles toward the back of his head and coming to rest on the nape of his neck. Nico shivered again, but he never took his eyes away from Alex. Alex pulled him down and pressed his lips lightly against Nico's mouth. He stood up, gathering Nico in his arms and applying firmer pressure. He edged his lips along the crease of Nico's mouth and when Nico gave a soft gasp, Alex made good use of the open mouth, delving his tongue inside, teasing and touching, and tasting and testing. Nico relaxed into the embrace, opening wider and using his own tongue to do some tasting himself. Alex allowed him to lead the kiss for a few moments before he took control back. He moved his hand back up to Nico's nape and he massaged the muscles until he felt Nico relax. He moved his mouth to Nico's neck, nibbling on the skin there before moving on to savor an earlobe. He pulled at the lobe with his teeth, keeping his touch light, just the faintest of sensations.

"Oh," said Nico in surprise, melting into the embrace.

"Oh?" asked Alex, continuing with soothing kisses along the line of Nico's jaw, edging his way back to the enticement of those luscious lips. Another deep kiss, more ardent and forceful. He moved his hands to frame Nico's face, holding him in position as he elicited a response better than he could have hoped for. Nico was returning his embrace with fervor and enthusiasm. Alex felt a rush going through his body as the kiss continued. Nico was intoxicating, and Alex felt heady with the thrill of it all. They broke the kiss, both needing air, yet eager to continue.

"Are we going to have sex now?" asked Nico shyly, his cheeks blushed pink.

"Soon." Alex smiled. "Let's get to know one another first. I want to explore every part of you and weren't we making you more comfortable?" He moved to the buttons of the wedding coat, working the top one open and then continuing down.

"It will come off over my head," interjected Nico. "It would be much quicker. That's how I put it on."

"Ah, but I want to take my time." Alex continued with the buttons, widening the opening so he could drop a kiss on Nico's collarbone. Nico shivered again. His reactions delighted Alex. When the coat was fully open, he slipped his hands inside, feeling his way around Nico's body. His skin was smooth as silk, so soft, so delectable. He loved the sensation on his hands and stroked the boy's sides, easing round to stroke his back and then back to the front again. He could feel Nico trembling, little jolts shuddering through his body. Alex's mouth returned to Nico's neck as his hands freed Nico's shoulders from the wedding coat. It slithered down Nico's arms and fell to the floor to be forgotten by them both.

"Oh," said Nico, and he received a kiss for his effort. Then a deeper kiss, more rousing, more commanding. Nico's arms went around Alex's shoulders, and he clung there as the kiss developed further. A sense of urgency crept in, growing slowly as it built in momentum. Alex wrapped his arms around Nico, pulling him closer. He could feel Nico's erection against him and moved his hands to Nico's buttocks, kneading the flesh he found there.

"Oh." A groan this time and Nico began to move his hips, grinding against Alex.

Alex laughed. "Oh no, I've got more to explore yet." He picked Nico up and dropped him on the bed, enjoying his startled gasp. Pulling off his shirt, Alex joined Nico on the bed. "Now, where do I want to go next? I know, let's have a look at this." He ran his hands over Nico's chest, feeling the shape of his shoulders and tracing down his arms with light strokes of his fingertips. Nico quivered, his breath coming in short pants, and his eyes half-closed. Alex placed a string of kisses along Nico's collarbone whilst he moved his fingers in ever decreasing circles across the boy's chest. He was surprised and extremely pleased to discover that Nico had defined muscle tone, firm to the touch. Alex couldn't resist. He had to keep touching. So much lovely smooth skin encasing some very appealing muscles. He moved down Nico's chest, kissing his way until he paused just above one nipple. Nico's breath was coming faster now, his chest rising up and down in a fervent rhythm. Alex bent down and touched his tongue to the nipple, one light quick stroke.

"Oh." Nico's voice was higher, a spasm running through his body. Alex did it again and again. He alternated between quick flicks of his tongue and blowing cool breath across the nipple. It stood up to attention as though begging for more. He moved over to the other nipple and began to do the same there. Nico's body went taut, and he took a deep shuddering breath as he lifted his chest closer to Alex's mouth.

"Oh please," he whimpered, "please." Alex continued rubbing his hands over Nico's sides, his shoulders. He played with the creases in Nico's elbows, loving the tingles that shook Nico's frame when he did. He wanted the boy so whipped up that his whole body vibrated. He moved back to kissing Nico, feeling his way and then thrusting his tongue in and out of Nico's mouth. He wanted Nico to know just what he was going to do to him. Nico groaned and, wrapping his arms around Alex's shoulders, pulled him closer. Alex was delighted. His boy had passion. He moved his hand down to Nico's belly button, and then slipping his hand under Nico's clothes, he tangled his fingers into the trail of hair below. It wasn't enough, and he quickly undid Nico's trousers and pushed down his briefs. Nico's cock was revealed and what a cock it was. Alex's mouth watered but he held himself back, only tracing light circles on the flesh above it, not touching the cock itself, though Goddess knew he wanted it in his mouth. He went back to kissing Nico, the stab stab stab of his tongue building up into an age-old rhythm. He moved his hand closer and closer, eliciting more trembling, more gasps.

Nico began to struggle, moaning against Alex's mouth and then pulling himself away from Alex. "I'm going to… I'm gonna…."

"That's right, baby," Alex crooned. "Come for me. Let me see you, baby. Show me."

At his words Nico went stiff beneath him and come erupted from his dick, spurting all over his abdomen. Alex held the boy throughout, his eyes never leaving Nico's cock.

"That's right, baby. You're so hot, babe, so hot." He moved his fingers through the come, placing gentle kisses on Nico's lips, and Nico's breath slowed and his body began to relax. Alex lifted his fingers to his mouth and licked them. "You taste good, babe. Can't wait till I get you in my mouth." He bent down and licked the come from Nico's stomach, feeling Nico's heart start to slow, his breaths evening out. He smiled to himself when he felt Nico's hand in his hair, stroking his scalp softly, tentatively. Was there anything sexier than this, he wondered, looking at the feast beneath him. He raised his head.

"Feeling good?"

"Feeling so good," sighed Nico as he dropped his hands to the sides, eyes closed. Suddenly he sat up, eyes wide open and horror-struck.

"Was that a premature ejaculation?"

"No, baby, there was nothing premature about that."

"But you haven't…."

"We've got all night, baby, all night."

NICO'S SHOULDERS slumped and he relaxed back on the bed. It wasn't premature, thank the Goddess. It hadn't hurt either, so why would the Grand Seers… oh. He remembered why. They hadn't done *that*. He wondered if that might be the more formal sex. Goddess knew there'd been nothing formal about what had just happened. He closed his eyes, vaguely aware that Alex, er, the duke, had left the bed. Should he still call him the duke? It seemed a bit ridiculous considering the intimacy they'd just shared. Alex didn't seem right, though, not yet. Perhaps if he called him "duke" in public and nothing in private. That could work.

Calling him the duke wouldn't work in private situations, that's for sure. *Please put my cock in your mouth, Your Grace.* The blood rushed to his face at the thought, and his dick sat up and took notice. Was there something wrong with him? He lifted his head from the pillow and looked down his body. Traces of come remained smeared over him and his dick thickened even more when he remembered Alex... the duke licking it from his body. He sighed. He was going to have to drop the "duke." It just wasn't working. The man in question appeared at the side of the bed holding a damp washcloth. "Come on," he said, "let's clean you up," and proceeded to do just that.

Nico lay back and wondered if he could blush any hotter. Surely Alex could see that he was getting erect again.

"Is there something wrong with me?" He spoke when he should have thought instead.

Alex looked at him in alarm. "Why would you say that?"

"I'm getting hard again." He should have kept that to himself too. He cursed his innate need to be honest.

"That's not a bad thing, Nico. That's a really, really good thing." Alex finished cleaning him up and lay down on the bed next to him. It was nice, comforting, to feel the warmth of another person's body. Nico didn't think he'd ever experienced that before. It felt special. He wanted to hold on to the moment, cherish it. He didn't want it to end.

His dick was starting to throb, though, and Alex's hands on his body only made the situation worse. Rising, he turned to face Alex and reached out to touch his cheekbone. He had haughty cheekbones, Nico decided. Sharp angles on a strong rectangular face. Alex really was Perfect Man, in looks at least, and right now all Nico was bothered about was looks. His own character would have to have depth when he was out of bed because right now, right this moment, all he could see was a beautiful man, a powerful man, and a man fully in control of all of that power. He reached out to touch Alex's biceps, stroking down his arm and then traveling back up again. He couldn't take his eyes off Alex's chest and moved his hand to feel there. Strength lay coiled tightly in the kissable muscles, and Nico didn't resist. Moving forward he dropped lots of tiny kisses, summoning up his courage to go closer and closer to that delectable flat nipple. When he finally kissed there, Alex groaned. "Suck, boy, suck." Nico did as he was bid, feeling deliciously naughty. He rolled his tongue around the nipple and then sucked on the point, thrilled as he felt it grow in his mouth. This sex stuff was seriously good. He could feel Alex's groans rumbling through his chest, urging Nico on and sparking off a totally unexpected response. His blood pounded and his breath quickened. His hands followed a path down Alex's sides and he felt the warrior shudder. Victory hummed in Nico's blood, and he lazily licked at the nipple whilst his hands investigated Alex's hips, pushing down at his trousers.

Alex rolled him onto his back and kissed him. Nico relished the feel of Alex's tongue in his mouth. He could do this all day. He pulled Alex closer, fingers entangling in the hair at Alex's nape, feeling and being possessed by a lust he'd never known before. He needed to keep riding the sensation, needed to keep building up this incredible excitement. It was stopped when Alex pulled away, and Nico reached out for him, desperate to bring him back close. "Shh," murmured Alex. "I'm coming back." He got off the bed and stripped out of his trousers, pausing by the side of the bed to allow Nico to look at him. Nico sat up and looked. His mouth fell open and his eyes widened. Alex smiled. The blood left Nico's dick and traveled up to his cheeks.

"You're not putting *that* in me," Nico said, moving back on the bed. "You can forget it. The Grand Seers were right. That's going to hurt. I thought they were exaggerating when they talked about medical assistance, but dear Goddess, no. Just no." He shook his head vehemently, grabbing at the covers on the bed and hauling them over him as though they were armor.

Alex grinned as he climbed back on the bed. "There's lots of things we can do, Nico, lots of things that feel real good. Didn't you feel good before?"

"Yes," Nico admitted reluctantly. He didn't let go of the covers, hunching them up tighter to his chest, but Alex pulled them away with no effort at all. He drew Nico into his arms and cuddled him tight, rubbing his back and dropping kisses on his head. Nico began to relax again. They didn't have to do "it"? That sounded good to him. His dick started to thicken again, and he lifted his face for more kissing. Kissing was good. Alex didn't disappoint him and for a few moments there was nothing but that fervid communion and the sound of their gasps and groans. Something inside him started to build and his breaths turned into pants, his heart palpitating. Alex moved down the bed and dear Goddess, he took Nico in his mouth. For a moment Nico couldn't breathe, couldn't believe the feeling of that hot mouth on his throbbing dick. Alex took him to the root, and Nico's hips lifted off the bed of their own accord. Nothing had ever felt this good. Every time that Alex pulled off his dick, he wanted to thrust it back into the man's mouth. When Alex started to lick around the glans and crown, Nico thought he'd go through the roof. So many feelings and sensations flooding through him. He started to pant heavily, his body out of control and the desperate need to rut overtaking all other feelings. That wonderful mouth took him back down to the root, and a warm hand cupped his balls, rolling them gently. It wasn't enough; the intensity and awe of the moment were all sending him dizzy, but he knew that it wasn't enough. His movements increased in tempo, and he grabbed at Alex's head, demanding more, never ceasing in his determination to reach the summit. To go over the summit. The hand at his balls moved farther back, stroking over his skin there, adding more fire to the flame. His whole body felt as though it was glowing. He could barely breathe anymore, and when Alex pressed one finger against his anus, he yelled out, coming so strongly that he spasmed with each wave. Alex caught it all in his mouth, swallowing down the come and not allowing a drop to spill. He moved back up the bed and kissed Nico deeply, allowing him to taste himself on Alex's tongue. Nico was surprised to discover how sexy that was and wallowed in the kiss as his heart rate slowed and his muscles relaxed. Then he felt Alex's penis erect against his hip and he reached down to touch.

Alex laughed and rolled onto his back. "Come on, baby, show me what you've learned," he encouraged. Nico didn't need to be told twice. Hadn't he always been a good student in the classes that mattered to him? He worked his way down Alex's body, learning his way with his hands. When he got to the magnificent dick, he paused, wanting to take his time. Alex's dick was fully erect and proud, jutting out from his body, beckoning Nico closer, tempting him with its allure. Nico leaned closer, reaching out with his tongue to lick at the crown and relishing the consequent shudder that went through the warrior. His warrior. He opened his mouth, taking in the whole of the head and trying to go down smoothly. It didn't go well at the first attempt, and Alex guided Nico's hand to the root of his penis. "Use your hand, babe."

Nico wrapped his hand around the dick, holding softly at first but gaining in confidence with each dip of his head. He moved more fluently, learning the language of Alex's body, firming his grip but not by too

much, just until Alex began to groan and move his hips. Having his hand
at the base of Alex's penis meant he didn't have to choke, but he still
wanted to go down farther. To do to Alex what had been done to him.
Why in the Goddess's name had he never paid attention in Eros class? He
should have made more of an effort with that banana. He bobbed down
again a little farther this time, loving the feel of dick in his mouth, using
his tongue as he teased around the crown. He couldn't decide whether
he liked licking around the head or feeling the fullness of an erect cock
right at the back of his throat. Saliva flooded out of his mouth making the
movement of up and down easier. It was thrilling, liberating. If this was
what marriage was like, then he was all for it.

Giving was every bit as exciting as receiving, he discovered. Alex
murmured and moaned, and Nico felt powerful. He'd never known a
feeling like it, and he wanted more. Using one hand at the base of Alex's
cock and continuing to stimulate with his lips and tongue, he reached
down with his other hand and cradled Alex's balls in his hand. The
delicate sensitive skin there called to him, and he moved his mouth down,
needing to feel it against his tongue. The scent of Alex was stronger now
and filled him with more lust, and he took one of Alex's testicles into his
mouth, sucking gently before turning his attention to the other one and
doing the same. His fingers sought the space behind Alex's balls and he
stroked there lightly, trying to copy the way Alex had done this to him.
He used Alex's moans to let him know whether he was getting it right or
not. When Alex started to breathe quicker, he thrilled once again at the
sensation of power that flooded through him.

Once again he took the cock in his mouth but he didn't stop stroking
Alex's perineum, loving the feel of the taut skin and the way Alex
trembled beneath his hands. He knew without warning that Alex was
close to coming, and he wanted to see that. Wanted to watch the way Alex
had watched him come earlier. His own dick was throbbing again and
he rubbed himself against the sheets, wanting friction, needing friction.
Alex's hand suddenly came down on the back of his head and urged him
to continue bobbing down, taking more and more of the dick until Alex
cried out and come shot into Nico's mouth. The exhilaration of the hot
spunk spurting to the back of his throat brought on another climax for
Nico, and he was overwhelmed by the emotions that rushed through his
body. Nico couldn't swallow quick enough, and Alex's semen dripped out
of his mouth, only adding to the lust still coursing through his blood. He

fell back panting, sweat dampening his hair and his chest, semen dripping from his dick. Alex wrapped his arms around him, holding Nico to his chest as they both allowed their pulse rates to slow.

"Hell, babe, you're one fast learner." Alex exhaled heavily. "Are you sure you haven't done that before?"

"Only with a banana and I choked on that."

Alex lifted his head, obviously confused. "A banana?"

"It's what they taught us in Eros class," yawned Nico, snuggling down and closing his eyes. Now that he was replete, he realized how tired he was. It had been a very long day, and he felt quite exhausted. He pressed a kiss to Alex's chest. "I liked that," he said drowsily. "Can we do it again?"

"As often as you like, babe" came the reply. "As often as you like." A reciprocal kiss landed on the top of his head, and Nico drifted away into sleep.

PART SEVEN

WAKING ALONE and in a strange bed, it took Nico a moment to remember where he was. He couldn't ever remember being so refreshed. He stretched out, luxuriating in the feel of the linen sheets. Last night had been incredible. This marriage business was proving to be a really good idea. No wonder the Grand Seers had raved about it. But then, none of them were married, so how would they know? He dismissed the thought out of his head and turned to look at the empty space beside him. Where had Alex... the duke gone? Nico wanted to snuggle up some more. A noise from the doorway disrupted his thoughts.

"Ah, you're awake," said the duke, carrying a tray into the room. "How did you sleep, babe?"

"Like a log." Nico yawned and sat up. "Is that breakfast?"

Alex placed the tray on the bed, then leaned forward to drop a kiss on Nico's mouth. "Eat up, and then go and get showered and dressed. We leave for the Sixth Land in a couple of hours."

"But I can't go, I don't have any clothes," Nico protested as he took some fresh melon from the tray. He ignored the coffee and looked to the fruit juice instead. "And I have to get all my things from Academia Hall."

"It's all been done, Nico. Your clothes are packed and on their way to the Sixth Land. There's an outfit ready for you in the dressing room." Alex sat on the side of the bed and gave Nico another slice of melon. "Anything else you need you can get from the Commercial Web once we're in Tarn."

"Tarn?"

"Yes, it's the harbor at the bottom of the Sixth Land. We'll fly there and then travel by land to the castle."

"There's a castle?"

Alex laughed and took a sip of the coffee. "Yes, there's a castle. It's said to be something of a folly. We'll live there as long as we like it. If we don't, we'll build something else."

"You shouldn't drink that. It's very bad for you."

"What? Coffee? I drink it every morning," replied Alex, somewhat taken aback. "Why? What's wrong with it?"

Nico sighed. "It's a stimulant and can be addictive. How much do you drink?"

"A cup, maybe two." Alex looked into the cup as though he'd be able to spot the dangers.

"That's not so bad, then. I've known people who drink thirty cups a day." Nico smiled brightly. "If it's only one or two cups it won't be so hard to stop." He munched on some grapes and took a sip of his fruit juice. Elderflower mixed with apple juice created the taste he loved so much. "So good," he breathed in satisfaction. "How did you know I loved this?"

"The Grand Seers have been very helpful," replied Alex, still looking deep into the cup of coffee. "So I have to give this up?"

"Don't think of it as 'giving up,' think of it as 'stopping,'" advised Nico, returning his attention to the fresh fruit.

"So why did the founders bring it with them if it's so bad?"

"They had to bring a complete ecology. Besides, it's not always bad. Sometimes it can be a very helpful medicine. You shouldn't drink it every day, though. Don't worry, it won't be that hard to stop. You can drink some herbal tea instead. I have lots of good recipes."

Alex didn't look convinced but put the cup back on the tray. Nico beamed at him.

"A couple of your tutors are here," said Alex, standing up. "Come out when you're ready."

"Tutors?" Nico placed his fruit juice back on the tray and started to get out of the bed. Then he remembered he was naked, turned bright pink, and pulled the covers back over himself. This earned a grin from Alex, who went over to the huge mahogany wardrobe and pulled out a robe.

"Probably too big for you." He handed the robe to Nico. "But it will protect your innocence for a little while longer," he added with a wink. Nico blushed harder but accepted the robe.

"I'll be downstairs. Take your time," Alex said, dropping another kiss on Nico's head. He turned and left the room.

Alone again, Nico slipped on the robe and got out of the bed. The robe was far too big for him, but he loved the way it wrapped around him and it carried Alex's scent. Once showered, he found clothes laid out and ready for him. Not his favorite suit, but not the worst by a long mark. He really had to get his own clothes. He'd had enough of frills and lace. He looked in the mirror. The curls would have to go too.

Making his way downstairs, he followed the sound of voices and found himself in a beautifully proportioned room. Alex was there along with Grand Seers Lucy and Amos. They all stood when he came into the room, and both of the Grand Seers bowed to him. Nico blinked. He was never going to get used to people bowing to him. It just wasn't natural. He bowed to other people, not the other way around. Alex held out his hand, and Nico went willingly to his side. He felt more secure standing next to him.

"Your Highness," began Grand Seer Lucy. "I trust we find you well?"

"Yes, thank you. I'm very well."

"I'm delighted to hear that, Nico. I mean, Your Highness."

"Please, call me Nico. You've always called me Nico, and please, sit down."

"Your situation has changed now, dear," Grand Seer Lucy said kindly. "But if you insist. We're here to discuss your future, Nico. We must make plans."

"We've already resolved that," Alex said coldly. "Nico is coming to the Sixth Land with me."

"Of course, of course," said Grand Seer Lucy. "We have no problem with that. We do need to go over his responsibilities with His Highness, though. We want only to guide his path."

"Indeed," agreed Grand Seer Amos. "Nico will need guidance in his new role. We intend to see to that. In fact, if we may have some privacy with His Highness, Your Grace?"

"Why do you need privacy?" demanded Alex, pulling Nico against his side.

Nico placed one hand on the duke's chest. "It's okay," he said. "It's probably something to do with the priesthood. I'm sure it won't take long." Alex didn't look convinced but didn't speak further when Prince Elias strode into the room accompanied by Prince Jael. The Grand Seers stood up again. More bows all around the room, and Nico wondered if he'd ever get used to it.

"We're here to see our brother," announced Prince Elias grandly.

Alex rolled his eyes. "You'll have to wait in turn. The Grand Seers got here first."

"That's all right," interrupted Prince Jael. "We could do with speaking to you first, anyway."

Alex sighed heavily. He kissed Nico on the head. "I'll be in the room across the hall," he said. "If you need me, just yell."

NICO WAITED until the three men had left the room and turned to the Grand Seers. "May I get you some refreshments?" he asked politely, sitting down when they shook their heads.

"Nico," Grand Seer Amos began, "we must talk about a situation of great delicacy."

Nico immediately blushed. Were they going to talk about sex? *Dear Goddess, don't let them talk about sex.*

"There's a growing problem in the Sixth Land," continued Grand Seer Lucy, and Nico relaxed. Thank Goddess for that. It wasn't about sex. "We've known of troubles for some time, but it's getting worse and the news from the parish there worries us."

Nico listened politely. What did this have to do with him? Oh yes, the priesthood.

"As the head of our religion, you have an important role to play, Nico. You must be a presence in the Sixth Land. You will be leading the people there. You must be active in the parish."

Head of the religion? When did that happen? Oh yes, the Prince thing.

"I'm not sure that I should be seen as the head of our religion, Grand Seer Lucy. After all, you all know so much more about it than I do."

She dismissed his words with a wave of a hand. "Nonsense," said Grand Seer Lucy. "You have been chosen by the Goddess. This is only the second time that it has happened in our history. You must take your rightful place. The Grand Seers in the Sixth Land are depending on you. But listen closely, Nico. There are enemies everywhere, and you must be careful who you place your trust in. Events are overtaking us and we must pray for resolution."

"Em, if I may?" asked Grand Seer Amos. "Nico, we have a message we want you to take to our brothers and sisters in the Sixth Land. It must be a secret, Nico. Tell no one and let no one see the message. Do you understand?"

"Er, yes, I think so." Nico was mystified. Why didn't they just send a letter or an e-mail? Were they always so paranoid? He'd never noticed it before. Still, if he could help the Grand Seers, it was undoubtedly his duty to do so.

Grand Seer Amos stood up and took a letter from his pocket. "Remember, Nico, this is only meant for the Grand Seers in the Sixth Land. Do not allow anyone else to look upon its contents." He thrust the envelope toward Nico, who took it and looked blankly at it.

"Hide it, Nico," cautioned Grand Seer Lucy. "Don't allow anyone to know that you have it." Nico stuffed it in his pocket, ensuring it was fully hidden. The Grand Seers stood, and Grand Seer Lucy came forward and kissed Nico's cheek. "Now, dear, you know that we're only a call away. This is an exciting time for you, and we want you to enjoy it, but if you need any guidance at all...."

"I'll call you," promised Nico.

ACROSS THE hallway, the conversation between Alex and Elias wasn't going so well.

"You must understand our position, Alex. At a time like now when the monarchy is under threat, and I don't say that lightly, we need our brother with us."

"Well, you can't have him. He's mine and he's coming with me."

Elias threw his hands in the air and turned to Jael for help. Jael shrugged. "Who knows, Elias? Perhaps the Sixth Land is where we need Nico to be."

"I'm not so sure, Jael. The situation is escalating every day. Nico is the head of our religion now. The people need him here."

"If the rumors are true, then the people of the Sixth Land need him more," inserted Alex, folding his arms across his chest. "Either way, I need him. I need a diplomat as well, you know. The fact that he's a priest and healer can only be of added benefit. As for being head of the religion, well, there's always the Social Web. People can see him on that."

"Really?" Jael looked shocked. "I thought you didn't approve of the Social Web for all you have a presence there."

"I don't, and I don't intend for Nico to have anything to do with it, but I can arrange for my staff to see to his Social Web presence just like they see to mine. We'll control his page and whatever is put on it. That will have to do. Now as far as I'm concerned, this topic is closed. Nico and I leave for the Sixth Land in an hour. If you want to spend time with your brother, I suggest you do it now."

"And teach him what? In the space of an hour?" Elias protested. "He needs to learn our ways. He hasn't been born to it like we have."

"He's been a student of Academia Hall for eight years, Elias. What else does he have to learn? He understands and is fluent in High Speech—believe me, he's very fluent. He understands the priesthood, he understands society, and he understands his role in it. There's nothing more for him to learn here."

"We must know our brother." Elias was adamant, but Alex wouldn't be moved.

"So talk to him over comms."

"Look." Jael spoke up. "We're going around in circles. Elias, you're not going to win this argument. Nico is going with Alex whether you like it or not, and you know—" He paused. "—I think Alex is right. The problems lie in the Sixth Land and any resolution must come from there. We can stay in touch through comms. If Nico needs to speak to us, if he needs advice, then we're one call away. Plus, I'm going to be following them over there in a couple of weeks. Our immediate concern must be Alphy. You know that, and there's nothing Nico can do to help with Alphonse."

Elias looked at him. "If our father—"

"If anything happens to your father, then I can fly Nico straight back. He can be here in a matter of hours," Alex promised.

Elias didn't look convinced but gave up the argument. "We Must Trust in the Goddess," he said.

Alex laughed. "You and Nico are like twin peas in a pod. He reverts to High Speech when he can't get his own way too. Come on, let's see if the Grand Seers have finished with Nico." He led them out of the room.

They found Nico alone in the sitting room. He was staring out of the window, deep in thought, and Alex went straight to him.

"Everything okay?" he asked, cradling Nico's cheek with one hand.

"Yes, everything is fine." Nico smiled up at him.

"What did the Grand Seers want?"

"It was just priesthood stuff, nothing to worry about," replied Nico, looking over at the princes. He bowed politely but both men ignored him and came across the room to hug him instead.

"Brother," said Elias. "We will miss you."

"You've only just met me," protested Nico.

"And we want to get to know you. You're one of our family now," replied Elias, taking hold of Nico's hands. "If you need us for anything, *anything*, we are only a call away."

"You're very kind, Your Highness. Thank you."

"Elias, please, I'm your brother now."

"Elias, then. I look forward to getting to know you."

Jael came forward. "Me too, I hope."

"Of course," said Nico with a smile. "I'm so sorry that there isn't anything I can do to help your father. I know the healers are making him comfortable."

The other two men nodded. "It's in the Hands of the Goddess now," said Elias sadly. "She Will Guide Us as She Sees Fit."

There didn't seem to be anything else to say to that, and Alex saw the two princes out.

THE FLIGHT to Tarn took four hours.

Alex liked to travel with his own city, or so it seemed to Nico. When they got to the docks, he'd been fascinated by the huge cargo trailers being off-loaded from the ship waiting there. When he'd found out it was all their belongings, he'd been astonished.

"Best to be prepared, lad," said Watkins. "Best to be prepared."

"What are we preparing for? Alien invasion?"

"Wouldn't be the first time they tried." Watkins shrugged and walked away. Nico stared after him. Surely he wasn't serious? There had never been any aliens in the Eight Lands or indeed on the planet. The aliens had never come closer than a few planets over. Nico couldn't remember the name of the planet; he wasn't really interested in that stuff. A war may have raged over ten years but it had little effect on life in the Eight Lands and therefore on Nico. The fighting had been half a solar system away. There was peace in this part of the galaxy now; everyone knew that. Alex was the one who'd won the surrender.

Tarn proved to be a delight. Cottages and houses were scattered about the hillsides, all painted in blues, pinks, and reds. The docks were a mass of ships, yachts, and boats. Everywhere was color. Everywhere was noise. Tarn was the start of the Sixth Land, and the land itself was bisected by the River Breede, which ran the country's length before finally joining the sea. A welcome party waited for them on the dock. There was even a brass band. Alex scowled when he saw them. "Just what we need," he said. "Watkins, I don't suppose—"

"No chance, lad," returned Watkins. "You've no choice but to go and meet them. Best to get it over, lad."

Alex looked resigned and took Nico's arm. "Come on, put your best behavior on. We're to meet the local dignitaries, it seems." Nico got the feeling that he had a lot more experience dealing with dignitaries than Alex did. Which seemed odd. Then again, he was a warrior, and everyone knew that warriors thought of no class but their own.

They made their way down the dock to meet the people waiting there. A crowd had gathered, but they were keeping a respectable distance from the small welcoming party and seemed to be in good spirits. A cheer went up as Alex and Nico got closer, and a small girl ran toward them with a bunch of flowers almost as big as she was. She came gasping to a halt and did her very best to curtsy. Nico bowed back whereas Alex dropped down to the child's height, smiling as he did so. He took the flowers from her and with a flourish, presented them to Nico. Nico grinned and bowed, and then he too dropped down to speak to the child directly. They both gave her a hug, and she ran back to her mother, giggling.

"Your Highness, Your Grace," shouted a small man dressed in a red cloak. "If you would be so kind. I am Alfred Jones, and I have the privilege of being the mayor of our little town. It's a pleasure to meet you both and a privilege too."

"A privilege indeed," said another man as he moved forward and subtly shifted the mayor to one side. Not so subtly that Nico didn't notice it, though. He wondered why the major didn't push back, but bowed instead to both gentlemen.

"Er, if I may introduce Lord Haven. Lord Haven is the head of our Chamber of Commerce," said the mayor, still hanging back.

"How do you do?" Alex sounded bored and Nico smiled.

"It's a great pleasure," he said to the men. "You have a beautiful home."

"We do indeed, Your Highness, and we'd like to show you more," said Haven. "In fact, we have a feast waiting at the Town Hall. We'd like to welcome you properly."

"No," said Alex. Nico quietly trod on his foot.

"We'd be honored," he told the lord with another smile.

"If we're to stay for the feast, I shall have to make arrangements," Alex said brusquely.

Nico beamed at him, well aware that their every move was being filmed and photographed. "That would be excellent, Your Grace. Will we travel together?"

Haven appeared at their elbows. "If I may? I would be pleased to accompany His Highness to the feast. We could leave straight away."

"No," said Alex.

"Why, I'd be delighted to have the pleasure of His Highness's company, Your Grace. It would be no bother, believe me."

"No. We'll be leaving together," Alex said to Nico. "Wait here. I'll be back in a moment."

Within minutes a sleek black car appeared on the dock and Alex climbed out of the back of it, holding the door open. Nico was glad to see him. There was only so much socializing with dignitaries that he could put up with. At least at the feast there would be the distraction of food. And Nico was itching to see what the local produce was like. The fish should be excellent.

"So," began Alex when they were sitting in the back of the car. "Why the big need to go to this feast?"

"There's something going on here," said Nico, looking out of the window. "I need to speak to the priests and healers to find out more. Besides, it's the politest thing to do. These people are your people now. If they go to the trouble of preparing a feast, the least you can do is attend it. The King Must be True to the People."

"I'm not the king."

"It's a saying," Nico said with a dismissive wave of his hand. "It means your debts are to the people."

"I know what it means, Nico."

"Then why did you ask?" Nico looked at him in confusion. "Never mind. It's more important that we find out what is wrong, anyway."

"I'm here to solve any problems. You will bring your concerns to me."

Nico laughed. "Yes, almighty master. You're so funny." He'd discovered on the flight that Alex had an excellent sense of humor.

BY THE end of the day, Alex still couldn't work out why Nico had laughed. He didn't mind the boy laughing at him. It was good to see him laugh. He just hoped that Nico understood it was Alex's role to protect him. Alex would sort the problems out, not Nico. Nico's role was to be cherished. He was a priest and a healer too, but Alex wouldn't mind if he spent an hour or two on those. He had to pay his debts, when all was said and done. If there was something wrong in the Sixth Land, though, Alex didn't want Nico to have any part of it. Who knew how bad it could get? Alex had seen war, but there was no way he'd allow Nico to.

They'd attended the feast, which was an all-day affair and involved meeting hundreds of people. Alex had given a speech on his debts to the people, which had gone down well, and Nico had given a blessing for the town. His boy had a majesty about him when in priest mode. His language became poetic and he used rhythm to build the power, mold that power, and finally release it in a climatic finish. Alex had been impressed. He could feel the power in the room and knew everyone else could too. Well, if Nico was that good, perhaps Alex should let him have a couple of hours every other day. Except weekends, of course. And holidays. He supposed he'd have to allow the High Days.

Nico fell asleep in the car on the way back to the ship where they'd be staying for the night. He woke up when Alex was carrying him over the gangplank. "Oh, I'm so sorry," he said, opening sleepy eyes. "Put me down. I can walk."

"Shh, go back to sleep. I like carrying you."

"It's the ritual." Nico yawned. "Makes me sleepy afterward."

Just a couple of hours a week, then, Alex decided. He rethought the High Days. How many High Days were there, anyway? He'd have to ask Nico in the morning. Right now he wanted to get him to bed.

Safely in the bed, Nico fell back asleep immediately. Alex was glad. He needed time to think about the night's information. According to Nico, before he'd fallen asleep, the priests and healer were reporting unexplained illness, poverty, and crime reaching unheard-of levels in the areas around Tarn. Tarn was a prosperous town and whilst there had always been crime, it had never been to this degree. Poverty too was almost unheard of. The sea provided enough work for the population and always had. The illnesses seemed to have no rhyme or reason. It was a mystery to the healers as to why people were ill. The priests reported bad omens and heavy black vibrations lying over the town. Nico hadn't appeared to give much credence to the bad omens. He said that in his experience, people were willing to see anything as a bad omen, and why should priests be different? Priests were people too. He was less revealing on the subject of the reported heavy black vibrations, merely stating that he'd need more time to study. Which wasn't going to happen, thought Alex, because they were out of here at first light. Nico didn't need to get into heavy black vibrations. That couldn't possibly be good for him. He turned his attention to the information he'd heard himself. It hadn't been difficult to persuade the mayor to open up, although Haven had been a more difficult character. Alex hadn't liked him. The man struck him as sly, and he didn't like the way he bullied and patronized the mayor. He also appeared a bit too interested in Nico, wanting the first dance of the night. Alex had made it very clear that Nico only danced with him, which had momentarily shut him up, but he wasn't quiet for long. He commented on how good it would be to spend a few moments with Nico, just to get to know him. Alex couldn't see any reason why he should and said no. Later on in the evening, he'd tried again, saying it would be his pleasure to tell His Highness some of the history of Tarn. Alex said he thought the priests had that covered. It hadn't stopped Haven from approaching Nico directly and trying to pull him to a quiet corner. Alex had been ready to intervene, but Nico had extracted himself from the situation without needing any help at all. And if Haven had been pissed off, he didn't show it. It was the diplomacy training, Alex was sure.

A quiet knock sounded at the suite door, and Alex got up to answer. Watkins stood at the door ready to make his report. Motioning him to be quiet, Alex closed the door to the bedroom and led Watkins into the lounge. "Drink?" he asked, holding up some whiskey from the bar. Watkins nodded, sitting down on the sofa and lying back against the cushions. He looked tired, and Alex realized Watkins was starting to show his age. When had that happened?

"It's been a long night, lad. I'll be glad to get to my bunk," Watkins said, sitting up and taking the glass of whiskey.

"News?"

Watkins nodded, sipping at his whiskey. "Aye, there's news. I met Carlton and Evans down on the wharf. They've been poking their noses around for a week or so now. News is that there's something wrong with the food, but that's seen as ridiculous."

"More conspiracy theory?"

"Aye, lad, perhaps. Then again, there's stories of unexplained illness all over the place. Poverty, too. Discontent is mounting, though more in the country than the towns, it seems. The twin cities are said to have their share of problems, and there's talk that it's the Elites who have a hand in it."

"They always blame the Elites," replied Alex with a shrug.

"Perhaps so, lad, perhaps so." Watkins placed his glass on the table and leaned back against the cushions again, his eyes closing for a moment.

"Time for bed, old man," said Alex standing up. "We can talk more tomorrow."

"Long journey tomorrow, lad, but I'm not arguing. Bed's where I need to be. You should go to bed yourself, lad."

Turning off the lights, Alex made his way to bed. He climbed into the bed and pulled the sleeping Nico into his arms. He remembered Haven and wondered what the man had said to Nico. He'd be sure to ask in the morning.

PART EIGHT

MORNING CAME all too soon as did the journey they'd undertaken. Alex stared out of the window as town gave way to countryside. It would be faster by ship, but Alex wanted to see the land. He wanted to see how much truth there was in the rumors of poverty in the countryside. He'd never known the countryside to have poverty. The countryside was where the Goddess was at Her strongest, Her most gracious. The people were gifted with fertile soils and seas. Woodlands full of game. How could they be living in poverty?

At first the villages along the way didn't look too bad. Nico and Alex waved at the people who came out to see the procession of cars and trailers passing by. People who looked tired but nevertheless willing to come out and cheer for the new duke. People who waved ribbons of green and cream and held up handmade banners of welcome.

"What's with all the green and cream?" asked Nico.

Alex shrugged, but Watkins spoke up from the front. "Those are the duke's colors," he said.

They passed more villages. Fewer and fewer people were coming out to greet them. The cottages started to look more worn, with some bordering on derelict. At one, Nico sat up straight and yelled at the driver to stop the car. As soon as it slowed, he was out the door and heading to the village. Alex rushed after him, and two men from the car behind rushed after both of them. Watkins took his time.

Nico was examining a small child when Alex caught up with him. He was persuading the little girl to stick her tongue out, showing by doing and making the child giggle. When he'd finished, he picked the child up and balanced her on one hip.

"Is there food in that trailer?" he asked Alex, nodding toward the luxury vehicle, which was part of their convoy.

Alex nodded.

"I need food to be prepared."

Alex looked around the village as more and more people came out of the deteriorated cottages.

"As much food as possible," continued Nico. "We have to feed these people. This child is suffering from malnutrition. Who is in charge of food?"

Alex looked to Watkins.

"I'll take you to him, boy," Watkins said gruffly.

Nico looked around himself. He spotted a woman, and recognizing the mother bond, took the child over to her, pausing to say a couple of hurried sentences. The woman smiled, relieved, and Nico took his leave to follow Watkins.

Alex took the time to look around him. It wasn't a very big village, but it was clearly in need of repair. Holes in the thatch on some of the cottages were obvious, and he wondered what tenant was in charge of all this. He'd certainly have something to say to them on the subjects of looking after subtenants. Half a dozen cottages clung to the main road next to the village green. Another half dozen could be seen over on the other side of the green. Farther back from the green, cottages were placed aimlessly. The different paint colors showed that some effort had been made in the past, but now the paint was old and worn. A couple of the cottages had boarded-up windows. The people sat outside their doors looking tired and defeated. It reminded Alex of the ravages of battle and soldiers who could take no more. His anger rose. Why was this happening? He looked for some sort of village leader but could find no one.

He was walking deeper into the village when Nico shouted for him. He spun round immediately, concerned for the boy's safety. Relieved to see Nico striding toward him, he relaxed slightly, a smile on his lips.

"The people need to hunt and fish. You must overrule the law that prevents them from doing that."

Alex studied Nico, slightly taken aback by the direct order. He wasn't used to taking orders. Nico positively sizzled with anger, so he paused, but before he could answer, Nico pointed a finger at him.

"The people have *no food*," Nico explained with grim emphasis. "They're not allowed to hunt or fish because some local Elite has decided they won't allow them to. This is not acceptable. It goes completely against the given rights. Change the law!"

Alex looked over at Watkins, and the older man made little attempt to hide his amusement. Alex arched an eyebrow, and the man coughed and straightened up.

"You do own both the forests and the river, Your Grace. It's well within your rights to change the law."

"Then the law is changed," Alex said smoothly. "See to it, Watkins." He turned back to Nico. "If the people are hungry, perhaps we should send some men to the cities and back to Tarn to get food. We can arrange a distribution program." He smiled, proud of his plan. It was bound to soothe all those ruffled feathers.

"Oh, I've already done that," Nico said with a dismissive hand as he turned back toward the village.

"What do you mean, you've already done that?" Alex demanded, halting the exit with a step forward. Surely to the Goddess Nico hadn't commanded his men? "How did you do that?"

"I told him to do it," replied Nico, nodding toward Watkins.

"You gave my man orders?" Alex was incensed.

"Well, yes." Nico shrugged indifferently. "I don't know why you're so surprised. It's what you always do. You say 'see to it, Watkins.' Heaven knows I've seen you do it enough. In fact, it always amuses me that people say you're in command of vast armies. From what I can see, you command only one." And with that he started off once more in the direction of the village.

Alex was dumbstruck; he couldn't think of a word to say. He turned to look at his Sergeant Major, his mouth agape. It didn't help that Watkins was leaning against the tree, laughing. "You took orders from him?"

"Of course," laughed Watkins. "Would you rather I ignore him?"

"I'd rather you came to talk to me."

"Why would I do that? So you could tell me to do the same? It was a good plan. I didn't think it needed your tuppence worth."

"Tuppence worth…?" Alex roared, looming over Watkins.

Unfortunately, it just made Watkins laugh harder until he bent over, slapping his knee. "What would you have me do, lad? It was a good plan."

"You should have cleared it with me."

"And you'd have said go ahead. I just skipped that bit." He grinned at Alex. "Give over your whinging, lad. Be glad the pretty boy has a brain, aye, and a good heart. Be very grateful. It could be very different. Meanwhile, I'll sit back and watch him run rings around you. I shall enjoy that."

IT WAS nighttime again before Alex could get hold of Nico. The boy had never stopped. Whilst Alex hadn't been able to discover the village elders, Nico had had no trouble at all. He'd spent quite some time with a very elderly lady who was bedridden in one of the cottages. Alex had wanted to go in but he'd been waved away by Nico, and from what he could tell, some sort of priest ritual was being conducted. It didn't feel right to interrupt, so Alex had stomped back to the village green. There he'd found tables set up and groaning with food. His men were feeding the villagers and even more people than that. He realized people were coming from all directions to the village, hungry people. Where did they all come from? Where did they all live?

He finally caught up with the boy in the trailer designated for their use. Nico was getting ready for bed and had just left the shower. He was drying his hair with a towel and wore sleep pants and nothing else. He smiled when he saw Alex. All of Alex's resolve to discuss the issue of Nico's giving orders to his men went straight out the window. How could Alex ignore that smile?

Taking Nico in his arms, he looked down into his eyes. "Hard day?"

Nico sighed, relaxing into Alex's arms and resting his head on Alex's shoulder. "Very hard," he breathed. "I never expected to see an actual case of malnutrition. That poor child's development may have been badly damaged. Worst of all, I don't know what's caused it. Well, I do know what's partially caused it. The ban on fishing and hunting. Thank you for revoking that law, Your Grace." Nico gave a sleepy smile, closing his eyes. "But in truth, she shouldn't have been that bad. They've been eating corn from the fields. Oh." He opened his eyes and stood up. "We need to talk about the corn. People are saying there's something wrong with it."

"Didn't you look at it?"

"No one would admit to having any. Apparently they've been stealing from the nearby fields to feed their families. If they're discovered they get put in prison. That's something else we need to talk about. We shouldn't be putting people in prison for doing what's necessary to feed their families." Nico yawned and placed his hand in front of his mouth. "There's probably other stuff I should mention too, but I'm just too tired. Can we talk in the morning?"

Alex picked him up and placed him very carefully on the bed. He pulled the down quilt up over Nico, tucking him in. "We can talk in the morning, babe. You can tell me all your worries then. Go to sleep, now."

For the second night in a row, Alex found himself alone, waiting on Watkins's report. It was their second day in the Sixth Land and already they'd discovered that the rumors were true. The people had nothing.

In the immediate future he could have food transported in. Revoking the hunting and fishing law would help too. The people needed to know he would look after them. They needed a figure that they could put their faith in, someone who wouldn't let them down. Alex was determined to be that person. He'd wanted to make an entrance in the country, and now he had the perfect vehicle. And a whole lot of Elites to deal with. What sort of people left their own tenants to starve?

The soft knock indicating Watkins had arrived sounded on the door, and Alex let him in.

"Local lord is never here," began Watkins when they both sat down. "Name of Leicester. Spends all his time in the capital land. Locals say he turned all the farming over to corn and didn't grow any other crop. He keeps himself in fish and game and has it flown to his house in the capital. It's said his friends are all kept high on the hog too. The people are kept from hunting and fishing by some rule or other but no one knew what. They just know they end up in prison if they break it. I'm told that many good men are gone from this village. Aye, and women, too. You'll be wanting to see to their release?"

"Yes," agreed Alex. "Don't think the boy will settle for anything else."

"Quite right, too," harrumphed Watkins. "The boy is turning out to be a better idea than I'd thought. The Goddess guided you there, lad."

She did indeed.

FOUR DAYS later they arrived at the castle. Or at least they thought they did. It had been four days of seeing poverty and destitution, setting up distribution lines for food and ensuring that all the people understood they could now hunt and fish. Glad he'd brought an army with him, Alex was even happier to finally get to the top of the Sixth Land. The castle wall was a shock. Their first glance had come from the top of a hill. The hill gave way to a lazy long roll of countryside before the castle wall itself. They'd stopped the car and got out to look. "Good grief," said

Alex, taken aback by the sheer size of it. It seemed endless, with tall turrets on either side of the gate and then at intervals along the walls and the corners.

Mountains dominated the left hand side of the castle, their tall peaks providing the best defense the castle could hope for. Alex knew from studying maps of the area that the sea was the defense at the back of the castle. The rolling fields and lack of trees between where they stood and the wall itself was its third line of defense, allowing no enemy to be hidden from sight if they approached from there. Casting his eye across the horizon, he realized the right side of the castle complex was similarly empty of either buildings or trees for miles. What had the old duke been worrying about, to build such a monstrosity? There had never been a modern war or battle in the Sixth Land. Nor anywhere else in the Eight Lands Kingdom for that matter. All the wars and battles had taken place off-planet. So why build this?

The first gates into the castle were derelict, one leaning against the wall itself, and Alex had his men clear the entrance so they could drive through.

They were greeted by wide grass fields and in the distance another curtain wall, more turrets, and more enormous doors. And so it went on. As they got through a set of doors, another curtain wall appeared in the distance. They got through that and yet another wall, again in the distance. They eventually discovered five curtain walls and a distance of some four miles before they got to the innermost space. It was almost a relief to get there. Alex had visions of being caught in some black magick maelstrom where they'd be breaking through doors for eternity.

"Don't be silly," Nico told him. "I'd be able to tell if there were any black magick in the area and there's certainly none here."

Alex looked at him, shocked. He was certain he hadn't said anything aloud. Watkins looked a bit taken aback by the words too, and looked to Alex for an explanation. Alex shrugged, looking around him instead. To one side of the space stood a huge mansion with the remains of formal gardens around it. The other side appeared to house billets and working space. A large courtyard stood in the middle. More than enough space for military training.

Nico made his way straight to the gardens, stopping to inspect a plant or flower every so often. A man and woman came out on the steps of the mansion, waiting for them to approach.

"Good morning," Nico said with a smile whilst Alex pulled him back cautiously. The man stepped forward protectively in front of the woman.

"I take it you're the new duke?" he shouted over to Alex.

"I am, and this is my spouse, Prince Nico."

"A prince, eh? No one said anything about that. I should make my bows," he added, though he failed to do so. "If you'd have told us you were coming, I'd have opened the gates."

"That would have been helpful," said Alex, calmly walking forward and holding his hand out to the man. "So who may you be?"

The man looked surprised but shook the offered hand. "I'll be Higgins, the old duke's majordomo. This 'ere is my sister. She's housekeeper and cook. There's us and a gardener. No one else left, so you shouldn't be expecting too much. We've done our best."

"And I can see you've done a wonderful job," Nico said, moving forward and shaking Higgins's hand. "Did you say your sister is a cook? How wonderful. I'd love to speak to her if I may?"

Higgins moved to one side and encouraged his sister forward. "This 'ere is Daisy. She's a fully qualified chef for all that there's been no use for her talents here. She's more than capable of running the kitchens for Your Grace and Your Highness."

Daisy came forward with a shy smile and shook their hands. Nico beamed at her. "Perhaps you can show me the kitchens, ma'am," he said. "I'd love to see them." Alex was impressed by his thoughtfulness. It couldn't be much fun to visit a kitchen for him but he was obviously determined to put Daisy at her ease.

"Is the house safe?" Alex asked Higgins.

"Glass missing from the skylight, but that's about the sum of it. Old duke did it, firing up an old rifle one night."

Alex nodded at Nico that he could go in, and the boy disappeared with the cook.

"Seems to be a procession of all kinds of vehicles coming in from the west. You'll be wanting those gates open, I'm thinking?"

"My men can handle that. It will be the rest of our belongings coming from the docks in Thetis. Tell me about the house." Alex indicated that Higgins should enter the house before him.

He walked into a large square hall, fireplaces at both ends of the room. An oak staircase wound its way up to the next floor. Looking farther up, Alex could see the damage done to the skylight, which seemed to hover about them. A series of buckets sat on a spread-out tarpaulin directly below the skylight and right in the middle of the hall's polished wooden floor.

"Why hasn't it been repaired?" he asked Higgins.

"By who? Once old Hugbet died, everything went to the Crown. The Crown didn't see fit to come here. Nothing has been done since, except the stuff that Daisy and I could manage, and the gardener, of course. Not that you see much of him. You do see that gardening has been done, though," he added hurriedly. "The man certainly pays his debts. He's kept us in fruit and veg this whole time. That's more than some folks have got since old Hugbet died." He pronounced the name as "hug bit," and Alex hid a smile. He only knew the Elite pronunciation "ooh bare." He decided he preferred Higgins's version better.

"What was he like?"

"The old duke? He was mad at the end. Any fool could see it. But he had been a fair man in his time, bit too decadent for my taste, but he made sure that the people were fed. He paid his debts in the best way he knew how."

"That's as good an epitaph as any," commented Alex thoughtfully. He paused, gathering those thoughts together. What would the people say about him when he died? Was he up to the role? He knew how to command thousands of soldiers. Knew how to bring them together so they could fight the common foe. He knew the strategies of combat, what tactics to use when going into battle. He could lead soldiers into war, but could he lead a people into peace?

"Show me round." He came out of his reverie and spoke to Higgins. "Watkins?" he shouted, knowing the man wouldn't be too far away. Within a minute he appeared from the direction Nico had taken to see the kitchen.

"What?" he shouted back from across the hall.

"Skylight needs fixing. See to it, Watkins."

NICO LOOKED around him and relaxed against the cupboard. The kitchen was immense, everything he'd ever dreamed of. Truly the Goddess was Good. He was beginning to think that perhaps she did have a tender spot for him. It needed updating, of course, and he'd have to discuss money with the duke. He was quite sure the priesthood gave him an allowance, but that probably wouldn't amount to much. He'd never had to deal with actual money before other than pocket money. It was another new thing he'd have to get used to. He was sure the duke would allow him the money to update the kitchen. After all, it really came under household expenses, not Nico's private dream. His eyes gleamed with the thought of all those pans. Pans of every shape and size. A pan for every aspect of cooking. It made him itch to start cooking.

"Perhaps Your Highness would like to see the rest of the house," said Daisy, who had been waiting patiently at his side. She was an older woman, a bit on the large side, but with the sweetest face. Her personal space was filled with love ready to attach itself to whoever was with her.

"Nico. Please, Daisy, call me Nico. I suppose I'll have to. It will be expected of me, won't it?"

"I think you should see the house, yes. Then you'll know if you want to change anything." She looked concerned at the thought.

"Well, I shall certainly need to update this kitchen," he said brightly. "But I'm going to need you to tell me what should be done. Do you have any ideas of what you'll like?"

"What I'll like?" Daisy looked confused. "Don't you mean what you'll like?"

"Not at all. It's your kitchen. It should be updated in accordance with your likes and needs. I'd like the chance to have my own little corner, though, if that would be okay?" She looked blankly at him and he waved at the kitchen.

"I like to cook," he explained. "I find it very enjoyable. I haven't been trained, of course, but I've had some lessons. I'd like you to continue with them if you will. Teach me what you know and let me have my own little corner of the kitchen so I can practice, if you would, that is." He looked at her hopefully.

"You want me to teach you how to cook?" she said. "Really?"

"Yes, really. I'd be honored if you would teach me. I can tell you are a woman of great skill."

"Well, I have learned a lot over the years. I suppose I could teach you. Are you really sure?" She looked doubtful and Nico laughed.

"I'm really sure. You have no idea of how much I like cooking," he said. "Now, whilst we look around the rest of the house, you can tell me all about the local produce."

THEY MADE their way into the main part of the house and eventually found their way upstairs. Nico was surprised to find Alex and Higgins in the master bedroom. Like the rest of the house, it was heavy on wood paneling and thick silken drapes. The furniture loomed like monsters beneath a wealth of dustsheets.

"We won't be able to sleep in here tonight," Alex announced. "It all needs to be cleaned out. It's full of dust. We can sleep outside."

"Outside?" Nico looked horrified. "Isn't that illegal?" Alex looked at Nico, his head cocked on one side. He turned to the siblings and thanked them for their help but said he and Nico would be fine now. With that dismissal, he turned back to Nico.

"Why would it be illegal to sleep outside, Nico?" he asked patiently.

"Well… erm… you're supposed to sleep inside, not outside," he said. "Inside is where everyone sleeps. It really won't take long to clear this room. I could do it myself." Nico went over and pulled the dustsheet off the bed. A huge cloud of dust blew up into the room, making him sneeze. "I may need some help, though," he said, rubbing at his eyes and sniffing suspiciously. "But I'm sure it won't take long. We'll be fine in here." He sneezed again, twice.

"What are you afraid of, Nico?" questioned Alex, still patient and making no move to get closer to the cloud of dust.

Nico sighed and straightened his shoulders, stepping away from all the dust. He had his nose in his handkerchief and was blinking quickly.

"Snakes," he spat out. "Snakes and snakes and creepy-crawly things. Things that live outside, not inside. Things we're not supposed to cohabit with. The outside things." He continued to sneeze and sniffle.

Alex walked over and took him by the hand to lead him downstairs and out into the spring sunshine.

"Aren't you dedicated to Arachne?" he asked once Nico's sniffles calmed down. "She Who Weaves The Web," he tacked on in the same pompous manner Nico used whenever he was trying to distract Alex.

"Amongst others, yes," agreed Nico. "I don't have a problem with spiders. Spiders are nothing like snakes. They don't look like snakes, they don't act like snakes. Really, it's impossible to confuse the two."

"What are you really afraid of, Nico? Are you worried that I won't be able to protect you?"

"I'm worried that I'll get bitten and die." Nico was scathing in both his reply and the look he gave Alex.

Alex grinned, folding his arms over his chest. "There are no poisonous snakes here, baby," he chuckled. "Just a couple of harmless grass snakes."

"Only two?" Nico perked up immediately. "Then we may have already passed them. This is a big land. They could be hidden anywhere. Have you got them monitored in some way? A tracking device or similar? It could tell us exactly where they are."

Alex blinked in confusion until he realized what Nico was talking about. "When I said there were only two, babe, I meant that there were only two types, not that there were only two snakes."

"You mean there's more?" Nico moved closer to Alex, looking around him as though a horde of snakes were about to come slithering forward out of the grass. He moved closer again.

Alex stepped forward and closed the last of the gap between them. He placed his hands on Nico's shoulders, manipulating the stiff muscles he found there.

"Nico," he said softly, trailing one finger along Nico's collarbone, up Nico's throat until it could tilt his chin. "Nico," he whispered now, staring into eyes that were luminous in intensity. "I won't let a snake get you. I want you all to myself, and I don't share." He bent forward and lightly touched his lips to those of his spouse. "We can stay in the trailer again, babe. We won't let the nasty things in. It will be just you and I." He nibbled on Nico's ear and Nico shivered. He loved making the boy shiver and the ear thing did it every time. He'd never known anyone to have such sensitive ears.

"In fact," he breathed, "let's go and check on that trailer now."

SADLY, THEY didn't make it to the trailer, and being apart proved to be a pattern for the next few days. Nico would fall asleep long before Alex came back, and he found himself waking alone. Of course, he could see how busy Alex was. The castle complex was rapidly turning into a mini city. The wide-open fields within the curtain walls were overrun with housing trailers and mess halls. Over a thousand men and women had accompanied Alex and Nico, with another thousand expected within the month. Nico wondered why Alex needed so many men. Weren't they at peace? Alex had explained that the kingdom still needed an army and it was his responsibility to ensure that army was properly trained. The army was there to stay, it seemed.

He himself concentrated on the house and the gardens. Having discussed finances with Alex, he'd discovered he had an unlimited fund for the house, which was music to his ears. He went into deep conference with Daisy, and they spent hours poring over the Commercial Web, ordering anything that attracted their eyes. Nico also found time to order some clothes more to his taste and even started to look at furniture for the rest of the house. Especially the bedroom. He wanted the bedroom to be complete.

He stopped himself from obsessing over their bedroom. There was too much to do. Every morning he allowed himself an hour on the beach. It had been discovered that whereas the front, left, and right of the castle had five curtain walls, the back only had one. The tall wooden gates led directly to a pristine white sand beach. There was the odd family of rocks with pools full of life. Nico found himself entranced. He loved the roar of the water as the sea pounded against the sand and rocks. The smell of the sea and the calls of the sea gulls. The white tips of the waves made him long to just dive in.

It was still a little too cold for him, but Nico had seen soldiers swimming in the bay. During the day they played a variety of ball games too, and some creatives had taken to making sand sculptures. Nico had been impressed by the artfulness of the designs and the skill. At this time of the morning, though, he always had the beach to himself and it felt good to walk along the water's edge. He found balance there, all of his worries and fears placed in perspective, all his thoughts and imaginings allowed to soar free. He breathed the air in, calming his heart rate and becoming one with the scene.

He realized it would soon be time for the feast of Tethys, Goddess of the Sea. A time to pay his debts. He pictured leading the celebratory power build here on the beach. It would be so easy to do; the power was all around, on the beach and in the sea. The rock formations echoed with centuries of history and contained their own power. There was one tall rock formation perfect for carrying a statue of the Goddess. He would have to see if there was one in the house and if there wasn't, he'd go to the city and commission one. Or perhaps he should ask some of the soldiers. Those sand sculptures were quite incredible. He did need to do a trip to the city, though. He wanted to see the place and visit the Grand Seers. He still had the letter for them hidden amongst his socks. He thought it safe enough there, but he needed to hand it over as soon as possible. The Grand Seers had stressed urgency.

When he returned to the castle, he found that he had no need to take the trip. The Grand Seers had come to him.

Higgins was waiting for him on the step. "Been waiting for you, Your Highness. You have visitors."

"What sort of visitors?"

"Grand Seers from the city. Very full of themselves they are, didn't feel the need to confide in me so don't be asking me what they want. They wouldn't tell me. Bunch of stuck-up, self-satisfied buffoons. Want me to get rid of them?"

Nico was taken aback. "No," he replied. "Really, it's fine. I'll go and find out what they want. It may just be a courtesy visit."

Nico found them in the long sitting room, which was one of the few usable rooms. He made a mental note to hire more staff. There were five Grand Seers and one acolyte, a young man who was trying desperately to sit still and failing miserably. All six stood up and made deep bows when Nico walked into the room.

"Good morning," said Nico formally with his own bow. "It is a pleasure to meet you."

"Your Highness," began one of the Grand Seers with another bow. "I am Grand Seer Joseph, and it is my pleasure to welcome you to the Sixth Land. If I may introduce you to my companions?"

"Of course." Nico beamed at them all, and a sense of relief ran through the visitors.

He was introduced to Grand Seers Jenny, Saffron, Niles, Edward, and finally to Patrick.

"Most people call me Trix, Your Highness," he said to the Grand Seers' disapproval.

Grand Seer Joseph spoke up again.

"*Patrick* is here to wait on you, Your Highness. He's a priest in training but is taking, er… some time out. He'll be your manservant, Prince Nico."

"Manservant? I'm not sure that I need a manservant, Brother Joseph. I really don't see what he could do."

"Well, I know he doesn't look like much, Your Highness, but I can assure you of his loyalty. He wants to be your manservant, don't you, Tri... er, Patrick?"

"Oh, yes," Trix enthused. "It's the Greatest Gift the Goddess could Give Me."

Grand Seer Joseph nodded and smiled benevolently at the boy. Nico paused. Clearly the boy wanted to be there, but it seemed the Grand Seers wanted Patrick there almost as much. What was going on there?

"Well, I suppose there's always room for one more," Nico replied. "Though I really don't see what you could do...."

"I'll do anything," vowed Trix, placing one hand on his heart. More benevolent smiles from the Grand Seers, and Nico gave in. Perhaps he could find him something to do in the kitchen. Then again, perhaps he could help with preparations for the High Days. His background was the local Academia Hall, of course, so he'd know a lot about the High Days.

"Then I'll be delighted to have you, Trix," said Nico with a smile. He tried not to laugh when the boy started to clap in joy.

"Quiet, Patrick," scolded Grand Seer Saffron. "Now go and arrange refreshments. Make yourself useful."

Nico blushed when he realized he hadn't offered any refreshments. He didn't want to make a bad impression on his guests. He was representing his own Academia Hall, after all. He made to apologize, but Grand Seer Saffron waved his concerns away.

"You are only just moving in, Your Highness. We don't expect you to have everything ready for our arrival. In fact, we should have allowed you more time to settle, but events do not allow us that luxury. I believe you may have a letter for us, my Prince?"

"I do indeed, but you must allow me time to fetch it, ma'am. I do not have it on me."

"You don't have it on you?" She looked aghast. "But surely the Grand Seers told you of its importance? If it should fall into the wrong hands—"

"They wouldn't understand a word of it, ma'am. It's written in Latin, and Latin has been dead for centuries. Only a member of the priesthood would be able to decipher it. Or a Grand Seer, of course."

"Well I suppose so but... are you sure no one has intercepted it?"

"No one, ma'am, although something strange did happen on the way here. We were in Tarn when one of the local dignitaries asked me if

I'd brought anything with me. I claimed to have no knowledge of what he was talking about, of course, but I was surprised that someone would even ask."

"Our enemies are all around us," said Grand Seer Niles with a shiver. "They grow ever near."

"Don't be so melodramatic, Niles. It doesn't suit you," interjected Grand Seer Jenny. "Can you tell us the name of this man or woman, Your Highness?"

"I believe his name was Haven. He has something to do with the Chamber of Commerce there."

"Ah, yes, we know all about Haven," Grand Seer Jenny said. "See, Niles? No need for the dramatics, it's just Haven."

"He is one of our enemies," Grand Seer Niles defended himself. Nico excused himself so he could go and fetch the missive. By the time he returned, Daisy was handing out tea and fruit juice. Trix was handing out breakfast rolls. Nico could smell the cinnamon in the air. Remembering how Higgins had been treated, he made a point of introducing Daisy as Miss Higgins and said what an integral part of his life she was. Daisy had gone bright red but appeared pleased with his statement, and he got the impression that the Grand Seers changed their behavior toward her. He made a mental note to discuss the ridiculousness of snobbery if he was ever asked to lead a power build at the academy.

Once the company was settled with refreshments, Daisy left the room, and Trix returned to his seat with the Grand Seers.

"I have the letter here, Brother Joseph," said Nico, handing it over. The Grand Seer looked like he was about to read it but heard a noise from the hall and placed it hurriedly in his pocket instead. Nico looked around to see Alex stride into the room. He waved at the visitors to remain seated as he walked across the room to Nico's side. He took Nico's hand and kissed the back of it. Nico blushed but smiled and made room on the couch for the duke to sit.

"Allow me to introduce our guests, Your Grace," he said politely and proceeded to do so. Alex nodded to each person in turn but made no effort to shake their hands or bow to them.

"And what brings you here, ladies and gentlemen?" he asked. "I'm afraid His Highness is far too busy at the moment to be doing any rituals, if that's what you're after." His tone was brusque, and Nico was as startled as the Grand Seers looked.

"Er, no. That is, of course not, Your Grace," stuttered Grand Seer Joseph. "We're well aware that His Highness needs time to settle in. Though we'd be honored if he were to lead any rituals at Academia Hall, of course."

"We rather thought His Highness would want to conduct his own rituals here, to be honest," said Grand Seer Jenny. "We didn't think he'd want to come into the city."

Alex looked delighted and Nico wondered why. What difference did it make to Alex? He decided to intervene. Alex was looking so pleased that it was downright rude.

"I would be honored to lead a ritual at Academia Hall. But I will need some time to settle in. There's so much to do."

The Grand Seers nodded both in sympathy and relief. They continued to eye the duke warily. He in turn had sat back, apparently pleased.

"You must tell me about the city, Brother Joseph," began Nico, and the conversation turned to the people and institutions of Tethys. Nico learned that there were two cities, one on either side of the river. Tethys was the older of the two, and home to the government buildings, religious and academic realms, and the courts and justice system. In fact, all the institutions of society were in Tethys, leaving Nico to wonder who inhabited the sister city Thetis. It wasn't long before he was informed. The Grand Seers didn't approve of Thetis, and they encouraged the duke to keep Nico well away from it. It was a place for drunks and ne'er-do-wells, they said. A place of disorder and no law. Really, what was needed was a more effective watcher force, but funding was a problem.

Alex didn't look concerned, Nico noted. In fact, he seemed almost bored. Nico trod on his foot.

Alex glared at him and sat up.

"I'll be looking into all your concerns over the next few days," he said. "If there is a problem that needs policing, then I can assure you it will be seen to. Now if you will excuse us, there is much to see to."

Since that hint couldn't be ignored, the Grand Seers made their bows and left. Trix was sent to the kitchen to talk to Daisy. Nico looked at Alex.

"What?" asked Alex. "Higgins told me you needed rescuing."

"I didn't need rescuing. I'm more than capable of looking after myself."

"Yes," agreed Alex, kissing him lightly on the lips. "But you don't have to. You've got me, now."

PART NINE

THE LAST rays of sun slanted through the window, casting across one corner of the room and leaving light shadows. Nico looked around the bedroom. He was pleased. The wood paneling was newly polished and added warmth. The bed had been covered with a deep red silk quilt and white sheets. Nico knew Alex would look gorgeous against it. He was also hoping the saying that red was for passion was true. He wanted tonight to be very special.

A corner of the room held a small round table just big enough for two to sit at, and Nico had thrown a red cloth over it and placed a candle and flowers in the middle. He looked over the crystal glassware and the silver cutlery. He'd ordered it all new from the Commercial Web and was pleased with his purchases. Tonight he'd wanted something special and had prepared dinner himself. It was just left to Trix to serve it. Once the duke arrived, that was. Nico looked to the clock. Five past the hour. He'd asked the duke to be there at quarter past, so he still had ten minutes. He'd spend it making everything perfect.

He checked his outfit in the mirror. His new clothes had arrived from the capital and this was the first chance he'd had to wear them. No more bright vivid colors, he'd decided, and his suit jacket was a pale gray, set off by a black waistcoat and a white linen shirt. His tie was also pale gray, and he'd tied the knot in the simplest way possible. It was a classic look, he felt, perhaps more somber than he usually dressed, but he liked the feeling of maturity it gave him. He hoped Alex liked it too.

This was their first night in the bedroom, and he wanted to make it memorable. Trix rushed into the room, his ever-present minicom in his hand.

"Is he here yet? Have I missed him? Should I start serving dinner now? Oh, wow, what are you wearing? You look so trem, is that silk? I've never had a silk suit. I'd love to have one, though. Silk is just the best, isn't it?" Trem? Nico was mystified. What was "trem"? Trix skipped across the room and felt Nico's lapel. "It is silk!" he enthused whilst looking around the room. "Where's the duke?"

"He's not due for another ten, no, five minutes. I'm just checking the room."

"I can help." Trix brightened, if it was possible to get any brighter. "What should I look for? The table looks delish, so that's okay. The bed…." He grinned widely. "Well, that looks good too. Did you check the balcony? Should I do that now? You definitely chose the right curtains. Are you glad I suggested pink?"

"They're not pink, they're red," replied Nico.

"Close enough. I think you could have gone pinker, but it was your choice. Pink would look great in the long sitting room, though. We should get onto that."

Nico hid his grimace. He could just imagine Alex's face if he suggested pink for the long sitting room. It would be almost worth doing. Except he wouldn't be able to live in a pink sitting room even if it was Trix's favorite color. No doubt Trix would want to add sequins and glitter. It dawned on Nico that Trix should probably be distracted from decorating the house, and Nico thought he knew the best way to do it.

"You should decorate your own room, Trix. How about I give you a budget and you can get on with it?"

"Really?" squealed Trix. "Do you really mean it? I'd be so happy." He began to dance around the room. "Oh, just let me go and tell my friends." He rushed to the nearest chair and started to tap furiously at his mini comm screen. "They'll be so excited for me. I'm going to do it all in pink. Pink with glitter and sequins. Oh, I can't believe you're letting me do this." He looked at Nico with his eyes shining. "It's going to be wonderful. Everyone will love it."

"Good." Nico smiled. "Why don't you go and do all your com work and come back in, erm, best make it forty minutes, to serve dinner. You can go on the Commercial Web and start planning things."

There was more squealing and tapping as Trix left the room with a skip, completely forgetting to close the door behind him. Nico sighed and went to shut the door. He went back to the window and lit a joss stick. The scent of freshly cut cucumber drifted into the room. Perhaps not the most obvious choice, but Nico had his reasons. He took a deep breath and looked around the room again. Perfect.

The duke arrived right on time, striding into the room and heading straight for Nico. He was pulled into the man's arms and kissed soundly. "Goddess, I've missed you," said Alex, breaking the kiss.

Nico beamed at him. "That's why I insisted we have an evening together. It's our first in the house. I thought we should celebrate." He nodded toward the champagne waiting on the side table. That earned him a quick peck on the nose.

"Are we having dinner?" Alex asked, looking around the room. "You've done a great job in here. I wouldn't have recognized it. Are our things here? Then I'm going to take a shower. Give me ten minutes."

When he returned Nico was surprised that he was wearing a suit. The black jacket had been cut beautifully against those broad shoulders and the waistcoat was a pale shade of green. Both contrasted with the whiteness of his linen shirt and tie. He looked breathtaking. He took Nico by the hand and led him over to the table, where he pulled out Nico's seat and helped him to sit down. Sitting down himself, he said, "This is the first time we've dined together since the boat."

Nico nodded whilst he took his mini comm from his pocket and sent Trix a message. "I know."

Alex poured the champagne and the conversation was light as they waited for the first course. Waited and waited. Nico realized it had been fifteen minutes and got his mini comm out of his pocket again. "Sorry about this," he said to Alex. "I'll just send another message." They continued to talk about the estate and how much work was to be done, but within five minutes came the expected knock at the door. Nico shouted, "Come in," which didn't feel very graceful but there was no way Trix would hear him otherwise.

The door opened and Trix practically fell through dragging a food trolley behind him. "I'm so sorry, Your Highness. I didn't get your first message. I was on the comm telling my friends about my bedroom and I lost all track of time. I do apologize. It's a good thing the food's cold anyway." He pulled the trolley up beside the table and beamed at the duke. "It's so good to see you again, Your Grace, and you look particularly good tonight. Can I take a photo? Or one of the two of you would be better. Please? Can I?"

"No, you can't," said Nico bluntly. "Serve the food, Trix."

"Of course, Your Highness, of course. I'll do that now and perhaps I can take a photo after that. The two of you together on your first night in the castle. It's a momentous day. It should be recorded. Don't you agree, Your Grace? Wouldn't you like a photo of the two of you together on your first night in the castle?"

"You know," said Alex slowly, "I would like that, yes."

"Oh goody!" squealed Trix. "I have my mini comm here, and it's going to be the best photo, I promise, the best photo I can do, and I'm quite good if I do say so myself." He continued to trill like a rabid canary as, food trolley completely forgotten, he ushered them over to the door leading to the balcony. "Now if you could just stand in the last of the sun's rays. Yes, that's right, move over to your right… or is that left? I can never remember the two; just go that way." He gestured as he lined the camera on the mini comm up. "Yes, yes, you put your hands around His Highness, Your Grace. Now if you can both relax and smile. Yes, that's very nice. Do that again." He took several more photos before Nico moved forward and put an end to it. He and Alex returned to the table and sat down. "That's wonderful!" shrilled Trix. "We'll get the two of you together at the table. The flowers set it off beautifully. Was that your design, Your Highness? Now if the two of you could just hold hands."

"Enough," said Alex loudly. "Serve the food."

It made Trix stop taking photos but didn't shut him up, and he chattered happily as he served up the two meals. Nico had to tell him to leave when he was midanecdote but it didn't seem to faze Trix. He just gave a bow and a giggle and started singing on his way out of the door.

"Who the hell is he?" demanded Alex, watching in disbelief as the young man left the room.

"That's Trix. You've met him."

"I'm sure that I haven't. I'd remember meeting him."

"He was here with the Grand Seers. You met him then."

"That was him?" Alex hadn't lost the look of disbelief. "But he was so quiet."

"Yes," said Nico darkly. "That's how they drew me in. I had no idea of what I was taking on."

"Taking on? What are you talking about?"

"The Grand Seers left him here. He's supposed to be some sort of manservant for me."

"Manservant?" Alex said. "I suppose that's not a bad idea, but do you really want *him*?"

"I know," agreed Nico. "But I can't send him back. It would be a terrible thing to do to him. He'd be seen as a total failure. And he's so happy here. Really, I couldn't send him away now."

"I can," retorted Alex grimly.

"No, I don't want you to do that. He'll calm down eventually. He's just so happy to be here. Now, forget Trix and eat up. We've got another two courses yet."

"Will he be serving them all?" Alex looked wary.

"Yes, but don't think about that. Think about the food," advised Nico. They turned their attention to the first course. Nico had spent a lot of time making it look as beautiful as he could. Fat slices of oozy goat cheese with quarters of figs arranged around them. An arugula salad with spears of asparagus completed the dish. He picked up a spear of asparagus and placed it to his lips, nibbling at the top. Alex dropped his fork, staring at Nico's mouth. *Oh good*, thought Nico, *it's working*. He concentrated on nibbling, paying close attention to Alex's reaction. He slowly worked the length of the asparagus into his mouth using his lips to slightly caress the vegetable. He started to thicken in his trousers. What was hopefully working on Alex was definitely working on him. He finished the piece of asparagus and gave Alex what he thought was a seductive smile. He'd never seduced anyone before, so he felt very new at it. With luck and the Goddess, he was doing it right. Alex gave back a slow sure smile that was pure seduction, and Nico blushed and turned back to his food. With a grin, Alex did the same.

Within a couple of minutes, though, Nico noticed that Alex was rooting through his salad and kept looking over to Nico's plate.

"Is there something wrong?" he asked.

Alex looked up at him. "I haven't got any cucumber. Do you have cucumber?"

"Er, no. It isn't part of this dish. I can send for some for you if you'd like?" Nico suddenly felt ridiculous for using a cucumber joss stick. It should have dawned on him that the duke would expect to see the stuff on his plate.

"No," said Alex, looking mystified. "I just thought I could smell it."

Nico wondered whether to be honest or not. Should he stay quiet? Discretion was something to do with valor, but that didn't really apply in this case. It was a cucumber joss stick, not an international incident. Plus, honesty was the best policy. Well, it was sometimes the best policy. Ultimately they were talking about a cucumber joss stick, and if he couldn't be honest about that then he might as well give up the priesthood.

"It's a joss stick," he said.

"What's a joss stick?"

"The cucumber smell. It's a cucumber-scented joss stick."

"Do they make cucumber joss sticks? I didn't know that. Why would they make cucumber joss sticks? I've never heard of vegetables being used for air freshener. Is it something new? Or is it particular to the Sixth Land?"

Seriously? He wanted to know that much about a cucumber joss stick? Nico rolled his eyes. "It's just a joss stick. There's not much more to be said about it. Now, tell me, are you enjoying your food?" He'd been patient enough. He wanted to know what Alex thought.

"Very much," said Alex. "It was an excellent idea to keep the chef. This is delicious even if there isn't any cucumber. Perhaps we could tell her next time."

That damn cucumber. Still, on the whole, it was a compliment, and compliments were good. He liked compliments. "The goat's cheese is a local product, Your Grace. I think it's a very good one and goes well with the champagne."

"Yes, I suppose it does. We really will have to compliment the chef."

Nico beamed at him.

The second course of raw oysters served with just a touch of lemon juice and Tabasco sauce went down well in more ways than one, and Trix finally brought in the final course. Dessert. Nico knew Alex had a sweet tooth, and he'd invented the dessert with Alex in mind. After two days in the kitchen perfecting it, it finally got to make its debut. Nico couldn't wait to see the reaction.

Trix managed to serve without too much trauma to their ears, and Nico turned his attention back to Alex. "This is a coffee and chocolate roulade served with raspberries, strawberries, and cream," he announced proudly.

Alex perked up. "Coffee?"

"Coffee," agreed Nico, "and you get to have a cup afterward as well. We'll have coffee and mints." And more chocolate, thought Nico. He'd made the mint chocolates himself, of course.

Alex looked satisfied as he attacked the roulade. Chocolate sponge filled with coffee cream, raspberries, and strawberries. Nico didn't normally use fruit out of season, but this was a special occasion. The whole thing was rolled up like a swiss roll, and Nico had cut a particularly large piece for his duke.

"This is incredible," said the duke around a mouthful of sponge. "That chef is worth her weight in gold. We have got to have this again; it's just so… incredible." He dived back in again and demolished the dessert within minutes. "Is there any more?" He looked up hopefully. Nico smiled and nodded. This was going so much better than he'd planned. He served another piece of dessert, then handed his own plate over when that was demolished as well.

Nico suggested that they move to the seating area whilst he served coffee, and they both settled on the sofa. "You only get one cup," he cautioned Alex. "Make the most of it."

Alex pulled off his tie and shrugged out of his jacket before he sat down. "That was some meal, babe. Are we doing that every night?"

"No." Nico laughed. "It's a special occasion."

"Shame." Alex tugged Nico closer and began to undo his tie. "I could look forward to doing this every night." He pressed his lips to Nico's and Nico opened for him at once. It had been days since they'd last done this, although they'd never done what he had planned. He knew instinctively that it was the right time. It would be another commitment, but one that Nico was happy to give. He'd discovered that he quite liked marriage. He had far more freedom than he expected and he got this as well. This was probably the most important thing, in fact. He moaned against Alex's mouth, trying to move closer, wanting to feel Alex's body. Alex didn't disappoint, pulling Nico against him and easing the gray jacket from his shoulders. Alex paused to nibble on Nico's ear, kindling a shiver.

"That boy isn't coming back, is he?" Alex nuzzled at Nico's throat, the words like a rumbling purr against his skin. He trembled, loving the closeness, the connection growing between them.

"No," he said, content. "I've given him the rest of the night off."

"Very wise." Alex grinned, looking up at Nico. "The way you look tonight… hell, the way you look every day. I don't know how I've kept my hands off you."

He went for another kiss, starting slow with the mere flick of his tongue against Nico's lips. He gently probed Nico's mouth, gradually intensifying the kiss until Nico's arms were around Alex's neck and his breathing was coming in rapid little bursts.

"So good," gasped Nico when he finally came up for air and rested his head on Alex's shoulder. "You are so good at that."

Alex laughed, setting Nico back and undoing his shirt buttons. When he drew the shirt off Nico's shoulders, his eyes gleamed with appreciation, and Nico knew Alex was pleased with what he saw. It gave him confidence and he reached out to undo Alex's buttons, concentrating hard on unveiling that magnificent frame. He placed small kisses along the way, feeling the path down Alex's torso. He paused to play with Alex's abdominals, breathing deeper to fully gorge on Alex's delicious smell. He smelled of sandalwood and vanilla, and Nico reveled in it, the scent captivating him. Alex let him take the lead and he foraged farther down. It no longer embarrassed him to take down Alex's trousers and briefs. He'd lost his embarrassment within a couple of days of the marriage. Sex was just too good. It was one of the Goddess's greatest gifts. And when the Goddess gave you a gift, the debt was to be paid in the best way—by using the gift. All of which meant more sex for Nico.

He went to his knees in front of Alex and slowly caressed the blessing that he found there. Such strength beneath the soft velvety skin. Such power. He couldn't wait to get all that strength and weight into his mouth. Taking his time, he licked at the head first. He knew Alex liked that; he'd been paying close attention. It always made Alex quicken, as he did now. Nico grinned as he gave a few more licks. He could feel the power begin to rise in Alex. He ducked his head and took the whole crown in his mouth with one smooth move. He'd been practicing that too. Alex gave a shuddering breath and his fingers entangled in Nico's curls. Nico felt his own power tingle and come to life. Another part of him was also coming to life and feeling very crammed in his trousers. He ignored it in favor of eliciting another shudder from Alex before moving on to really arouse him. He manipulated, provoked, and challenged Alex with his tongue, wanting to spur the man on. Nico felt vitalized. He wanted to explore the full potential of the power building between them. He bobbed his head again and took the whole shaft down his throat. Another skill he'd been practicing and it was so much easier with the real thing than it had been with a banana. The real thing didn't break apart in your throat, for one thing. He choked on that thought and pulled away from the shaft, coughing as he did so. Alex reached down and helped him up. He used thumbs to wipe away the tears that had accompanied the coughing.

"Sorry," muttered Nico when the fit ended.

"Don't apologize," said Alex, lifting Nico's chin with one finger. "I was losing control anyway."

"I like you losing control," replied Nico. Alex's eyes were the most beautiful he'd ever seen, Nico decided. Beautiful emerald green, they sparkled with life. And lust, he was happy to notice. He was sure that look was lust.

"I like losing control too." Alex took Nico by the hand and headed for the bed. "But not right now. I haven't had you in days and right now I want to worship you." He stopped by the side of the bed. "You're so beautiful." The moments lengthened into a long pause. Nico couldn't speak, could only continue to stare into Alex's eyes. He was fascinated by the fire he saw banked there. He wanted to add more sparks to the flame and then fan them into an explosion. He loved it when Alex exploded.

So he was quite surprised when Alex picked him up and dropped him on the bed. The man grinned down at him, unrepentant.

"You're wearing too many clothes, baby. Time to take them off."

Alex divested Nico of his clothes and then joined him on the bed. Now they were both naked. Which had been part of his plan, Nico remembered. He mentally patted himself on the back for achieving it. Then he turned his attention back to Alex. Alex, who was skipping his hand back and forth along Nico's flank. Tiny touches that awoke Nico's skin as it tightened with each glance of those wickedly clever fingers.

He began to tremble and not just with lust. He knew he was going to take a big step and whilst he wasn't frightened, he was apprehensive. Would it hurt? The Grand Seers said it did but Alex had promised never to hurt him, and surely he wouldn't promise that if it wasn't true? Alex was an honest man. Plus the Grand Seers had said it *might* hurt. Which meant that it *might not*. Nico knew he wanted to try it. The thought of it excited him. Sometimes when they were having sex, Alex would press his fingers against Nico's anus. It never failed to tip him into climax. It whetted Nico's appetite for more.

Alex was gently massaging his arm now, each long continuous stroke a caress. Nico moved closer. He took a deep breath. "I want more," he said simply.

Alex stared down at him. "You want...?" The question was soft but the fire in his eyes said much more.

"I want more," repeated Nico. "I want you inside me."

He got the slow seductive smile in return. "Are you sure?"

Nico nodded but added, "Will it hurt?"

Alex bent forward to kiss his forehead. "I'd never hurt you, baby. I'm just going to make you feel real good. You're going to love what I do to you." He took Nico's mouth with his own, delving inside to explore, teasing and tormenting as he did. Nico's dick jerked, and he moved closer still, wanting to press himself against Alex, to feel skin against skin. Or hopefully dick against dick.

"I'll be back in a minute," Alex said.

Nico sat up. Where was he going? He watched Alex disappear into the dressing room only to reappear two minutes later. He was carrying some sort of bottle.

"What's that?" Nico questioned.

"It's lube, babe."

"Oh, I've heard of that. Isn't it called lubricant? It's supposed to make it easier? I think they mentioned it in Eros class, but I wasn't really paying attention. I should have paid more attention." He ended on something of a squeak, and he looked at Alex, contrite.

Alex slid on to the bed and cupped Nico's jaw. "Shh, babe, it's okay. I'm here to teach you, remember? It doesn't matter if you didn't pay attention in class. You're not in class now, baby. It's all okay."

Nico relaxed against him. It would be okay, he thought. Alex had said so. Alex kissed him again, and used his fingers to entangle Nico's curls. The feel of those fingers across his scalp was magical, and Nico felt the trembling begin all over again. He gave a contented sigh, giving himself up to the kiss. It became deeper, passionate in the questing of Alex's tongue. He wrapped his arms around Alex's neck, snuggling closer with his body, and allowed his eyes to close. One of Alex's hands drifted down to his buttock, fondling the flesh it found there. Nico felt swept along by the kiss. He felt his power rising, little whirls of electricity that incited his blood to heat, his body to shiver. Nico could feel Alex's power held tightly under control. It excited him that Alex had such self-control. He mastered his powers and Nico had never seen anything so sexy. All that might kept under such a tight rein. All that knowledge and all that skill, and all of it focused on Nico. It was like being a feast to the man.

Tremors racked his body as Alex trailed a path of kisses down his throat and over to his collarbone. A shock went through him when Alex teased his nipple, little light taps of his tongue, a scrape of his teeth, and then a tugging on the nipple itself. Nico came up off the bed with a sharply indrawn breath. The pressure on his nipple didn't cease but became intoxicating, and Nico knew he was leaking badly. He wasn't sure he could control the power anymore, wasn't sure he wanted to. He was rising in a cloud of impulses, unable to see his way through. He began to pant, pleasure making his body stiffen in small jolts. Alex held him firmly, held him still. He didn't allow Nico to pull away; he didn't allow Nico to do anything except feel.

"I can't." Nico tried to focus. "I can't… I'm going to…."

"Oh, yes," murmured Alex against his chest. "I'm looking forward to it." He started to move down Nico's chest, stabbing his tongue into Nico's belly button whilst stroking down his hips.

Nico tried to push him away. "No," he groaned. "I'm going to come. I don't want to come yet."

"Hush, baby. We've got all night. This isn't the end. It's the beginning."

His mouth continued to wind down Nico's body, and Nico surrendered to the feelings. His dick was aching with need, and his balls felt swollen. He pressed forward with his hips, longing for friction, movement, anything to take away this feeling of turmoil that roiled in his blood and left him screaming for more. When Alex finally took Nico's dick in his mouth, Nico cried out. He thrust his hips up, loving the way Alex swallowed him down. He wasn't allowed to move for long, though. Alex grabbed hold of his hips and held them tight as he bobbed up and down Nico's cock, using his mouth and throat to accelerate the blood pumping through Nico's veins. Nico could hear it pounding in his ears, could smell both his own arousal and Alex's. His senses were overloaded, unable to cope when he finally came, cascade after cascade flowing out of him. He groaned back against the pillows, riding the wave as long as he could until replete, then fully relaxed, a deep sigh emanating from his chest.

Alex moved back up his body and kissed him. Nico could taste himself in Alex's mouth, something that never failed to give him a thrill. It was so deliciously naughty. His eyes closed.

"Oh, no, babe. You don't get to go to sleep. We're just beginning." Alex tickled Nico under the arm and Nico jumped. He giggled, opening his eyes to look at his lover. His lover, Nico realized, the words having sudden importance. This was the man he made love with. Alex was his lover. For a split second he wondered if Alex felt the same, but he dismissed the thought immediately. Now wasn't the time for such thoughts. Now was the time for making his connection with this man deeper. It was something Nico felt instinctively. He knew the Goddess was guiding him here. Tonight was special. Tonight was a statement. Tonight was a new vow. And tonight started now.

Alex sat up against the pillows and tugged Nico until Nico's back was against Alex's chest. He wrapped his arms around Nico, patting and stroking wherever his hands fell. Nico leaned back against him, snuggling up and resting his head on Alex's shoulder. The quiet was nice, tranquil. He could hear the distant roar of the sea. Smell the lingering scent of cucumber and feel the solid build of Alex behind him. He felt safe and secure. Protected. It wasn't long before Alex began to nuzzle at his neck, dropping tiny kisses and working his way up to Nico's ear. There was the barest touch of teeth and lots of sexy hot breaths. Nico gave his customary shiver. Alex nuzzled his way back down to his neck and took a deep breath.

"You smell hot."

"I smell of come," laughed Nico.

"Like I said, babe, hot."

Alex moved, sliding out from behind Nico to lie on top of him. Supporting himself on his arms, he pressed his erection against Nico's. Nico loved the weight of the man, the way he always felt so overpowered by Alex, so happy to give in to Alex's command. There was a dominance in Alex that made Nico submit every time. One hand found its way to Nico's buttocks and a finger pressed against his anus. And all the while Alex whispered sweet, hot words in his ear, that wonderful hot breath a rhythm that made him want to sing. "You want me inside, Nico? I want to be inside you so bad. I want to fill you up. My big cock squeezed into that tight little hole. I want that, babe. Do you want that?"

Yes, Nico wanted that. His body started to stir, his dick, already hard, went even harder. He lifted his head, looking for a kiss, and the kiss he got heightened every feeling in his body. Alex was in command of him, directing Nico's body as he saw fit. He reigned over Nico, and if Nico had ever wanted to see majesty, he was certainly seeing it now. It devoured him, and he happily threw himself into the maelstrom.

Alex began to move down his body again, more quickly this time. His nipples only earned the barest of kisses, his torso the lightest of touches. When Alex approached his cock, Nico breathed in expectantly but Alex still used the merest trace of his lips. He didn't deepen the touch until he reached Nico's balls and there he nuzzled the soft wrinkly skin with his nose. Bracing himself on one arm, he continued to nuzzle, whilst bringing his free hand in a smooth sweep along the back of Nico's leg. Strong manipulative fingers massaged the back of Nico's knee. Nico had no idea as to why that should be so exciting, but it was. It made him reach for more. He didn't want to stop this slow build of power that had overtaken him.

Alex lifted up slowly and opened Nico's legs so he could place himself between them. He pushed the legs up, making Nico bend at the knees. Nico found himself fully exposed to Alex's view. He knew a moment's doubt and alarm, but he pushed them both away. He wanted this. He felt more aware of himself, his body, and his senses. He could feel the smooth cotton of the sheet as he grabbed at it with his hands. He could feel Alex's eyes on him, studying him, those eyes half-closed as he took in the scene in front of him. Then Alex lowered himself down and began to lick Nico's perineum. Nico tensed; he'd never been licked there before. It felt unbelievable, heightening the tremble of his body, inciting flame into Nico's blood. He was being energized. Alex's mouth was energizing him, invigorating him, every nerve ending being stimulated and vitalized.

Alex grasped each of Nico's buttocks and spread his cheeks before moving his mouth over Nico's anus. Nico screamed out, unable to contain all the power within any longer. He felt electrified and on his way to a frenzy. He had to let some of the power out, so he moaned and he groaned and he gasped and he gulped. And still the power flooded through him, building and building until he was sure he would pass out from the sheer pleasure Alex bestowed on him. But the rhythmic motion of Alex's mouth and tongue only continued that mind-boggling bliss that made him beg for more. Made him plead with Alex to keep sweeping his tongue across Nico's asshole. He didn't want it to stop.

Then Alex changed the tempo. He moved to short sharp jabs with the point of his tongue. Nico was right on board with this. "Yes, yes," he cried. "Keep doing that, keep doing that." Then he was back to begging and pleading, searching for more. Not knowing what he wanted, only knowing that there was something he needed. He didn't just want. Want was too simple a word.

He reached for his dick but Alex pushed his hand away. "Gonna give you what you want, baby. Gonna give you what you need." His voice was rasping, the breath hot and heavy against Nico's hole. There were more licks, more thrusts, and then that deep sexy voice against him again. "I could eat you out all night, boy."

Nico didn't understand the thrill that went through his body with the word "boy." He couldn't deny it, though, as thrill became tremors and tremors became a full-blown tremble. He arched his body up to Alex's mouth, the pleas becoming whispers now, his throat parched from all the screaming.

Alex laughed. "Poor baby," he murmured before kissing Nico again. The kiss was soft and soothing, and Nico's desperation began to dissipate. He began to feel a bit more in control. It didn't last long. Alex slid one long finger between his buttocks and used just the tip to enter Nico. Nico stiffened against the invasion. Alex nuzzled him along his neck, and he immediately trembled. The finger was questing farther now, and Nico was aware of a burning sensation, not quite pain but not comfortable either. The finger withdrew, and Nico realized that Alex was applying lube to his fingers. All of his fingers.

"Alex?"

"Hush, babe. It's okay. Just relax."

The finger returned to his anus and this time it slid in easier, right through the thick muscle until it entered Nico fully. He gasped at the breach but the burn was gone and it felt so good. He wanted to bear down, to meet Alex's rhythm with his own. Alex's finger brushed against his prostate and he screamed, his hips lifting from the bed, searching for the feeling again. "Oh my Goddess" became a chant, a demand. It became ambitious as his body sought for more.

He didn't want this to stop, had never known such a feeling was possible. A second finger entered and Nico felt the burn again, but this time it was a promise that there was so much more to come. He welcomed it, loving the stretch of his hole, the easing of the muscle. He was begging for more when Alex added the third finger, and as he urged his lover on, he became aware once again of the power building in the room. It had never disappeared, simply sat dormant around them until it was called on again. His power and Alex's power swirled around them, enveloping them in their own private cocoon. Nico had never seen power like it. Had never experienced power like it. It rushed through his body even as it whistled around them. Alex brushed against his prostate again, and Nico forgot all about power and concentrated on matching Alex's movements. He felt full but not full enough. His body was greedy and he didn't know how to communicate that to Alex. He groaned in dismay when Alex withdrew his fingers, then watched in fascination when Alex lubed up his prick. Then Alex was back between his legs and that strong rigid dick was poking between his buttocks. Alex took a moment to line himself up, and then he smiled down at Nico. It was a feral, sexy smile, the smile of a man who knew he'd conquered. He looked deep into Nico's eyes.

"Ready?"

"Goddess, yes." Nico almost wept and cried out when Alex entered, pushing through the muscle and then slowly going deeper inside Nico. There was the burn, exciting now to Nico, who wondered how he could have ever found it uncomfortable. There was the sense of being filled, crammed, and overwhelmed. Once he was fully seated, Alex stayed still for a few moments. Nico's body adapted to Alex, relaxing the muscles and opening up. He automatically wrapped his legs around Alex's hips, urging him to move and go deeper. They both groaned when Alex did move. They worked in tandem to find the rhythm to time their movements for the maximum effect. Nico felt the fire flood through him, building him up. He opened his eyes to realize that his power and Alex's power had actually merged, and the intensity of the cocoon was heating up. He moved his hips with zeal, dedicating himself to the frenzy, when suddenly he erupted, come spurting out of him with a release that overshadowed every orgasm that had gone before. He yelled out Alex's name as his body pulsed with orgasm, his muscles tightening around Alex. The effect had Alex stiffening before he cried out in triumph as his own orgasm hit him.

Nico lay replete after what was probably the most staggering experience of his life. He welcomed the weight of Alex's body as it grounded him back to the now.

Eventually, Alex rolled on his back, taking Nico with him, but by the time he did so, Nico was fast asleep.

PART TEN

ALEX DRANK down the last of his herbal tea and grimaced. It was disgusting stuff, and he doubted he'd ever get used to it. Even though he'd had a cup last night, he mourned the loss of coffee. Worth it if it kept his boy happy, of course. Alex realized that he'd do anything to keep his boy happy. He'd never felt like this before. Lovers came and went, sometimes literally. He'd had the odd affair but always with other soldiers. Men who understood the system. Men every bit as focused on their career as Alex was. Or at least had been. He'd reached the pinnacle, career-wise, but life was about more than careers. Life was about love, home, joy, and happiness. His parents had taught him that and the lesson had stayed with him. He'd entered the Gleaning in the hope of finding the love his parents had, and he placed his full trust in the Goddess. It was all working out fine. He and Nico suited each other; they fit well. They'd certainly fitted well the night before. He grinned. They'd fit well tonight too. As long as Nico wasn't too sore. He had been gone when Alex awoke, but that wasn't unusual. Nico enjoyed his morning walk. Alex thought it was some sort of priest thing. He'd issued orders that Nico was not to be disturbed and no one was allowed on the beach until Nico had finished. Then he'd set men in the turrets to guard not only Nico's privacy but also his life. The rumors of discontent were gaining weight, and Alex had no intention of leaving Nico without guards. He hadn't told Nico. No reason to worry the boy. Not when Alex had everything in hand.

He looked at his empty plate and mourned the loss of bacon. Fruit was all well and good, but it wasn't meat. He was startled by the door opening with a great crash and looked around to see Watkins storming into the room waving a mini comm.

"Have you seen this, lad?" Watkins bellowed. "Have you seen this?" He threw the mini comm at Alex, who managed to catch it before it hit him in the face.

"What the hell…?"

"Look at it, lad. Look at the nonsense about you and the pretty boy that's all over the Social Web. There are photographs." His voice rose, clearly astounded that such a thing could happen. "Photographs! I thought you controlled your Social Web page. You told me you controlled it."

"I do control it," replied Alex, who was busy studying the mini comm. He frowned as a photo appeared of him and Nico. He recognized it straight away. It had been taken the night before. The photo led to an article where great effort had gone into describing the "romantic candlelit dinner for two," and had subparagraphs with headings like "First Night in Their New Home." All nonsense from what Alex could tell as he scanned down the columns.

"I didn't authorize this, but I really don't see what damage it's done."

"Don't see the damage?" roared Watkins. "It's turned you into a laughingstock, lad, but there's worse than that."

"What are you talking about, old man?" Alex narrowed his eyes as he turned his full focus on Watkins.

"Riots, lad. Riots! There's trouble in Thetis. The people there aren't happy about their duke paying more attention to his pretty boy than to them. I told you this would happen, lad. I told you where your attention should lie but did you listen to me? Did you?"

"I'm listening now, old man. Tell me about the riots."

"Started about five this morning; the watchers got it under control about nine. There's lots of property damage and a couple of minor injuries. No one dead, thank the Goddess."

"We'll go to the city. See if you can get me a meeting with the instigator of this riot. Let's see what they've got to say."

"And the rest of it?"

"What rest of it?"

"The stories, lad, the stories on the Social Web." Watkins looked at him in disbelief. "You have to do something about the stories."

"I don't see what I can do about them, Watkins," said Alex slowly. "If they're all over the Social Web, then there's no shutting it down. Besides, what have people learned? We had a meal and it was our first night in the house. Who cares?"

"The food, lad. He's turned you into a laughingstock. Look at the food."

Alex looked down on the mini comm in confusion.

"Aphrodisiacs, lad," Watkins yelled. "Aphrodisiacs. Everything the pretty boy served you was an aphrodisiac."

Alex grinned. "It certainly was."

Watkins threw his hands in the air and turned away on a grunt, muttering furiously under his breath.

"For Goddess's sake, old man. There's nothing I can do about the news on the Social Web. I can, however, make sure it doesn't happen again. I'll have to go and find Trix."

"Why will you have to find Trix, Your Grace?" Nico stood in the doorway, one eyebrow arched in question.

Alex smiled when he saw him and crossed the room to kiss his cheek.

"How are you feeling?" he asked softly so Watkins wouldn't hear.

Nico blushed but said, "I'm very well, thank you, Your Grace. I'm feeling very, er, satisfied today. Now why do you need to find Trix, Your Grace?"

"It's nothing for you to worry about, Nico," replied Alex smoothly. He didn't want the boy bothered by the riots. Knowing Nico's inherent need to help people, he'd want to be out there, and Alex wasn't going to allow that.

"Nevertheless, I'd like to know," Nico said formally. "If Your Grace would be so good?"

They were interrupted by a squeal from the door and Trix came running in, rushing up to Nico. "Have you seen it? Have you seen it? It looks so good." He waved his mini comm in Nico's face. "I couldn't believe it when I saw it. We're all over the Social Web. All over it." He laughed happily before turning to Alex. "Did you like the photo, Your Grace? I told you I was good. Some of my friends think I might get an award for it. Can you imagine? I've never won an award, and to get one on the Social Web, well, that would just be trem. Don't you think that would be trem?"

"I don't know what 'trem' means," said Alex, taken aback by the question. Didn't this boy realize what trouble he was in?

Nico looked up from where he was studying Trix's mini comm. "I believe it means 'tremendous,' Your Grace," he explained before turning his attention back to the mini comm.

"Does it?" Trix looked delighted. "I didn't know that. I'll have to tell my friends. Can I have the mini comm back, Your Highness, or do you want to read more of the articles? Don't you love the photograph? I do. I love it so much and if I win an award... I so want to win an award. It would just be so trem."

"Is this boy responsible for…?" demanded Watkins.

"Apparently," replied Alex.

Nico looked up at once. "What is he responsible for?" He handed the mini comm back to Trix and then maneuvered his position so he was between Trix and Watkins. And himself, Alex realized. What did Nico think he was going to do to the boy?

"He released unauthorized material onto the Social Web," Alex replied carefully. He didn't want Nico to dig too deep into this.

"Does that matter?" questioned Nico in surprise.

"Of course it matters, fool. Of course it matters," bellowed Watkins in disgust.

Alex wasn't going to let him get away with it, however. "You will apologize, and you will not call His Highness a fool again," he ordered curtly.

"I don't mind if he calls me a fool," said Nico. "Every Man is a Fool at the Beginning of His Journey." He added the last in High Speech, and Alex was startled to see that it shut Watkins up.

It wouldn't shut him up, though. "Well, I do mind, and Watkins will apologize."

Watkins had the grace to look shamefaced and muttered a quick apology. It wasn't the greatest apology, but Alex knew it was the only one Nico would get. Nico, bless him, accepted it graciously.

"Now," Nico started again. "Just why does this matter? It seems frivolous, but it doesn't seem anything to get upset about."

Alex suggested they sit down. He included both Trix and Watkins. He had to tread very carefully here. It would be too easy to give away the news of the riot. Nico sent for more tea and then served everyone—wasn't Trix supposed to do that? Trix was tapping away at his screen and Alex wondered what he was saying now. Was the whole world to know that Nico had ordered lemon balm tea on the grounds that it would calm them all down? He decided to take the screen away from the boy. Just until things were explained carefully to him.

"We have to control what information is given out about us," he began, carefully placing the mini comm on the table in front of him. Trix looked at it mournfully, and Alex realized that he probably looked like that when he was thinking about bacon.

"Whilst this seems to be a bit of a flummery, it was unauthorized and we cannot allow unauthorized information to get out."

"Okay," said Nico complacently. "Now we know that, we'll make sure not to do it in future. Trix? Do you agree?"

"Agree to what? Can I have my mini pad back now? I'm waiting on messages from friends, and I need to tell them about the lemon balm tea." He looked anxiously at the mini comm. Alex saw a look of concern come over Nico's face, and Nico leaned in toward Trix.

"Trix?" he said softly. "Listen to me for a moment." Trix turned to Nico and gave a smile.

"You can't have your mini pad back, Trix, until you agree not to write anything more about myself or the duke."

"Or anything about the Sixth Land," inserted Alex hurriedly, but Nico glared at him.

"I don't think we need to go that far, Your Grace."

"Not write about Your Highness and Your Grace?" Trix looked at Nico and then turned to Alex, huge tears welling up in Trix's eyes. Alex shifted uncomfortably, whilst Watkins looked disgusted. Nico was looking more concerned.

"But what will I write? My friends want to know all about you. More and more people want to be my friend since I started posting about you, and I thought you loved the photograph. Didn't you love the photograph?"

"We love the photograph, Trix." Nico took hold of one of Trix's hands. "Didn't we love the photograph, Your Grace?"

Alex nodded and when a glare from Nico made him realize that wasn't enough, he quickly added, "Yes, we loved the photograph. In fact, I'd like one to put in a frame. I think it's an excellent photograph." That earned him a smiling nod from Nico, so he didn't mind that he sounded like a sap.

Thankfully, the tears stopped and Trix looked at him with big blue eyes. "Really?" he said. "Do you really like it?"

"I do, yes," Alex began carefully again. "But you can't post any more." Hell, the tears were starting again. He looked to Nico. Luckily, Nico looked like he knew what he was doing. He was a healer after all. Didn't they have compassion? Alex didn't have compassion. He was a warrior. Warriors didn't do compassion. Not often anyway, he thought, remembering a couple of occasions. He brought himself back to the moment. Nico was giving Trix a handkerchief and telling him that everything would be okay.

Alex started anew.

"It's a question of safety, Trix. You want to keep His Highness safe, don't you?" Trix nodded. "Then you can't post anything about His Highness's movements. What he does, for example, what his routines are. You'll be leaving him open to attack."

"Why would anyone attack His Highness?" asked Trix between sobs. "No one would want to hurt him. Everybody loves him. You can see how popular he is on the Social Web. Look, just look." He waved toward the mini comm, clearly becoming more agitated.

The sobs got louder and Nico sighed. He took a deep breath and set his shoulders back. "I think that I may just go and have a chat with Trix on my own, Your Grace." He stood up, encouraging Trix to stand up too. Nico placed one arm around Trix and allowed him to cry on Nico's shoulder. Compassion, thought Alex. His boy had compassion. He hid his grin of pleasure because now really wasn't the time. Trix was still sobbing as Nico led him out of the room. Alex couldn't pretend he wasn't relieved. He'd seen men crying before, but they were soldiers. They cried out of the sheer horror of war. But they weren't young boys. Young boys shouldn't have anything to cry about.

Nico stopped at the doorway, still holding Trix. He turned back to Alex.

"I shall be about an hour, Your Grace," he said. "I suggest you arrange some transport for us. We need to visit Thetis."

ALEX WAS still walking up and down the breakfast room an hour later. No, no, no, he kept repeating. Absolutely no way was Nico going to Thetis. Over his dead body would Nico travel to Thetis. He looked at Watkins and turned back to trace his steps. No, no, no.

"Well, you've got yourself in a mess now, lad," observed Watkins. "How are you going to get out of this? Can't take the pretty boy to Thetis; pretty boy can't look after himself. Have to keep him safe."

"I know that, thank you," retorted Alex, annoyed at everyone and everything. The day had started so well, too. "I don't need you to tell me how to look after him. He isn't going to Thetis."

"So why don't we leave now?" scorned Watkins. "What are we waiting for? The people in Thetis need to see you. They need to know that you're going to act. What are we waiting for, lad?"

"We're waiting to explain it to him. I'm not just going to disappear without talking to him. What sort of husband would that make me? I'm going to explain things to him and then we'll leave for Thetis. It's still early. One hour isn't going to make a difference."

Watkins grunted and muttered under his breath. Alex left him to it. He had to work out exactly the right way to put this to Nico. He had a feeling the boy wasn't going to react well.

The boy in question came back into the room. It was a relief that he didn't have Trix with him.

"Have you arranged transport, Your Grace?"

"Sit down, Nico." Alex smiled. Nico put his head on one side, studying Alex. He seemed to come to some sort of understanding and nodded.

"All right," he said and took a chair at the table. Alex sat next to him and took one of his hands.

"Is Trix okay?" he asked, stroking Nico's hand.

"He will be," replied Nico. "It's going to take some time and effort, but we must discuss Trix later, Your Grace. I believe that we have other, equally important news."

"Er, what news would that be?" Alex groaned internally. He'd hoped to avoid this.

"The riots in Thetis, of course. We must go there immediately. The King Will Be True to the People, Your Grace. I believe we've discussed this before."

"You don't need to go," Alex said, deciding the simplest argument would be the best. Nico always appreciated brevity when it came to explanations. In fact, Nico picked things up very quickly. Alex had never had to explain anything to him in depth. He hoped that would be true now.

"You can stay here," he continued, keeping his attention on Nico's reactions. "I can go. You'll be safe here."

Nico laughed. Actually laughed. Alex sat back in confusion. Didn't Nico realize the dangers? Thetis was a firework waiting to go off. Tensions there were high. There was no way he was going to allow Nico to go to Thetis.

"I'll be perfectly safe, Your Grace. I am a priest and a healer. I have free pass amongst the people."

Alex wanted to squirm. Strictly speaking, that was true. Both priests and healers were able to go about their business with no fear of assault, regardless of how bad an area they might wander into. No one would hurt a priest or a healer. The trouble was that Nico was so much more than a priest and a healer. He was a Royal Prince of the Goddess, he had taken vows with the Duke of the Sixth Land, and since the rumors were undoubtedly true, that made him the enemy of a large number of people. He pondered his words.

"Whilst we *hope* that is true," he said, "we don't *know* that it's true. I won't take a chance with your safety."

"You really think that I may be under threat?" Nico asked calmly. Alex wanted to shake him. Of course he was under threat and he shouldn't be taking that so lightly. He took a deep breath before he responded.

"I won't take a chance with your safety," he repeated. What else was there to say?

Nico nodded. "You'll feel better if I don't go?"

Alex let out his breath. The boy understood. Thank the Goddess. "Yes, I'll feel much better. I won't be long and I'll tell you all about it when I come back."

"That would be very kind of you, Your Grace. However, I may not be here. If I can't go to Thetis, then I must go to Tethys. I need to see the Grand Seers there. It is a healing matter."

"You want to go to Tethys?" Alex wasn't sure he liked that any more than the idea that Nico would go to Thetis. Tethys was the larger of the two cities, and Nico would be open to attack. It was true that the riots had taken place in Thetis, but that didn't mean that it wouldn't kick off in Tethys.

"I'll be perfectly safe, Your Grace." Nico was beginning to sound annoyed. "I'll go straight from here to Academia Hall and I'll be inside Academia Hall until I come straight back here. What could possibly go wrong?"

"Don't say that, boy!" shouted Watkins immediately. "We don't use that phrase, boy. Never use that phrase."

Nico turned to him. "Really? Why ever not?"

"You're tempting Fate, boy. We don't tempt Fate. Now turn around three times and spit over your left shoulder," Watkins advised. Alex nodded.

"Seriously?" Nico looked astounded. "You want me to turn around three times and spit over my left shoulder?"

"Yes." Alex nodded. "It appeases Fate."

"I'm not spitting in the breakfast room," Nico objected, but he was smiling too. Alex felt a flash of annoyance. The boy was a priest, for Goddess's sake. Surely he understood Fate?

"Then go outside," bellowed Watkins. "But do it now."

If Nico was taken aback, he didn't show it. He stood up and went to the door that led out onto the veranda. There he turned three times and spat over his shoulder. He returned to the room and sat down as though nothing had happened.

"Do you feel better now, Your Grace?" he asked with a small smile.

Alex felt a bit stupid. "Yes, thank you," he muttered.

"Good. Now, my trip to Tethys. I expect you'd rather I went with a guard."

Alex realized that Nico had neatly placed him in a corner. If he objected to the trip now, he'd look unreasonable. In truth, he couldn't think of any reason why Nico shouldn't go to see the Grand Seers. If he was going to be safe anywhere, it would be in Academia Hall. Plus with *two* guards in the car, he should be safe enough on the journey there and back. He knew he wouldn't feel happy until Nico was at the castle, though. He'd stay in touch with the car through comms. He'd make it very clear to Nico's guards that he was to be told if anything… anything happened at all. He was going to give in, and decided there and then that he should do so with good grace.

ALEX RETURNED from Thetis five very long hours later. Thetis had been a nightmare. It was like entering the remains of a war zone. The commercial docks dominated the shoreline. They rose like black monstrous shadows, casting a pall over their surroundings. Wasteland stood all around them. They'd driven past run-down hotels and flophouses, bars, gambling dens, brothels catering to all types. Everywhere was in a state of disrepair or even falling down. Large empty lots told of buildings long gone and forgotten.

Alex was shocked to see that the healing center included what they called a soup kitchen. In his mind, soup kitchens belonged to Old Earth along with the poverty that had occurred there. In today's world and on this planet, there had never been poverty. Why was it happening now? The healer they were introduced to said it was lack of food. There just wasn't enough. There was also a problem with wages. People couldn't afford to rent a house and earn enough to eat. The subsequent overcrowding that resulted was bringing a whole host of illnesses with it. He was open about the fact that the healers couldn't cope with the masses flooding into the city looking for work or for food and shelter. He was vitriolic about the distribution of money in the twin cities. Tethys had luxury beyond belief whilst Thetis had nothing. He believed that it was not surprising the people were rioting and it could only get worse.

Alex was given a tour of the surrounding area and could have wept for the people. The housing stock was derelict; there was no other way to describe it. Most of the streets had boarded-up buildings and there was rubbish piled high on the streets. The people themselves were run-down, apathetic for the most part. Children dressed in rags played among the rubbish, whilst old people sat on the house steps watching them. No one approached them or even paid attention to them. The whole atmosphere was one of neglect and lethargy. He was shown the damage that had been done to a couple of the houses during the riot. Empty houses, he noticed, and he asked why they had been targeted. The landlord preferred to keep houses empty rather than lower the rent, and the people had objected in the only way open to them. He made a note of the landlord's name.

After a quick deliberation with Watkins, he arranged for food to be shipped into the area and promised to have soldiers help distribute it throughout the city. He also promised more healers in the immediate future. Finally, he said he'd look into the housing situation and the job situation. He couldn't understand why wages were so low. The biggest employer was the docks, and they were clearly busy, so why weren't the workers getting paid?

It was a relief to get back to the castle, but the relief didn't last long. He'd kept in touch with Nico's guards throughout the day and everything had been fine. So it was a shock to discover Nico hadn't returned home.

PART ELEVEN

ACCOMPANIED BY two guards, Nico left the castle. Trix had wanted to come with him, but Nico had felt he would do better at the castle. It would be a lot easier to talk about Trix with the Grand Seers if Trix wasn't there. He'd given Trix some hands-on healing and left him with a pot of chamomile tea. He'd also obtained Trix's promise that he wouldn't post any more information on the Social Web. Trix hadn't been happy about it, but when Nico had pointed out that he could post all he liked about his bedroom design, the boy had been happier. Now Nico had to get to the bottom of the problem, and he firmly believed that the Grand Seers could give him the answers he needed. It wasn't too long a journey to Tethys, and Nico was looking forward to it. It was the first time he'd left the castle since they'd arrived, and he soon discovered that there was lots to see.

Tethys was a beautiful city. Clean, open, and green, it spoke of luxury in its buildings and parks. Academia Hall was huge with its own parkland and several graceful buildings on the campus. Nico went straight to the main building, surprised to find that the guards followed him in. What did they think would happen to him in Academia Hall?

It wasn't long before Grand Seer Joseph came hurrying down the corridor to meet him.

"We're most honored, Your Highness, most honored. Did we… er… expect your visit?"

"No, not at all, Brother Joseph, and please, call me Nico. Is there somewhere we can talk?"

Grand Seer Joseph led them to a side sitting room and Nico recognized the layout and furniture. It was much the same as the side sitting room in his own Academia Hall. He was pleased when his guards, having checked the room out, opted to stay outside and posted themselves on either side of the door.

"I need to talk about Patrick," began Nico. "How long has he been having mental health issues?"

The Grand Seer shifted uncomfortably in his seat. "We weren't really sure it was a mental health issue," he prevaricated. "We thought he might have attention problems."

"It's definitely a mental health issue, and he doesn't have any attention problems when he's on the Social Web. What can you tell me about his background?"

It was a sad story. Abandoned on the step of Academia Hall when he was a toddler, he'd been adopted by the Grand Seers because there had been nowhere else to send him. At one stage they hoped that he might be eligible for the Gleaning, but that proved not to be so. However, those with foresight had emphasized the importance that he stay in Academia Hall because he was favored by the Goddess. The Grand Seers had taken that to mean he should be one of the Priest class. That too had failed, however, and it wasn't until Nico and Alex appeared that they decided he should serve the Prince. Trix's own enthusiasm for that post had encouraged the Grand Seers into thinking it was the right move.

"Do you want him to return here, Your Highness? I can appreciate you don't want your personal affairs all over the Social Web."

Nico was shocked. "Of course not. I want him to stay at the castle. It seems to me that Trix thinks his friends only exist online. That isn't true, of course."

"It isn't?" questioned the Grand Seer doubtfully.

"No, it isn't," confirmed Nico. "I'm his friend, and I don't just exist on the Web. Never fear, Brother Joseph, Trix will be quite happy at the castle. I shall see to his healing myself. Now tell me, brother, do we have healers in Thetis?"

On that subject Grand Seer Joseph was much more verbose. His dislike of the inhabitants of Thetis was obvious and it was also obvious that he never actually spent any time there. Nico decided he didn't like what he was hearing. If there was a need for healers here, then it seemed to him, they should be in Thetis. A modern hospital existed in Tethys but no such facility in Thetis. Instead, it appeared there was a small healing center staffed by very few healers. Nico asked if he could meet them, and the Grand Seer looked shocked.

"Meet the healers?" he asked. "Why would you want to meet the healers in Thetis? Very rough and inferior people, Your Highness, they wouldn't be able to find employment here in Tethys, believe me."

"But they are healers?"

"Oh, yes. They passed the exams, wouldn't be able to practice otherwise, but no decent hospital would employ them. Do you know that some of them have tattoos? Quite unacceptable."

Nico realized that snobbery was very much alive and kicking in Tethys. If he'd had an inkling at the castle, he was fully convinced now. He also realized he wasn't going to get much further with Grand Seer Joseph. He'd have to attack this problem from another angle.

"Perhaps I can meet the healers here," he suggested. "Is the healing center close?"

"Why yes, Your Highness, it isn't far at all. However, would you not like to tour Academia Hall first? I know that our candidates for the Gleaning would love to meet you."

Oh, Goddess, thought Nico. Really? The last thing he wanted to do was tour Academia Hall. He wanted to get to the root of the problems in Thetis.

"I'd like that very much, Brother Joseph, but I feel that I should have the duke with me for such an important event and it would be very wrong of me to just turn up and expect a tour. Perhaps we could arrange it for another day?"

"Er, yes, of course, Your Highness. In truth it would probably be better to arrange a day when we've had time to prepare. It's very thoughtful of you to consider us. Erm, would you like me to accompany you?"

"That's kind of you, sir, but unnecessary, I assure you. I know that you must have a busy day ahead of you, and I've already taken up too much of your time. I'll just take my leave now."

Nico was relieved to leave Academia Hall. Was everyone in this city a snob or elitist? Hopefully he'd fare better at the healing center. Healers were trained to treat all patients and not to consider their backgrounds. Unfortunately, the trip to the healing center wasn't any better, and Nico was left frustrated and angry, though he didn't show either emotion. The elitism was in total contrast to the ethos of healers, and Nico didn't understand why they couldn't see that. They talked of the inhabitants of Thetis as if they were the dregs of society, and one or two of the healers had made it known that they would never lay healing hands on someone from Thetis. Nico was appalled at their attitudes. He took note of the fact that it was the weakest of the healers who held this view, but that was no excuse. If they'd passed the healer exam, then they knew all about the ethos, so why weren't they practicing it? The rumors spoke of mysterious illnesses in both the city and the countryside, but these people didn't seem to know anything about them. Nico knew he had to go to Thetis and see for himself. He wasn't going to get any help from Tethys. He was tempted to go straight away; it was only over the bridge and would take an hour at most. He couldn't go, though, because the duke had made it clear he wouldn't be safe. Nico didn't believe that for a moment, but he'd promised the duke. Had he actually promised? No, he didn't think he had, but it would be splitting hairs. He'd allowed the duke to think he wouldn't go there today and so he couldn't go. It wouldn't be right to break his word. No one had said anything about tomorrow, though. Tomorrow he would travel to Thetis whether the duke liked it or not. Just because he was married to the man didn't mean he should allow the duke to dictate his movements. In fact, the duke had promised to let him pursue his own interests, and right now his interests lay in Thetis. He said a quick prayer to the Goddess to ask Her to send someone from Thetis to him in the meantime. If he could talk to one of them, he might get some answers.

Suddenly, he wanted out of the healing center and away from all these elitist bigots. He needed some air. Spotting an exit, he made some excuses to the healer accompanying him on the tour and headed straight for it. Closely followed by his guards, of course.

They exited the healing center somewhere near the side of the building, and Nico found himself opposite the Watchers Station. It was a new building done in the style known as minimalist. Nico hated it on sight. About to suggest to the guards that they should return to the car, he was distracted by a bellow from over the road. Two watchers were trying to capture a dog who had escaped. The dog was leading them on a merry chase around the car park in front of the station. When one watcher got close, it would run in a different direction. The other watcher would approach and off the dog would go again. Nico smiled. The dog had character, and he liked that. He didn't like the way the watchers were speaking to the animal, though, and made his way across the road, shrugging off the guards' concerns.

"Excuse me," Nico said loudly to the two watchers. "What are you doing?"

"You mind your own business, boy. This is nothing to do with you. This is watchers' business."

"And I'm making it my business."

"Just stay out of it. Who do you think you are getting into watchers' business?"

Nico signaled to his guards to stay back when both men tried to move in front of him. He walked closer to the watchers and tilted his head to one side. "Does it matter who I am? I'm asking a simple question. I'm not doing any harm."

"I've told you to stay away," barked the first of the Watchers. "If you don't move back, you'll be feeling the weight of my baton."

The guards hurriedly tried to get in front of Nico, but once again, Nico signaled them to stay back. He couldn't believe the way these watchers were speaking to him. Not that he expected special treatment, but they shouldn't be speaking to anyone like this. All he was doing was asking a simple question. He looked at the dog, who was observing them from the far side of the car park. The two watchers appeared to have forgotten it and had all their focus on Nico. Nico gave a short whistle and patted his thigh. The dog came running over and wound its way around Nico's legs. He bent down to stroke it.

"Get away from that animal," ordered the first Watcher. "He's dangerous."

"Don't be ridiculous," snapped Nico, losing patience. "He's not dangerous at all. Look at him."

The dog had lain down at his feet and rolled onto his back, exposing his stomach. Nico reached down and rubbed his belly, and the dog squirmed in delight.

"I said get away from the dog," warned the Watcher. "And mind your own business. We're the Watchers, not you."

"No," replied Nico. "I'm the Prince of the Sixth Land, and I'd like to see your manager."

"Yeah, right," sneered the second Watcher. "And I'm the duke. I bet you're from Thetis, aren't you? Scum, we don't put up with your sort here in Tethys. Now run along or I'll be arresting you."

"Then I suggest you arrest me, but I'll be taking the dog with me." Nico was furious now. The dog sat up and whimpered at his feet, and he leaned down to stroke him, patting his head gently.

The guards were at his side immediately. "For Goddess's sake, Your Highness, don't do this," said one quietly. "The duke will be livid. The dog's not worth it."

"All of the Goddess's creatures are worth it," replied Nico. He took a step forward. The guards and the dog both took steps forward too, which ruined the effect Nico was trying to make. He sighed, took a deep breath, and squared his shoulders. He would not be bullied, and the two Watchers were obviously bullies. Nico hated bullies.

One of the Watchers also took a step forward whilst the other brought out a baton. The dog began to growl, and the guards uncovered their guns. Things were rapidly getting out of control, and even the Watchers seemed to realize it. They glanced at each other uneasily and moved closer together. The first Watcher got his baton out as well.

"My guards have guns," Nico pointed out. "Batons aren't an effective weapon in comparison." He hoped the guards had the guns set to stun, but he wasn't going to let the Watchers know that. One of the Watchers took a step back.

"Just give us the dog and you can go," he said. "The dog's got to be put down. It's dangerous."

"He's not dangerous at all," retorted Nico, "and you're not going to put him down. I'll take him."

"Then you're a fool. That animal came over the bridge from Thetis. Goddess only knows what diseases it's got."

The conversation went no further when half a dozen Watchers streamed out of the building. Carrying guns, they formed a semicircle in front of Nico. Nico's guards sprang into action, getting in front of Nico despite his protests. "Stand down" came the order from the Watchers. The guards took no notice, keeping their guns aimed at the men. Nico focused all his energies. He felt the power build and released it with a rush. The Watchers all dropped their guns with yells and shouts. They looked at their hands in horror. Nico knew they expected to see burns. He'd made the guns very hot after all. He strode past his surprised guards and approached the Watchers.

"I want to see the person in charge," he commanded. One of the men ran back into the station. Within a minute, he was back accompanied by an older man who did not look happy to be there.

"And you are?" asked Nico

"I'm the Head Watcher here, and I want to know what you think you're doing," the man said. "Who the hell are you?"

"My name is Nico DeVrie, and I'm the Prince of the Sixth Land. I'm also a healer and a priest, and I expect free passage in this land. I do not expect to be bullied and threatened as I go about my business. Explain the actions of your men, sir."

The man paled and came forward bowing. "Your Highness," he said. "I'm sure it's a simple misunderstanding. If we go inside, I'm sure there will be a good explanation for this." He looked to the two original Watchers, who looked nauseated at his words. "Yes, I'm sure it's just a misunderstanding. Come inside. I can send for refreshments and find out what's been going on, and I'm certain we can resolve this issue, Your Highness. I assure you no harm was meant."

"Harm was meant to this dog," retorted Nico. "And I can only presume that harm was meant to me when your men threatened me with batons."

"Of course, of course, but a misunderstanding I'm sure. If you'll just come inside...."

"No, I don't think so," said Nico. "I think I would rather just leave. I'll be taking the dog with me."

"You want the dog?" The man looked confused. "But this dog is from Thetis. We've been trying to catch it for days. Full of disease you know, not at all suitable for someone of your eminence. Not at all."

"Nevertheless, I will be taking the dog. If he has any illness, I shall consult a vet. You do have vets here, I presume?" Nico allowed the scorn to show in his voice. The snobbery apparently extended to animals. He despaired for the people of Tethys. What sort of society was this? Would the vet even agree to treat the dog? He leaned down and patted the dog's head again.

One of the guards interrupted his thoughts. "Your Highness, we must leave. We were expected back at the castle an hour ago."

Nico nodded in agreement. He looked down at the dog. Despite being muddy and bedraggled, he was clearly a beautiful dog. His ears flopped down at the tips and Nico thought it was adorable. He'd always wanted a dog. He realized he'd asked the Goddess to bring a native of Thetis to him and She'd done just that. He smiled. Let She Who Weaves The Web Write the Story, he thought. He turned his attention back to the Head of the Watchers. "I'm going to take the dog. If my husband was available, then I'd suggest you explain your actions to him, but I know that he is busy in Thetis today so we won't disturb him. However, in the future I don't expect to be accosted by your men. I trust that you will make that clear?"

The man went even whiter but nodded in agreement. "Of course, Your Highness. It won't happen again. You have my word."

Nico took his leave, pleased that the dog came with him. He even walked to heel. Someone somewhere had trained the dog well.

Settled back in the car with the dog next to him, Nico pondered what to call him. The name came at once. Oliver. Oliver was a great name. It owed its existence to the olive tree and symbolized fruitfulness and beauty and dignity. Nico was sure that once he was cleaned up, Oliver would be both beautiful and dignified. He expected their relationship would be very fruitful indeed. The Goddess had given him Oliver, and Nico knew that Oliver was a true gift.

"You're going to be very happy with us," he cooed to the dog. "No more nasty Watchers for you." Oliver looked up at him, eyes gleaming. Nico was very surprised to see the dog wink. Had he imagined it? Did dogs wink? He'd never heard of that. Perhaps it was just a one-off thing, he thought, and turned his attention to giving the dog a good cuddle for the rest of the journey.

BY THE time they arrived back at the castle, it was getting dark. Alex was waiting for them on the steps of the mansion house. He was accompanied by Watkins and Higgins, and none of them looked happy.

"Where the hell have you been?" demanded Alex, coming over to the car. Nico climbed out with a sigh.

"I've been in Tethys, Your Grace, as I said earlier." He encouraged Oliver out of the car. "This is Oliver, Your Grace."

Alex looked down at the dog in surprise. Oliver looked at Alex warily. Alex looked at Nico for explanation.

"I rescued him in Tethys. I think we have much to talk about, Your Grace, but if you'll excuse me, I need to organize a vet for Oliver."

"Is he ill?" Alex got down to his haunches and beckoned to the dog. Oliver went toward him still wary but willing to accept a pat on the head. He sniffed at Alex and decided to lie down and roll on his back. Alex gave him a rub and then used the opportunity to run his hands over the dog.

"There's nothing broken," he said, still examining the dog. "Looks like he needs a good bath, though." He stood up again and turned to Watkins. "The dog needs a vet. See to it, Watkins." He turned his attention back to Nico. "The conversation isn't over, Nico, but we'll see to the dog first. I take it you want to keep him?"

"I'd like to, yes, but I think an owner may turn up. He's clearly been trained. We need to talk about the Watchers in Tethys. I'm not happy with the way they act. In fact, they're the reason that I'm late."

"We'll talk inside. Let's get the animal settled first."

Nico could have kissed him but settled for giving him a huge smile. He should have known the duke would understand putting Oliver first.

They headed straight for the bathroom, and Nico ran a shallow bath just warm enough to be comfortable for the dog. To their surprise Oliver got straight in it. He stood patiently whilst Nico soaped him up, washing the mud off the dog. Nico noticed he liked having his tummy soaped up but seemed disinterested in the rest of the process. He required several applications of the soap interspersed with rinses from the shower attachment. As soon as he was rinsed off, he'd shake his coat out and both Nico and Alex got soaked in the process. Laughing, they finally got Oliver out of the bath and gave him a good rubdown with a couple of towels.

"You're really good with him," Nico commented as Alex brushed the dog.

"We always had dogs when I was a kid," explained Alex. "It was my job to look after them. I've missed having a dog."

"We might not be able to keep this one if his owner turns up," cautioned Nico. "The Watchers said he came over the bridge from Thetis. They wanted to put him down."

Alex looked at him in horror. "They wanted to put him down? But he's a beautiful dog."

"I know. I had to, erm, argue the point with them."

"What are you not telling me, Nico?"

Nico sighed. "Let's get changed and go down to the kitchen to see if we can find Oliver some food and a bone. I'll tell you all about it then," he said, noticing that Oliver's ears had perked up at the mention of the word "bone." Really, the dog was proving to be very intelligent. And stunningly beautiful. He had a caramel and blond coat that shone under the lights and seemed to be in great condition. The tips of his ears flopped forward in a way that was both cute and charming. They settled in the long sitting room, with Oliver on the rug before them gnawing on a large bone. He was a large dog and covered most of the rug, and Nico was glad that he was fully grown. He did look a little underweight, though, and Nico wondered how much he'd been fed recently.

"Now, tell me what you meant earlier," began Alex, only to be interrupted by the arrival of the vet. Watkins brought the man in and introduced him as Finbar Valdez. He was an older man with a petite frame and graying hair. Nico and Alex both stood when he came into the room, and Alex introduced himself and Nico, using their first names and not their titles. Nico approved.

"Good Goddess, is that Oliver?" said the vet. "It is Oliver. I wondered what had happened to him."

"You know this dog?" questioned Alex. "How do you know his name is Oliver?" He looked to Watkins for explanation, but Watkins just shrugged.

"How do I know?" repeated the vet in surprise. "I've been treating him since he was a puppy." Oliver had noticed the vet and abandoned the bone in favor of a good stroke from him. He licked at the man's hands and raised up on his back paws to lick at his face.

"Then you know who he belongs to?" Nico tried to hide his disappointment. He'd been secretly hoping to keep the dog. Oliver was a Gift of the Goddess.

"I know who he did belong to," said Valdez. "His owner died about a week ago. I've been looking for Oliver ever since. The neighbors said that he'd run away. Where did you find him?"

"In Tethys," replied Nico.

"Tethys? Then he must have come across the bridge. Were you looking for me, boy?" He spoke directly to the dog. Oliver perked his ears up and gave a loud woof. The vet laughed. "I'm glad to see you, boy. You had me worried. You could do with gaining a little weight, though."

"So Oliver is from Thetis?" said Alex.

The vet looked up sharply. "Is that a problem, Your Grace?" he asked pointedly, all friendliness gone from his eyes.

"No. Why would that be a problem? I just wondered why a vet from Tethys was treating a dog from Thetis," replied Alex with some confusion.

"Ah." The vet relaxed. "There aren't any vets in Thetis. I go over once a week to run a free animal clinic. I'd like to make it more, but I have to earn a living as well."

"We can help with that," Nico said instantly. "A free clinic for animals is an excellent idea. I'm sure the duke and I could contribute something." Alex nodded in agreement and Nico's heart gave a flutter at his generosity.

"Really?" It was the vet's turn to look surprised. "Well, I must admit that would be very helpful, but are you sure? I've lost a lot of clients because of my work in Thetis. People can be very bigoted when it comes to that city."

"Yes, I've noticed that," Nico replied, "but it's important work. Animals shouldn't be suffering. The Goddess Gifts Us All with Her Creations. It would be wrong to ignore those gifts."

The vet smiled. A relaxed, genuine smile. "I'm delighted to hear that, Your Highness. There is much work to be done in Thetis."

"Please call me Nico. Now can you give Oliver a proper examination? If he needs any treatment at all…."

The vet got to work, checking Oliver over and taking a couple of blood samples. Oliver seemed perfectly at ease with the man and didn't even flinch at the needle.

"From what I can see, he's in fine health, but the blood samples will tell me more. I can have results for you in a day or two. Will you be keeping him?"

"We'd like to, yes," Alex answered. "Is there anyone who might have a claim to him?"

"Only me," said the vet, "and to be honest, my wife would have a lot to say if I brought another animal home. She's not too happy with the amount we've got already. I'd be very grateful if you could give him a home here."

"Then he's ours," said Nico, smiling widely, pleased to note that the duke was smiling too.

"Well, I can tell you that he's a wonderful dog. Mr. Thomas trained him well and he has a great temperament. He'll need a lot of exercise, though, as he's a border collie and he likes to play. He has a tendency to try and herd cats. Do you have any cats?"

"No," said Nico, "but I'd like to one day. I like cats. Well, I like all animals, really. We were never allowed any at Academia Hall."

"Perhaps we should start with just Oliver for the moment," said the duke dryly. "We can talk about other animals at another date."

Nico smiled.

PART TWELVE

"THEY DID *what*?" Alex roared loud enough that the whole castle probably heard them. "They pulled guns on you? They dared to pull guns on you?"

Nico stretched out to pat his hand. "I was never in any danger. I had the guards with me, and I have the Power of the Goddess. They couldn't hurt me. I think we should send for some tea. Wouldn't you like a soothing cup of tea?"

"I don't want any tea, although a good stiff whiskey would go down well." Alex got up from the sofa and stomped over to the sideboard where a decanter and glasses sat. He poured a small amount into a glass and swallowed it down in one. "I'll kill them. How dare they pull a gun on you. Did you tell them who you are?"

"I tried. They didn't believe me, but that's not the point, Your Grace. They shouldn't be training guns on people just because they asked a question. Well, in fairness, they came out with guns because my guards pulled theirs. But they only did that after I was threatened with batons. No one should be threatened with batons simply for asking a question. That's not acceptable."

"What were their names?" Alex started to pace up and down the room.

Nico looked at him blankly. "I have no idea. I didn't ask. Eventually the Head of the Watchers came out, and he did recognize me or at least he recognized the uniforms of my guards. He wanted me to go into the station but I refused. I told him that I was taking Oliver and left. Do you know that even animals are subjected to the most ridiculous bigotry here? They wanted to put Oliver down simply because he was from Thetis. They said that he had all sorts of diseases, but it's easy to see that's not true. I don't think you need to be a healer to see it. Really, Your Grace, I despaired of Tethys. Everywhere I went there was bigotry."

"What do you mean 'everywhere you went'?" demanded Alex. "You were supposed to go to Academia Hall and come straight back. Where else did you go?"

"I went to the healing center and from there I could see the Watchers Station, but that's not the point, either. The point is the awful bigotry and snobbishness that's going on in Tethys. Do you know there were healers in the healing center who said that they would never lay healing hands on someone from Thetis? That goes directly against the ethos of the healers. I must go to Thetis tomorrow and find out what's happening from the healers there."

"Absolutely not." Alex was incredulous. "You're going nowhere near the place. Leave Thetis to me. I will sort the city out."

"No, Your Grace, I must insist. I need to see Thetis for myself. I cannot pay my debts properly without seeing it. I fear the healers there must be in need of assistance, and it's my duty to provide it. This is my final word on the subject, Your Grace."

"No, and that's my final word." Alex crossed his arms and glared at Nico.

Nico ignored him and picked up his mini comm. "You need some tea," he said and began tapping at the screen.

"I don't need tea," growled Alex. "I need to know that you're safe, and you won't be safe in Thetis."

"Nonsense," retorted Nico. "Didn't I prove that I could take care of myself today? Anyway, I can take some guards, and I may take Ollie with me too."

"You're not going."

"Yes, I am."

"No, you're not."

"Oh for Goddess's sake!" snapped Nico. "You can't stop me. I'm a priest and a healer and I demand to be allowed to pay my debts where they're most needed. If you're so bothered about it, you can come with me. You and all thousand of your soldiers, if needs be. Perhaps that will make you happier."

"I'll be happier if you stay here. You have no idea of what the situation is like in Thetis."

"And why is that?" asked Nico. "You haven't told me what's going on in Thetis. You've been there all day and you haven't said a word about it. Well, I've had enough. This marriage is supposed to be a partnership. We're supposed to share things. The Sixth Land needs both of us, not just you with me in reserve. I need to be out there, helping the people, and it's very clear that the place that needs the most help is Thetis."

"You could work in Tethys."

"No, just no. I couldn't stand the snobbery. Believe me, I have plans for the people of Tethys, but my immediate need is to go to Thetis. I'll be going tomorrow and there's nothing you can do to stop me."

Alex growled and started to pace up and down the room again. Oliver whined, looking up at him.

"Now you're upsetting the dog!" snarled Nico. "I won't have, it Your Grace. Do you hear me?"

"Oh, I hear you. How could I not?" Alex retorted, but he bent down to comfort Oliver all the same until the dog, satisfied, went back to his bone.

"If you're determined to do this, then I'm coming with you and we'll take a full quota of guards." He scowled at Nico, but Nico ignored him, choosing to answer the knock at the door instead. It was Trix with a tea tray. Trix took one look at Alex, handed the tray to Nico, and disappeared back out of the door. Nico brought the tea tray to the coffee table and set it down.

"I have no problem with being accompanied," he said haughtily. "The Tree of Life has a Branch for Everyone."

Alex grunted and sat back on the sofa. He accepted a cup of tea from Nico. "What's this?" He looked into the cup.

"It's passion flower, Your Grace," Nico replied smoothly. "It will aid you in a restful sleep. You look like you need it."

"Don't push, boy. I'd have a better night's sleep if I knew you were staying safe in the castle tomorrow."

"I can think of something else that might help you sleep." Nico gave a small smile and slid along the sofa to be closer. He laid his hand on Alex's thigh. "It'll help me sleep too," he murmured, sliding his hand farther up.

"Now that," said Alex, "is a much better idea. Let's go to bed."

ALEX WOKE up earlier than Nico and left him sleeping in the bed whilst he showered and got dressed. The boy was still sleeping when he left the room, and he made his way downstairs and sent a message to Watkins. He also sent a message to Nico's two guards. He wanted to hear their side of the story. He didn't care if they were still in bed; they could come to the castle and explain themselves.

Watkins arrived first and Alex told him what had happened the day before. "Best be doubling up the guard, then," he commented. "Though what those Watchers were about, I don't know."

"I'll have an explanation from the Head Watcher," said Alex, "and I'll have it today. We'll go there on the way to Thetis."

"You're really going to let pretty boy go to Thetis?" asked Watkins. "Is that wise, lad?"

"I'll be with him, and you will too. Plus we'll take a lot of guards. I want the healing center surrounded whilst Nico is in it, and I'll want guards on the inside too. I'm taking no chances. I want you by his side every minute."

"Will do, lad, will do."

"Hopefully he'll just want a quick tour, meet the healers, and we'll be done. In the meantime I'm going to find out what happened from his guards. They should be here soon. I want to know why they didn't contact me the minute it happened. There can be no excuse. Their instructions were clear."

It turned out there was an excuse. The Watchers Station or at least the car park was a dead zone, and the guards hadn't been able to make contact. Once they got onto the road, they'd decided it would be better to get straight back to the castle as quickly as possible. They'd sent a message to give their estimated arrival time as per instructions, but both men felt the incident itself was better done in person. They had both made a full report and given it to their immediate superior.

"In the future, you give it straight to me," Alex told them. "I want anything to do with His Highness to come straight to me. See to it, Watkins." He nodded at the man, who rolled his eyes in return. Alex ignored him and turned to dismiss the men.

"We need to find out where all the blind spots are," he said.

"We're already on it, lad. Had men searching them out since we got here. We knew about the Watchers Station, but no one expected pretty boy to go there. Have to say, lad, he handled it well, though. Never would have thought to say that but it's true. And that's a great dog."

Alex nodded. Oliver was a great dog. He'd taken to Watkins immediately and was now sitting at the man's feet. Watkins leaned down to stroke him.

"Breakfast is ready, Your Dukedom." Higgins strolled into the room without bothering to knock. Oliver's ears pricked up at his words. Alex had given up asking the man to call him by his first name. He was quite sure that Higgins had never called old Hugbet "Your Dukedom," but it didn't bother him. He'd been called far worse by Watkins.

"Must say I don't like the look of yours," Higgins continued. "All that fruit, a man needs meat for breakfast. Can't work if you don't have meat. And I've told His Nibs that, so I have." Alex wondered how Nico felt about being called "His Nibs."

He asked Nico just that when they were on their way to Tethys. Nico wore one of his pale gray suits, with a plain pale blue waistcoat and crisp white linen shirt. His tie was knotted simply and the only jewelry he wore was his wedding ring. It dawned on Alex that Nico never wore the other jewelry Alex had bought him. He always wore the ring. Alex picked up Nico's hand and gently rubbed his thumb along Nico's palm.

"Do I care if Higgins calls me His Nibs?" said Nico in surprise. "He never calls me His Nibs. He always calls me Nico." He went back to staring out of the window but his hand tightened around Alex's. "I like his nickname for you, though. Your Dukedom sounds right. After all, you are the dukedom, aren't you? It isn't the land or the castle or the holdings or the money. It's you."

"Me?" Alex said in surprise.

"Yes," said Nico. "You are the dukedom. It is your privilege."

"But what if…." Alex bit the words off. Did he want to expose his fears? A knot tightened in his stomach.

"But what if what?" Nico turned his attention to Alex. "What if you do the wrong thing? What if you make things worse? What if you *fail*? You're not going to fail, Alex. The Goddess Has Chosen Well. You may make mistakes. The Tree Of Life Has Many Tangles after all, but you will always find your way back. I have faith in you." Nico took both of Alex's hands in his. "You wouldn't have been chosen if you couldn't do it. The Goddess Does Not Make Mistakes."

Alex stared into Nico's eyes and saw the truth there. In that moment he fell in love. Before he could stop himself he asked, "Did she make a mistake about us?"

Nico stared back at him solemnly, paused, and then said, "I don't think so, no." Alex felt the power build between them. Why couldn't they be home in bed? Why couldn't they just be alone? There was no privacy here, and there wouldn't be all day.

"The King Must Be True to the People, Alex. It will be nighttime soon." Nico smiled and turned his attention back to the window, holding on to Alex's hand. Idly stroking Nico's hand, Alex fell into a reverie. Two momentous things had happened, he realized. Nico had said that he understood their marriage to be a Gift of the Goddess, and Nico had called him Alex. Outside of the bedroom, Nico never called him Alex. His was a formality that was natural. Princeliness looked good on Nico, and he wore it well. He could talk to Grand Seer or commoner and act in the same easygoing natural way. He made people feel welcome and included, and he did so with grace. And now they had the beginnings of something big. Something larger and deeper than anything else Alex had known. Alex had a feeling he'd be hearing "Alex" a lot more in the future. Nico was bringing down one of the walls between them. And he had his boy's faith. He felt exhilarated, eager to grasp the future, impatient to solve the problems of Thetis and to bring back balance to the Sixth Land.

They arrived at the Watchers Station in Tethys, and Watkins sent four men in to clear the facility of any dangers. The Head Watcher met them at the door.

"Your Grace, Your Highness," he stuttered. "We weren't expecting you, er, if you'd like to come in, Your Grace?" he babbled as Alex walked straight past him through the door.

"Who's in charge here?" he demanded.

"Er… I am, Your Grace, I am." The man started to bow repeatedly.

Not another one, thought Alex. "Where's your office?" he asked wearily. He couldn't stand obsequiousness and all this ridiculous bowing business. Unfortunately, he saw far too much of it. The man led the way to his office and standing at the open door, started to bow again.

"For Goddess's sake, man, stop bowing," snapped Alex, going into the office. He stood to one side to allow Nico to sit down. Nico refused, saying he'd rather stand. Alex preferred to stand too. He glared at the man in front of him. The man looked to his chair and then to Alex and then to his chair. "Sit down, man," said Alex. "Now, I want an explanation as to why my husband, who is a priest, a healer, and a Prince of this land, had weapons drawn on him yesterday."

"A total misunderstanding, Your Grace, a total misunderstanding. The Watchers didn't recognize the Prince. They thought he was interfering in Watcher business. Well, we can't have people interfering in Watcher business, can we? And the dog was dangerous. The People Must Be Protected. However, I can promise you that the two individuals concerned have been sacked. The matter can be considered over," he finished pompously. It was clearly a preplanned speech, practiced heavily.

"I don't want those men sacked," said Nico from the corner of the office. He came farther into the room. "I think you've missed the point, sir. The Watchers shouldn't have acted like that with anyone, regardless of who they are. I only asked a question. However, I wonder how responsible they are for their actions. What are the rules concerning Watchers? How is it that two men would think it permissible to raise a baton to a fellow citizen?"

"Well, they've been sacked," objected the Head Watcher defensively. "What more can be done? The matter is over," he repeated again as though mere repetition made fact.

"The matter is not over," Alex responded. "The matter is far from over. Your Highness, what would you like to see done here?"

Nico gave him a smile. "I'd like to see a completely different attitude from the Watchers, Your Grace. I'd like the person responsible for that attitude to be reprimanded, perhaps encouraged to retire. We have a New Dawning in Tethys, Your Grace. It's time the people remembered that Thetis is the granddaughter of Tethys and must be treated accordingly. I abhor bullying, and I want it stopped."

Alex bowed to him, his own smile wide. "Then it will be my pleasure to see to that for you, Your Highness."

He turned to the Head Watcher. "I expect you at my office in the castle tomorrow at nine o'clock in the morning. You will bring me a full report of how this station is run and who is responsible for what. I will also want to see your arrest record for the past five years. I don't know who you report to on the council, but I suggest you bring them with you."

The man began to puff and pant, sitting upright in his chair, furious and defensive. "Now just a moment, Your Grace," he spat. "You can't talk to me like that. I have an elected position. The people chose me, and I only answer to the Head of the Council."

"You answer to me," said Alex. "You swear your allegiance to me. You will attend tomorrow at nine o'clock and you will bring the reports I have requested. If you don't, I'll send out a platoon of men to pick you up. How do you think the people would see that? Nine o'clock," he ordered before gesturing to Nico to lead the way out. They left the man with his mouth open, spluttering and stuttering.

The trip through Thetis was sobering. The contrast between it and Tethys was startling. Nico was silent for the whole time they drove through the city toward the healing center. He gave his entire focus to watching the streets they passed through. When they pulled up in front of the healing center, he turned to Alex and said, "I never realized that poverty could be this bad. It's even worse than the countryside. Look at the people queuing, Alex. They're queuing for food and they're queuing for healing. They shouldn't be queuing for those things. The Goddess Feeds All, The Goddess Heals All."

He got out of the car and walked to the nearest queue. There he stood and talked with the people, two minutes here, five minutes there. Alex let him do it. He was surrounded by guards, and more guards had gone into the healing center itself to clear it. It was forty minutes before Nico was done and he'd worked his way to the front of the healing line. Alex was happy to see the food queue, whilst never ending, was moving quickly as people picked up the rations he'd had delivered to the soup kitchen. Soup kitchen. Such a horrible phrase. He wanted rid of this one, and he never wanted to see another one in the Sixth Land or elsewhere.

He joined Nico at the head of the queue, and they entered the healing center together. The receptionist looked shocked and quickly picked up a comms unit. Within minutes the healer Alex had seen the day before arrived in the reception. He held his hands up as he came forward.

"I'm sorry, Your Grace, but I do not have time to see you today. I spent quite some time with you yesterday, and I cannot spare any more."

Alex was quick to reassure the man. "And I gratefully thank you for the time you gave me, sir. May I call you Vincent? I'm here to accompany my husband."

"And I'm here to offer healing hands," said Nico. "If you could show me to a station?" He took his coat off and handing it to Alex, he rolled his sleeves.

"You're here to help?" Vincent looked at him suspiciously. "Why would the Prince of the Land help in Thetis?"

"I must pay my debts just like any other healer," Nico answered. "And it would seem that this is where I'm needed. Please, show me to a station."

Vincent quickly decided to take Nico at his word and led the way back to the cubicles. "Well, I'm certainly not going to refuse help, Your Highness. We've heard of your gifts even out here."

"The Goddess Gifts All. Please, call me Nico."

Both the healer and Nico disappeared into a cubicle and Alex was left holding Nico's jacket. He handed it to Watkins.

"I wasn't expecting him to actually work here," confided Alex. "What am I supposed to do now?"

"Excellent opportunity to go and talk to the people, lad."

"I suppose." Alex thought for a moment. "I'll leave you with His Highness, and I'll take a troop of men. I may go over to the docks, see what's happening there."

He got a grunt from Watkins in reply and left the healing center.

NICO LOOKED at his station and checked that there was everything he'd need. He'd brought his own crystals and incense, but he needed massage oil and certain fresh herbs. He was glad to see the most basic of herbs but wondered why there wasn't a wider selection. He made a note to ask Alex to arrange that. After that, the day flew by. The people coming in all spoke of the same problems. He saw evidence of their malnutrition in their eyes, their mouths, and their skin. He saw the secondary problems that accompanied the lack of proteins, vitamins, and minerals. Hair, teeth, and behavior all pointed in the same direction. There wasn't enough food, and the people had weakened immune systems. He got the chance to speak to Vincent during a quick break between patients. Vincent confirmed his diagnoses. Food was scarce, Nico was told, and what was available went for high prices. Most people couldn't afford to buy it. So the lines at the soup kitchen had grown.

"At least there is food now," said Vincent. "We have your husband to thank for that, and Goddess willing, we won't have to turn anyone away."

They returned to their duties and Nico started to ask a different set of questions. He learned a lot about corn. It was the only crop being grown, and it was all shipped out of the country at the docks. He heard of the huge lorries traveling the outside road up and down the length of the Sixth Land, all carrying corn. He heard of guards looking after the corn and people going to prison if they stole any. Which didn't stop them from stealing, or at least it stopped the ones in prison. There were plenty more people on the outside of prison who were willing to risk it if it meant their family was fed. But what was the obsession with corn in the first place? Who was growing it and why? Why didn't they sell it to the local people? Most of all, where was it going to and what was it being used for? He just couldn't work it out. He needed to talk to Alex. The work kept him busy, though, and he was feeling the exhaustion of raising so much healing power. It was getting dark when he started to flag. Watkins noticed immediately. He'd never left Nico's side for the entire day, standing just outside of his cubicle and insisting that the guards on the door search anyone entering for a weapon. Nico, having learned that there was no point in arguing with Watkins, left him to it. So he wasn't entirely surprised when Watkins spoke up.

"That's enough now, lad," he came into the cubicle to say. "You've paid your debts today. It's time to return to the castle." Nico protested that he was fine, but Watkins didn't believe a word of it. Nico slipped into High Speech, and Watkins threw it right back at him. In the end, they agreed he could see one more patient.

Nico was surprised that the man who came into the cubicle wasn't suffering from malnutrition or malaise. Instead he had a straightforward wound on his arm. He announced that his name was Felix and he was an artist. He'd injured himself whilst working on a piece of stone.

"You're a sculptor?" asked Nico in delight. "I've been looking for a sculptor. Are you any good?"

"Good enough," replied the man with a laugh. He looked Nico up and down. "So you're the new Prince? What are you doing here in Thetis, and why aren't you at that swanky castle of yours? I'll bet that's where your duke is."

"Not at all," replied Nico. "I'm not sure where he is, to be honest, but I'm sure he's out paying his debts just like I am. Why wouldn't we pay our debts in Thetis?"

"It's not the sort of place your sort visit," said Felix bluntly. "We know what Tethys thinks of us."

"I'm not Tethys, and neither is the duke."

"So what... you're the good guys? Here to save the day? I think the problems here are a bit too big for you and your duke to handle, pretty boy."

Watkins was through the curtain in an instant. He loomed over the man. "Show your respect," he snarled. "This is His Highness Prince Nico of the Sixth Land. Start acting like you know it."

The man sat up on the bench, eyes wide. "Hey," he said to Nico. "Call the guard dog off. I didn't mean any harm. You are a pretty boy."

Watkins punched him in the mouth.

Nico sprang forward, trying to pull Watkins off. "No, for Goddess's sake, no. We don't resort to violence. We don't."

"Some of us do, lad," said Watkins, unrepentant. "The man asked for it. Any man would have done it."

"I wouldn't," objected Nico quickly.

"Yes, you would. You'd have just done it in some priestly way. No difference. A man acts in the way he's taught, and you know I'm one of the warrior class, lad."

"Just move out of the way and let me treat him," said Nico reaching for some swabs. He checked the man's mouth and the lip was split and bleeding, the area bruised.

Felix laughed. "He throws a good punch for an old man. Thought he'd knocked out a couple of teeth for a moment."

"Say 'pretty boy' one more time and I'll do more than knock out your teeth," snarled Watkins. "Show your respect."

"Hey, I'm showing, I'm showing. Would you like me to bow? Here in Thetis we're made of stronger stuff. We believe that respect is earned."

"Quite so," Nico said firmly. He had no idea what Watkins's problem was. Watkins called him pretty boy all the time. Perhaps it was a strange "us and them" situation. Nico had seen that before. One of the chefs at Academia Hall had been choice in describing his staff but no one else had been allowed to speak of them in that way. The chef was fierce in defending his staff if anyone else was critical of them. Nico turned back to his patient. "I'll give you some arnica for the bruising and the cuts and some swabs for your mouth. If you'd like to make a complaint about Watkins, I suggest you seek counsel with the duke. Come to the castle tomorrow and I'll make sure he speaks to you." He paused and then looked at Watkins. "Can you arrange transport for Mr....?" He looked back at Felix.

"Just Felix. I don't have any fancy titles." The man grinned at Watkins. "Transport would be good, though. We tend not to have our own transport here in Thetis, and the public transport sucks."

"Oh, I'll arrange your transport for you, boy. I'll be happy to see the duke deal with you," Watkins laughed. "Now if you're quite finished using His Highness's talents, perhaps you'll leave. Or I can help you with that...."

"Nope." Felix jumped off the bench. "I can manage that all by myself. I thank you, Your Highness, for the gift of your talent, and I would like to speak to the duke tomorrow, perhaps early? I tend to get up early, morning light, you know."

"Then Watkins will make the arrangement, and do bring some examples of your art. I meant it when I said I was looking for a sculptor."

Felix looked surprised at that but gave a mock bow and said he'd see them tomorrow. Watkins advised him to leave his address with the guard at the door, and Felix left the room.

"You shouldn't have done that," said Nico when they were alone.

"Shouldn't have done what?" Watkins looked at him, eyebrows raised.

"You shouldn't have punched him," retorted Nico sharply. "As you well know."

"He was asking to be punched and he knew he was asking to be punched. He got punched. Served him right. Talking to you like that. Who did he think he was?"

"Now you're going to have to explain yourself to the duke," Nico pointed out shrewishly. Watkins put his head back and laughed out loud. He laughed so hard that tears came to his eyes and he started to slap his thigh in delight. Nico looked at him.

"Explain myself to the duke, lad? The duke will shake my hand. The duke would have my head if I hadn't punched him. The duke is a warrior. He knows the rules."

Nico realized with some regret that Watkins was probably right. Not that he'd wanted to get Watkins into trouble. He hadn't, but you couldn't just go around punching people regardless of the provocation. He was going to have to make that clear to both Alex and Watkins. He yawned and realized how tired he was. His lecture would have to wait until tomorrow. He needed to recover his energy tonight. He began to gather his things and looked around for his coat. Watkins handed it to him whilst tapping into his mini comm.

"His Grace will be here soon to pick us up," he said. "Go and have a cup of that tea stuff you like so much. It'll be ten minutes or so yet."

"Then I'll go and take my leave of Brother Vincent," said Nico. "There's a couple of things I want to clarify."

PART THIRTEEN

ALEX OPENED his eyes and groaned. Nico was gone. He'd wanted his boy to have a lie-in. He'd been horrified by how exhausted Nico had looked when he'd picked him up the night before. He'd fallen straight to sleep on the ride home and had only roused when they reached the castle. Then he had made his excuses and gone to bed. He'd been fast asleep when Alex got there. Watkins had given a full report on the day, and Alex had shaken his hand when he heard about the punch. Who the hell did that man think he was? Yes, Watkins frequently called Nico "pretty boy" but Watkins was family. It was different. Alex would certainly have something to say if the upstart turned up at the castle. He just wished Nico hadn't arranged it for such an early time. He had no problem getting up himself, but he knew that Nico would want to be there and Nico was in need of a lie-in.

Wasn't to be. Alex looked at the clock and knew Nico would be on the beach, playing with Oliver. It had become the morning norm. Nico took him for a run in the morning, and Alex took him for a proper run when he did his own exercise in the evening. Oliver was coming on in leaps, responding to both the exercise and diet well. It hadn't taken long for the dog to bounce back.

He got up and went down to the breakfast room. Trix brought him his breakfast, pulling his mini comm from his pocket when he'd laid the plate down on the table. "Good morning, Your Grace," he said cheerfully. "Have you seen the Social Web? The announcement His Highness made is all over it. I told you everyone loved His Highness. And I'm quite pleased with the photo I took. I think I do him justice, though I have to say he was very good and sat still like I asked him to. He even winked, which made me giggle because I've never seen him wink before. I didn't know he knew how to do that. Did you know he knew how to do that, Your Grace?"

Alex looked at him in bewilderment. What was the boy talking about? Who sat still and winked? Surely not Nico? What announcement? They hadn't made an announcement.

"What are you talking about, Trix?" he asked warily. Was this going to be another unauthorized press release? He didn't want to go through that again. If the boy started crying, then Nico wasn't here to deal with it. Besides, Nico had promised him there wouldn't be any more unauthorized releases.

Trix placed one hand on his hip and offered the mini comm with the other. He sniffed haughtily. "Don't be looking at me like that, Your Grace. This was authorized. His Highness authorized it himself. In fact, he actually came to me and asked me to do it. So I can't be in any trouble, can I?"

Alex took the mini comm and read the article on it. It was about the appointment of a vet to the Royal Household. Mr. Finbar Valdez had been appointed to treat all animals of the Royal Household. There was a heavy emphasis on "Royal Household," Alex noticed, and much written about Finbar Valdez in the highest of terms. In fact, it was just the sort of puff piece his own staff liked to hand out. When he let them, that was. "Did you write this, Trix?" he said, looking up.

Trix snorted. "Of course. And I took the photo too. I'm very proud of that photo."

Alex scrolled down and sitting still, looking very majestic indeed, was Oliver. He wasn't winking, though.

"It's very good. You've caught just the right tone. I think I may have a job for you, Trix."

"No thank you. I have a job. I wait on His Highness. He's going to let me post things to his Social Web account. In fact, I'm sort of a correspondent on his behalf. I Am Blessed By the Goddess." When Trix did High Speech there was a simple truth to it. He also noticed how calm Trix was. He was still bubbly, still enthusiastic, but there was no sense of frenzy about him now. He didn't look like he'd collapse into tears if Alex said the wrong thing. The boy grinned widely at Alex and took his mini comm back. He didn't ask for it back, he just took it out of Alex's hands. He turned to leave the room, telling Alex to be sure to eat all his breakfast. His Highness had worked hard to prepare it.

Once again Alex was forced to ask, "What are you talking about, Trix?"

"Why, His Highness prepares your breakfast every morning. Didn't you know that? It's the first thing he does before he goes on the beach." Trix left the room and Alex was left looking at his breakfast. The fruit was ripe and enticing. It was beautifully cut and arranged on the plate.

There were even small mint leaves scattered here and there. Alex picked up his fork. So it wasn't bacon? Who cared? His boy had made this. His boy had made him breakfast. He dug in, relishing every bite.

Watkins arrived on the dot of eight. "That sculptor chap is due in fifteen minutes," he said. "Where do you want to see him? I'll let Higgins know."

"We'll see him in the duke's office, Watkins," Nico answered from the door, Oliver following closely to heel.

Both Alex and Watkins looked at him. "I have an office?" asked Alex.

"Of course you have an office," said Nico with a frown. "How could you work without an office? It's next to mine," he finished, sitting at the table and pouring a glass of fruit juice from the jug there.

"When did that happen?"

"I believe it was finished yesterday whilst I was out at the healing center. Which reminds me, I need to get back there as soon as we've seen Felix. I do hope he's remembered to bring examples of his art. Or do you think I should wait until we've seen the Head Watcher? I thought I might leave you to handle that, but if you'd like my presence…? Not that it would do you much good. I said all I want to say on that subject yesterday." He drank the last of the juice and placed the glass down. "Have you finished?"

"Yes, thank you," said Alex politely and automatically. "I didn't realize that you'd want to go back to Thetis today. I thought we'd spend today in the castle."

"Good heavens no," said Nico, startled. "You saw the amount of work that needed to be done, Alex. I must go back there, today and every day that I'm needed. You're surely not worried about my security anymore? Send guards with me. We have enough of them."

"I can't spare Watkins."

"I don't want Watkins. He's the only man I've ever seen cause harm in a healing center. I think he should be kept out of them."

"Let's see to the sculptor and the Head Watcher first. Then we can discuss it again," reasoned Alex carefully. If he did it right he might be able to persuade Nico to stay at the castle. Then again….

Nico was happy to go along with his plan for now and led Alex to his office. It was a huge square room with the usual wood paneling and deep carpet. Green, he noticed. The ceiling was a work of art with groups of fruits and vegetables worked into the plaster complete with images of the Goddess painted in a crisp white.

A huge oak desk took up a good amount of room. There was a big leather chair behind it and an assortment of wooden chairs around the room. Nico took one of these for himself and placed it next to the leather chair. He suggested that Watkins do the same, but Watkins always preferred to stand.

"Did you say this room is next to your office?" Alex asked Nico.

"Yes, it's just through that door," Nico replied, pointing to a door at the side of the room. "Do you want to see it? We can go in there later if you like, but I think we need to see Felix first, don't you? You should sit down. I'll order tea."

Felix arrived on time and was shown in by Higgins. "Felix something or other here to see you, Your Dukedom. Do you want him in here, then? Wouldn't tell me his name, but I recognize him all the same. He's the Earl of Richmond's son. Often saw his father at the old duke's parties, and Goddess knows he's the image of the man. Don't let him be telling you any nonsense about being from Thetis. He's high-born, this one, which probably explains his fancies." With a grunt in Felix's direction, Higgins left the room. Felix looked horrified.

"I take it you didn't want us to know that information, Mr. Richmond?" Alex said, standing to greet the man.

"Not really, no," admitted Felix, "and call me Felix. I'm not a person who stands on ceremony."

"Are you here to complain about Watkins?" Alex was blunt and Nico rolled his eyes.

"No, I'm here to plead for the people in Thetis. Watkins was just a way to get your attention. I deserved the punch; it was rightfully given, and I do apologize for my words, Your Highness. I was desperate. The tenants of Thetis have suffered enough."

"Quite right," said Nico with a smile. "It's time for the suffering to end. We're quite with you on that one, Felix. Isn't that so, Your Grace?"

"Indeed. In fact, we'd be grateful for any help you can give us. What can you tell us about Thetis?"

It turned out that Felix could tell them a lot. He'd been living in Thetis for ten years and had seen the downfall of Thetis society.

"We never used to have poverty. The sea, the industry, all of it provided work for the citizens. There was plenty of food at realistic prices. Then slowly the wages decreased; men and women had to work longer and harder for less. Food became scarce as estate after estate converted to growing corn. Corn that wasn't sold to the local people but exported out." Felix didn't know where it was going but he did know that there were masses of it. Vans arrived at the docks every hour of every day. All to be loaded onto seagoing ships to leave the Sixth Land. The people got hungry and jobs paid less and less. The landlords of Thetis showed no mercy, preferring to keep a house empty rather than lower rents. It was said they were in collusion with the Elites and it was a new type of economy.

"Surely that's a conspiracy theory," Alex said with some derision. "What possible interest could the Elites have in landlords from Thetis? From what I've seen they wouldn't cross into Thetis in a million years."

"You'd think that, Your Grace, but the truth is that the Elites *are* the landlords. They've been buying up property for years and own huge swaths of it. They can afford to do without tenants because they also have access to the huge estates they rent from you. They argue that the corn earns them more money than normal crops. They ask why they should be feeding the people. They argue that it's their place to keep the standards high in society and that to do that, they need more money."

"You sound familiar with their arguments, Felix," observed Alex, and Felix gave a shrug.

"I've been arguing this with my father for the past five years," he said. "But I'm getting nowhere. It's a movement that's becoming more and more popular with the Elites. They're led by a most horrendous man called Lunette. Can't stand him myself, but I don't go into society these days. I moved to Thetis so I could concentrate on my art. The property there was cheap. It meant that I could pay my debts in the best way. Recently, though, I've been spending more and more time on social issues. Society isn't supposed to be this way. It must be made right."

Alex was impressed with the man's fervor and dedication. "Do you know who's behind the riots?" Alex asked.

"If I do, I'm not going to tell you," Felix grinned. "The riots are a way to attract attention."

Alex nodded thoughtfully. He looked at Nico, and Nico nodded. He looked at Watkins and the older man also nodded. They were in agreement, then.

"I want you to contact the instigators. I want you to tell them that they are in no trouble and that I want to speak to them directly. I will need good men and women if we are to solve these problems, but by the Grace Of The Goddess, we will solve them."

"The King Is True to the People," added Nico with a smile at Felix. "Now, did you bring some samples of your art? I do hope so. I've been looking forward to seeing them."

"Well, I do have some photos on my mini comm," said Felix shyly. "If you're sure...."

THE MEETING with the Head Watcher didn't go anywhere near as well. He arrived accompanied by three council members, all four looking incensed. Infuriated and defensive, they came on the attack.

"I'm the Head of the Sixth Land Council, Your Grace," spat one man. "And I'd like an explanation of your treatment of Council Member Anwell. He's an elected member of the council. An elected member, Your Grace," he spat the title again. Alex rose to his feet as Watkins came farther into the room.

"And he's failing miserably at his job," sneered Alex. "Tell me, did you notice?" Nico sat up straight.

"Notice what?" bellowed the man. "Council Member Anwell always pays his debts. There is no one better for the job and both the people and the council know that. I don't know who you think you are coming here like this—"

"He's the Duke of the Sixth Land," intercepted Nico before Alex could answer. "And you declare your loyalty to him, do you not?"

It stopped the man in his tracks but he quickly rallied. "I swore allegiance to Hugbet." He pronounced the word as "ooh bear" and Alex hid a smile. "I don't know that I'll be swearing allegiance to you," he said, looking directly at Alex.

Alex allowed a cold smile. "Then I'll have your resignation. Be so kind as to give your name to Watkins and make sure we have a signed copy immediately."

"What?" the man cried. "You can't demand that."

"Yes, I can. I own the land. I was placed here by the decree of our king. Surely you give your allegiance to our king, sir?"

"Well, yes, but—"

"There's no more to be said, then. If I do not have your allegiance, I certainly don't want you on the council. The people may pick someone else. Not you. Now I'd be grateful if you'll leave. I have business to conduct here. Watkins?"

"On it, Your Grace," said Watkins cheerfully. "If you'd just come with me, sir." The other man, who hadn't even given his name, might have been in a state of shock, but one look at Watkins had him leaving the room without another word. Alex turned back to the other three council members.

"Does anyone else have something to say?"

Since all three of them remained quiet, he instructed them to get some chairs and sit down.

"Perhaps you'd be so kind as to introduce yourselves," said Nico with a gentle but questioning air.

The only woman in the party leaned forward. "Erm, I'm Council Member Radclyffe and I'm responsible for the charitable affairs of our council. This is Head Watcher Anwell, who as you know is also a council member, and Council Member Johns, who is in charge of the treasury."

"A pleasure to meet you ma'am," Nico said with a smile. "I wish it was under different circumstances."

"Well as to that, Your Highness, I must admit we were shocked at the news that Head Watcher Anwell brought to us. It's unheard of for a council member to be treated in this manner. Head Watcher Anwell is very highly thought of on the council." Since her tone was respectful, Alex gestured that she should continue. "There have never been any complaints of his work and he has always maintained the highest standards. The council has been very happy with his work."

"Unfortunately that wasn't my experience, ma'am," Nico responded. "My experience was quite different, and I was forced to use the Power of the Goddess, ma'am. That isn't something I do lightly, believe me."

"My husband is a priest and healer, and he should be enjoying free passage in this land," said Alex sharply. "Instead he was threatened by the very people who are supposed to protect him." His eyes flashed with anger and the woman leaned back, clutching her hand to her chest. The Head Watcher was beginning to look nauseated and the man beside him was looking at Anwell intently.

"I can assure you, Your Grace," Council Member Johns said pompously, "that this is the first I've heard of this. Isn't that so, Council Member Radclyffe? There was no mention of this."

The woman looked at him askance. "Well, I think it was mentioned but it wasn't put in quite those terms, perhaps," she replied with diplomacy. "I'm sorry that you went through that, Your Highness. Obviously, we wish it hadn't happened. However, I must plead Head Watcher Anwell's case. This is the first such incident under his leadership and I believe it was a simple case of the Watchers concerned not recognizing you. Surely the Goddess Forgives?"

"She Does Indeed," said Nico. "But that must be true for the Watchers concerned as well. From what I can tell, the two men were dismissed immediately. If it was a simple mistake, why did that happen? Alas, I feel there is more going on here, which is why His Grace requested that Head Watcher Anwell attend today. I believe he was supposed to bring some reports with him?"

"I have them right here," said Head Watcher Anwell, speaking for the first time. "A report of the current management system at the Watchers Station and a report of every crime from the past five years. I can assure you that I have not been remiss in my administration. The figures are there for you to see."

"I'm delighted to hear it," said the duke, accepting the reports. "The fact remains, though, that men in your charge behaved like bullies. That is not acceptable."

"They've been *sacked*!" Head Watcher Anwell threw his arms up in despair. "What more can I do?" He looked to Council Member Radclyffe for support.

"There, there, Teddy," she whispered, patting his arm. "I'm sure the duke and His Highness are reasonable people. Don't be getting upset." She turned to Alex. "Really, Your Grace, surely there is some way through this? What would you like to see happen?"

Alex looked at Nico and gestured for him to answer the question. Nico was quiet for a moment, and Alex realized the atmosphere in the room had changed. It had gone from rage to an almost peaceful tranquility. Nico had done that. He waited to hear what his boy would say.

"I think we can have some agreement, Council Member Radclyffe, and I thank you for your input. Head Watcher Anwell, I understand now where your gifts lie. Yours is a position of administration. Perhaps I expected too much from you. I'd like to see the two watchers concerned taken back into employment. I'd like the ethos of the Watchers be developed. Watchers should be more accessible to the public, I feel. Perhaps we could work together to achieve that?"

Head Watcher Anwell looked astonished. He looked to Council Member Radclyffe in bewilderment. She patted his hand again. "I think that sounds excellent, Your Highness. Don't you agree, Teddy?" When the man remained silent, she patted his hand again. "Now there was nothing to worry about at all, so you can settle down. Really, the excitement isn't good for you, dear." She turned her attention back to Nico and Alex. "Your Highness, Your Grace, thank you for giving us your time. I'm so happy that we could reach a solution that pleases us all."

Alex acknowledged her with a nod. Nico gave her a smile. "If you'll just give His Grace the time to come up to speed, then I'm sure he'll have some very good proposals for you. The King Is True to the People," he finished.

Alex thought that was a bit over the top. He really didn't like being compared to the king, and yes, he knew it was a saying. It still made him uncomfortable. He remembered that Nico had faith in him and felt better. Standing, he smiled at Council Member Radclyffe and held out his hand. She smiled right back at him and took his hand. There was a twinkle in her eye that made Alex realize that she had basically gotten her own way. She'd achieved her objective, that was for sure. She bowed to him graciously and he returned the bow. This was a woman who interested him. He needed good people to enact change in Tethys and Thetis, and he was of the opinion that he'd just found one. "I too would be very interested in talking to you about charitable matters," he said and earned another smile.

"I'm delighted to hear that, Your Grace. Really, it has been a pleasure to meet both you and His Highness, a real pleasure."

"We shall be in touch very soon," promised Nico, who had also stood and was ready to shake hands and exchange bows.

Council Member Johns also stood and bowed deeply. "Your Grace," he began, "I can assure you of my allegiance, have no fear. Both you and His Highness have my fealty. Why, if there's anything at all that I can do…." He opened his arms wide as though to encompass the world.

When Alex interrupted him, he didn't do so politely. "Yes, yes, we'll be in touch." He dismissed the man carelessly, turning his attention to Head Watcher Anwell. "Anwell." He looked the man straight in the eyes. "Consider yourself lucky my husband is more reasonable than

I am." Then he sat down in his chair and leaned back. *Diplomat*, he thought, *I've got a diplomat.* It was an enormous weight off his mind and suddenly he didn't feel so alone.

HE FELT very alone when faced with an angry Nico fifteen minutes later. His suggestion that Nico stay at the castle wasn't received well, and he knew that he had to be the one who gave in. He couldn't argue with his boy any longer. The boy was right.

"You have to take Watkins with you," he bargained. "And as many guards as I say."

"If that's what it takes." Nico gave a sigh. He took a deep breath and straightened his shoulders. "We cannot be doing this every day, Your Grace. Decide what protection you think I need and accept that I'll be going to Thetis for as long as I'm needed."

"You have other duties, Nico," Alex said desperately.

Nico nodded. "I do have other duties. So it will be up to you to provide a decent quota of healers for Thetis, won't it? The sooner you do that, the sooner I'm not needed. I can contact my own Academia Hall for help if you wish."

Alex wondered why he hadn't thought of that. The boy was a genius. All he had to do was bring more healers in. He could have them flown in straight away. He looked at Watkins. "See to it, Watkins," he ordered, ignoring the roll of eyes that was too often Watkins's response. He didn't care how Watkins responded; he just wanted the man to get on with his orders. Watkins had never failed him in that regard. Or in any regard. There was no one Alex would trust more with Nico's safety. Finally, he saw both Nico and Watkins off and returned to his office.

Alex wished he could go with Nico himself, but there was just too much to do. He'd learned a lot at the docks yesterday, and Felix had confirmed some of his fears. Now he had to work out what the hell this new "economic model" was, and he didn't like the fact that he'd have to go into society to do that. He had little patience with fools, and his experience of the Elites was that's what they all were. He just had to work out the best way to get the information in the shortest time. He was delighted then when Higgins came into the room to announce that some jumped-up prince had turned up, and could His Dukedom possibly keep Higgins informed if this was to keep happening?

Jael strolled into the office with a wide grin. "Hello, Brother," he said. "Surprised to see me?"

"Delighted to see you," returned Alex, coming around the desk to hug the prince.

"Oh?" Jael widened his eyes. "Is the honeymoon over already?"

"No, it isn't," Alex retorted, giving him a mock punch. "But you've missed Nico. He's gone to do some healing."

"Alone?"

"Of course not. He has Watkins with him and enough guards to protect the king himself. Tell me, Jael. How does the king do?"

"Not well." The smile fell from Jael's face. "The healers feel it will be a matter of weeks, not months."

"I'm sorry, Jael."

Jael nodded but moved to sit in a chair. "Well, no point in worrying about that now. She Who Weaves the Web Tells the Story, and I'm hearing that there's a story to be told here?"

Alex moved back to his own chair. "There is. A long story. We're going to need a drink."

Minutes later, Higgins brought in some brandy and two glasses. "I got you the good stuff, Your Dukedom. It's the one I always help meself to when I fancy a tot. Hugbet had good taste in alcohol; you could say that about him." He nodded casually at Jael and left the room.

"Fascinating character," observed Jael. "Do you know he asked me if I was here to cause trouble? He said he wasn't letting me in if I was. Don't think I've ever been spoken to like that before. I like him."

"I do too," said Alex, pouring them both a brandy. They were soon deep in discussion.

"You know what you should do?" Jael said, sitting up. "You should have a ball. You need to gather the Elites, and you don't want to spend a lot of time with them, so a ball is perfect. It's all over and done with in one evening. You get to talk to the Elites and then they all go home. What could be better? Plus you have to give a ball anyway, to be honest. It's expected."

Alex thought about it. "I don't know how to go about setting up a ball," he admitted.

"No, but I bet Nico does. Isn't that what he's trained for? Plus, Higgins probably knows more than he's letting on. He seems to know Hugbet's business. If he knows what the man kept in his cellar, he probably knows a lot more. He knows how to recognize good booze, that's for sure. Do you have a chef? Don't you keep some for the troops?"

"We have a chef in the house. She's excellent, though I don't know if she has experience of balls. We can find out."

"Then it's done. You'll throw a ball, meet your expectations, and interrogate the Elite whilst they're here. We'll get the answers we need and then we can kick them out. It's a good plan, Alex."

They drank to its success.

PART FOURTEEN

THE PROPOSAL of a ball delighted Nico, but he pointed out to Alex that he was needed at the healing center. Alex had very smugly told him that ten new healers had arrived in Thetis and were beginning work at eight. He further suggested contacting Council Member Radclyffe for help. She was conversant with the social scene and could guide Nico.

Nico thought that was a great idea and immediately made for his office so he could make plans. His first call was to Trix. He knew the boy would be excited, but that proved an understatement. Trix was ecstatic. That he would be mixing with society? No one had ever wished for more. "And I'll do the photos," he said happily, having given an exhaustive list of how he would help plan the ball.

"Have to be approved before you publish them, Trix. Remember the rules."

"Oh, I will," agreed Trix readily before tapping away at his mini comm. "Now decorations, I'm thinking pink...."

After Nico had made it clear that the ballroom would be decorated in the duke's colors, he suggested Trix turn to the Commercial Web and start highlighting the things they would need. Higgins arrived five minutes later. "I'm too old for this, Nico. It was all well and good giving balls when I was a younger man, but I'm too old now."

Nico promised him lots of help and told him to do the interviews himself. "I'd rather the new employees come from Thetis," he said. "They'll live here at the castle, of course. The staff quarters should be finished by now." Higgins, taken aback at being able to choose his own staff, cheered up slightly.

"Your help is invaluable, Mr. Higgins," continued Nico. "Take on as many staff as you need. You won't have very long to train them, of course, but I'm sure they'll all do the best they can. People must accept us as we are."

"I'll get right on that, then," Higgins said more enthusiastically. He paused and then said, "You're a good lad, Nico. Your parents would be proud of you. Don't think I haven't noticed the difference in Daisy. She'd turned into a shadow of herself cooped up here, but you've brought her back. I thank you for that." Without giving Nico any chance to reply, the man left the room.

A black cloud floated in a couple of minutes later. Watkins was not amused. "Now, boy," he began. "You've got to rid His Grace of the ridiculous idea that there should be a ball. It's a lot of flummery and not something His Grace should waste his time on. Do you hear me, boy? Flummery! Sheer flummery!"

"I think it's a good idea," Nico proffered. "Besides, it's expected. We have to do one sooner or later."

"Bah! Expected? People need to accept that His Grace is a warrior, boy, and warriors don't do balls. And why are you doing one? You don't even dance. What reason have you got for having a ball? Tell me that, boy. What reason have you got?"

"I'm supporting Alex, Watkins. Whether you like it or not, Alex is a duke now. There are things he must do to take his place in society. You should be supporting him too."

"Support him? I have to *protect* him, boy, protect him. How am I supposed to do that if you fill the place up with fools?"

"I'm sure you'll find a way. It's not like we don't have enough guards. There's an army camping on the grounds."

"It's flummery!"

"It's necessary."

Watkins vented his frustration with a growl. "I thought you were the reasonable one," he barked before turning and leaving the room.

Finally Nico was able to phone Council Member Radclyffe. She was delighted to help, said she had a lot of experience with balls, and promised to be there in time for lunch. That gave Nico an hour. He headed straight for the kitchen.

Council Member Radclyffe turned out to be Lady Rose Radclyffe. "But you must call me Rosie," she said, patting Nico on the knee. "All my friends do."

She was an expert on balls and helped Nico to draw up a project plan. He also had to revise his time periods. It was going to take at least two weeks to organize this ball. And that was if he did without sleep. Regretfully, he tacked on another week. His suggestion of a ball in three weeks was met with approval, and the date was set. He was grateful for Rosie's help. He may have had some education in the subject, but theory and practice were two different things. He hadn't even considered half of the tasks she put before him, and he began to realize this was a huge undertaking. It wasn't just about the food. Along the way, he realized she was definitely an ally. She let it drop that she thought the situation in Thetis was despicable and contrary to the Ethos of the Goddess. She spoke of her small circle of friends who felt the same way. They were the only ones who grew crops for the people. She despaired of the other Elites and described a society that had changed beyond recognition. When gently pushed, she admitted that she'd been glad to see the back of the senior council member, as he was a boor who rarely thought of anything but his own position. He hadn't cared about the people at all. Teddy, though, was a different matter. Teddy's gifts lay in administration, and he was a thorough and fair man. Really, she'd been so pleased that they'd been able to resolve it all. She'd known at once what sort of people Nico and His Grace were. She now had hopes for the Sixth Land. Nico liked her immensely and knew they would become good friends. They started to draw up a guest list for the ball. As they added names of the scions and socialites of society, Nico became thoughtful. The ball was an excuse to interrogate the Elite for Alex, but what if it could also be used to build allies? Would there be enough time to do both? It was to be a huge affair with five hundred guests. They couldn't get any more into the ballroom.

Rosie grinned at him. "I shall look forward to this tremendously. There hasn't been a ball in the castle in many years. It will be the highlight of the season."

Here's hoping, thought Nico, waving her off. He turned to Higgins. "I think you may need to hire even more staff. I'll be in the kitchen if you need me."

IN BED that night, he told Alex all of his plans. He loved the time before they fell asleep. They could talk for hours, wrapped in each other's arms, snuggled up under the covers. It was when they shared their hopes and dreams, talked about their day, and settled down to the important business of getting to know each other. Sometimes they laughed, sometimes they got philosophical. Sometimes they got so close that Nico could feel the bridge of power between them. It was a sacred time for Nico, as important as his walk on the beach each day. He hated it when Alex was late and he fell asleep waiting, but he always woke up against Alex's chest, those strong arms holding him close. It made him feel loved. And it made him fall in love. He knew that he was definitely on his way to being in love with Alex. All the symptoms were there. His heart would race for a minute when he saw Alex; his body craved Alex's touch even if it was just to hold hands in the car. Alex filled his mind, his first thought in the morning, his last thought at night. Nico wouldn't have had it any other way. He knew he needed time to meditate on it, but time was in short supply. Planning his career started to seem pointless. Why would he want to build a life in the city when he could build such a good life here? He had lots of time in the kitchen, which was what he'd always wanted, really. He may have had plans for the greatest restaurant ever, but he didn't really need that. He just needed to cook, and he got to do that here. He'd have lots of opportunity to cater for large numbers of people and that would be enough. People would be eating his recipes. Trix would even publish his recipes. Not that he'd ever let it be known he was the cook. He had to protect Alex's place in society, and he couldn't be seen to be doing the cooking. No, it would all be anonymous, but it would be there. He'd be more than satisfied with that. If only he could get the chance to do some meditation. He'd be able to clear his mind of the multitude of thoughts whizzing around in it. He fell asleep thinking about it.

MORNING BROUGHT a new set of problems. Somehow Alphy had gotten wind of the ball and had contacted Nico through comms to invite himself and his party. A party that included Lunette. Nico was glad to end the call. He sent the new additions through to Alex's comms for his approval with a quick explanation of how it had happened. Nico was well aware that Alex didn't like Lunette. He'd been watching from behind the curtains when they'd met at the Gleaning, and the duke's body language had been clear. There was something odd about Lunette, though Nico couldn't put his finger on it. He'd also met him at the Gleaning, but it had been for two minutes whilst he was introduced to Prince Alphonse, and none of the Elites had been paying much attention to him. They were all very much wrapped up in themselves.

Nico returned from the beach with Oliver, and they made their way to the breakfast room. He could hear raised voices when he entered the corridor. Prince Jael, he thought, with Alex taking the role of peacekeeper. He got nearer to the door.

"It's not acceptable, Alex," roared Jael. "Alphy should be with our father, not tripping off to balls in the Sixth Land. What is he thinking? He can't just leave Elias to do *his* duty. If it weren't for the trouble in Thetis, I'd be there. But both my father and Elias felt that I would be better paying my debts here. Otherwise I wouldn't have left Father's side. But Alphy!" His voice started to rise again, and Nico felt that he should let his presence be known.

"Excuse me, Jael," he said, entering the room. "I did not mean to overhear you, but you were quite loud." Both men looked to Nico and stood up. The duke came across the room to kiss his cheek.

"I'm sorry, Nico." Jael stepped forward to give him a hug. "I shouldn't be shouting in your home. I'm just so frustrated. I can't believe that Alphy invited himself to the ball."

"Yes, well he did," said Alex bluntly, returning to his seat. "And now we've got to deal with having Lunette in the house. Ah well, it will be a good opportunity to interrogate the man."

"You're not going to interrogate our guests, Your Grace," admonished Nico, accepting the glass of fruit juice Alex offered him. "We're going to be very civilized. We're going to coax the information out of them. It shouldn't be too hard. The Elites do love to talk about themselves."

Alex grunted in reply, but Nico knew he'd made his point. He wished both men a good day and made his escape to the kitchen. There was so much to do.

ALEX LOOKED around the docks. They'd traveled to the far side of Thetis to the very end of the docks where they met the far road. Truck after truck had pulled in, and they were all full of corn. Alex hadn't realized there was that much corn in the world. Watkins had been talking with some of the dockers, but he now made his way to Alex's side. "Learn anything?" Alex asked.

Watkins sighed. "Nothing you want to hear, lad. Nothing you want to hear."

"What's that supposed to mean?" demanded Alex. "I listen."

"And then you cry 'conspiracy theory,' lad. Well, you know my feelings on the subject. Sometimes conspiracy theories turn into conspiracy fact, lad, conspiracy fact."

"We've nothing else to go on," said Jael with a shrug. "Everyone knows the corn is coming in, and no one knows where it goes. You'd think the ships would have to file some sort of journey plan. Aren't they supposed to do that?"

"Apparently the law of the Sixth Land doesn't require one," said Alex dryly. "According to the clerks, the ships go out full and come back empty, and they know nothing else. I've yet to find a ship's captain or member of crew willing to talk to me." He scowled in annoyance. "The people here are playing games and I don't like it. They know a lot more than they're saying. Well, I'll have the truth, one way or another. I'll have the truth. In fact, I have my own men on those ships, so we'll know where they're going soon enough."

"So what's the conspiracy theory?" Jael asked Watkins when Alex had nothing further to add.

"There's something wrong with the corn. It's not like natural corn," Watkins said.

Alex looked at him in disbelief. "Not natural? What else can it be? Of course it's natural. It grows in the field, for Goddess's sake."

"Well, the people are saying it's not natural, and I've learned to listen to what the people say, lad. How many times have the people saved our asses? More times than we care to remember. I'm telling you, lad, you have to look at the corn. Get it analyzed or something. Whatever it is that chemists do. Get them to look at it, lad. Let's get to the truth of it."

"Is that what it's going to take to shut you up, old man?" retorted Alex. "Fine! Get the guards to confiscate some of the corn and we'll have the stuff analyzed. Damn fool waste of time but if it will make you happy." He folded his arms over his chest.

THREE WEEKS flew by and the day of the ball approached all too quickly. Nico had been convinced that they wouldn't have that many guests because it was such short notice. But nobody had wanted to miss what was being seen as the event of the year, and Elites were known to be flying in to the Sixth Land to attend. Alex didn't see much of Nico during the week. He seemed to be spending all his time in the kitchen. It had concerned Alex until he realized his boy was enjoying himself. He heard all about it at night during that special time when they talked and talked. Alex loved that time of the day. He was falling deeper and deeper in love with his boy. Every new thing he learned was a fascination. A gem. Something to cherish. He had no doubts now that the Goddess had guided his path. Theirs was a sacred marriage. He was sure of it. He wanted his boy to be sure too.

PART FIFTEEN

NICO ESCAPED to dress for the ball with a huge sense of relief. Higgins had hired two dozen young people to help in the house and with the ball. Unfortunately, whilst they were all very enthusiastic, none of them had any training, and subsequently bedlam occupied the house. He wasn't sure how he was supposed to handle that, since the topic had never come up at Academia Hall. He was hoping Alex might have an idea or two. Wasn't he best known for his tactics? Or was it strategies? Both? Nico wasn't sure he knew the difference between tactics and strategies, but he was sure that Alex would be good at both of them. After all, he knew how to win wars. He was the one who had the skill set they needed.

The door opened and Alex appeared. "We're never doing this again," he said, his back flat against the door. "I think I've got PTSD. Do I look ill? Perhaps I should just stay here. I need a healer. You should stay here too."

Nico giggled as he went over to wind his arms around Alex's waist, and he laid his head on Alex's shoulder. "If only," he said, kissing at Alex's jawline. "We've got half an hour. How about we try and resolve some of your issues?" he whispered.

Alex laughed. "Now that's the best idea I've heard all day," he said. Nico pulled away from Alex and lost clothes rapidly as he made his way to the bed. Alex followed him, losing his own clothes just as rapidly. They fell naked onto the bed and turned on their sides to face each other. Alex leaned forward to nibble at Nico's jawline. His hand slid straight to Nico's cock and Nico gasped at the feel. He grew harder as Alex slowly stroked him. Long slow strokes that sometimes resulted in a quick rub of the head. He knew exactly how Nico liked it and drew the process out. Nico stared into those beautiful green eyes and fell deeper in love. Who else could he have this with? Nico felt their bond strengthen. He tipped his head to one side, allowing Alex to nibble along his neck. He stroked Alex's chest, feeling the power and the strength that lay there. He went readily into Alex's kiss. Alex moved their bodies closer together and aligned their cocks, holding both in one strong warrior hand. He whispered into Nico's ear, "You like this, babe. It's one of your favorites."

Nico smiled, reaching out to touch Alex's jaw. "I'm very fond of it, yes," he murmured softly, closing his eyes and settling into the pattern made by Alex's strokes. He wanted to urge it on, make it go faster. Now wasn't the time for long seductive lovemaking; now was the time for fast torrid sex. He moaned when Alex rubbed his thumb over the head of Nico's cock. He thrust his hips and leaned forward to capture Alex's mouth. Nico kissed him aggressively, pushing his tongue in and out, moving his hips to the same beat. It was Alex's turn to moan, and he took command of the kiss, so his tongue was the dominant. At the same time he increased the speed of his fist, holding them both with just the right pressure. Nico broke off the kiss, gasping for air, his hips still moving in time with Alex's hand. Goddess, he loved this. Loved the closeness, the way they accelerated together, gaining momentum together. He loved the rush, the eagerness, the swiftness. Sometimes he just needed it fast, the power between them taking over and hustling them to completion. Just as it was doing now. Nico gave himself up to the storm raging around them. He wallowed in the feeling, the force, and the fascination. Gave himself over to the exhilaration. Afterward he floated in beatitude.

He wanted to tell Alex that he loved him. But he knew it was too soon. Nico had no doubt that he was genuinely in love. He was a priest; he'd been trained to recognize love. But would Alex know it? Alex might well think it was just lust, that Nico was just a silly boy. He wanted a year and a day. Or had it been Nico who'd asked for that? Nico came back to reality. He looked at the clock. "Oh, Good Goddess." He sat up. "That was supposed to be a quickie. We've only got fifteen minutes to get dressed. We have to move."

Alex grinned and pulled him back down for a cuddle. "We can shower together, babe, plenty of time."

FIFTEEN MINUTES later they stood together at the ballroom entrance. Whilst not dressed identically, they did complement each other well. Nico thought Alex looked very handsome in his military dress. Blue wool jacket with gold braid at every edge and gold fringes on his shoulders. The uniform emphasized his height and breadth. Nico had also gone with a military air, but his was the fashion version. He'd chosen Alex's old colors of black and green. The ones he used when he won the war. Having seen battle lines drawn this weekend, he couldn't help but wonder if it had been a flash of foresight that had made him choose those colors. He felt like he was going into a war.

The Elite arrived en masse, and Nico soon tired of being looked up and down like a piece of chattel. He was also disconcerted to hear Higgins, who was supposed to be announcing each guest, instead saying, "Well, in you go, then. Come on, come on, plenty more want to get in, you know. We haven't got all day." He made the most of a quick break in the queue to go over and ask the man what he thought he was doing. Higgins looked at him in confusion. "I'm sending them in, Nico. What does it look like I'm doing?"

"But you're supposed to announce them."

"It's an empty room. Who do I announce them to? No, Nico, you must trust me on this, we need a few in there before we can start announcing them. Now you just go back to His Dukedom. He's looking a bit offended."

Nico looked over and saw that Higgins was right. Alex was starting to look angry now, and he rushed back to his side. He touched his hand to Alex's as he stood in line. The offending guest had no choice but to move up to him in the line. Alex had insisted he take lead place in the welcoming line, and Nico thought that was probably a good idea. People wanted to monopolize Alex, and he didn't have the greatest tact in moving them on. Nico was more gracious in his dealing with the guests and was able to move them on into the room in a much politer manner. It was unfortunate that he handed them over to Higgins.

"His Lordship and Her Ladybits," Higgins announced in a very grand and very loud voice. Elderly Lord Falcon and his trophy wife were very taken aback. "I'm sure you all know them," Higgins continued as he pushed Lord Falcon into the room. "Come along, haven't got all day," he said, fortunately in a much quieter way, and Nico was sure only the immediate circle heard it. He turned his attention back to the line and managed to filter out Higgins. There was nothing he could do about him now. He just hoped the Elites were too distracted by the crowd to pay any attention. Nico had never seen such colors and such glitz as on the people arriving. They dripped in jewelry and ribbons and expensive fabrics in a multitude of colors. All of the officers from the camp had been invited, and like Alex, turned up in military colors. Nico thought they looked stunning. It seemed an age before the last straggler made his way into the room. Prince Alphonse, naturally, liked to make an entrance, and Nico and Alex had been forced to wait for him when they should have been seeing to the guests. Alphy gave a wave of a hand and a lazy apology for being late. He shook Alex's hand, hugged Nico, and then he went and stood next to Higgins to wait for his announcement.

"There's another one!" shouted Higgins above the chatter of the guests. "Look everybody, there's another one!" He tugged on Alphy's arm and brought him forward. "Off you go, then. I've got better things to do than stand here, mate. My throat's parched. Oi," he shouted, causing Alphy to start and drop his heavily jeweled riding crop. Higgins waved at a server who was carrying a tray of champagne. "Over here, boy. That's just what I need. Now you just stand right there." He swallowed down a glass and reached for another one. "Three should do it, boy. You just stay right where you are." Alphy, askance, looked down at his ornamental riding crop and then around to see who would pick it up for him. In the end he was forced to do it himself.

Alex fell laughing amongst the curtains behind them, and Nico looked at him with a steely eye. It only made Alex laugh more and in the end Nico couldn't keep his face straight anymore. They ended up hiding behind the folds of the curtain and kissing deeply. "That's better," said Alex when they stopped for breath. "If this is how the evening is going to continue, we'll be spending a lot of time behind curtains." He chuckled. "Elias is going to love that story."

They entered the ballroom together with no one to announce them but soon found themselves separated as competing groups of people took over their time. Nico noticed that Alex always stood where he could see Nico and never allowed the distance between them to grow too great. Every so often he would excuse himself from his own group and come and join Nico's. He always stood by Nico's side and would hold his hand or place an arm around his shoulder. Such things were acceptable in society, and Alex made the most of them. It made Nico feel loved, and he smiled whenever Alex joined him. They'd share a brief glance and for a moment, they were the only two people in the room. The bridge between them was stronger.

All too soon the group divided and Alex and Nico were again separated. Nico spent a lot of time talking about fashion. Fashion, theater, and the Social Web were the main topics for most of the Elite. But only in how they themselves saw each topic. They talked constantly of themselves. He heard too many names and saw too many faces, and the Elites seemed to merge together in one clear stereotype. He was grateful for the relief of talking to Alex's officers. The Grand Seers too provided some sane conversation. Although Brother Edward had seemed to be in his cups. He kept apologizing and complaining of some dizziness. Nico arranged some coffee for him, made sure he was okay, and moved on to the next group of people. It was exhausting, hard work. He had nothing in common with these people, although they seemed to think he did. They talked of princeliness and majesty. They spoke of ratings and following. They spoke like the fools they were, and Nico found he had little enthusiasm for them. No wonder there were riots in Thetis. He was glad when Alex, once again, appeared at his side and held on to the hand that lightly brushed his. The group was talking about how artistic they were personally, and Nico was bored. He looked around the room and was surprised to see Haven, the man who'd cornered him at the reception in Tarn. Where had he come from? Nico was sure he hadn't been invited, so what was he doing here?

Before long the group he was with split up, and Nico took a moment to go and check on the kitchen. Supper had been served, dishes were being replenished, and he wanted to check that they had enough food. So far the ball was going much better than he'd thought it would. The dancing had been popular, and if it was thought odd that neither Alex nor Nico danced, then it was seen as quite sweet too. He had been surprised to see a couple of the servers waltzing with the best of them, but he supposed no harm was done. He slipped into the well-ordered bedlam of the kitchen, standing to one side to allow servers to carry out laden trays. Daisy was hot, bothered, and she was beaming. "I'd forgotten how much I like running a brigade," she said. "And these chefs are fantastic, a great team." Nico had commandeered the chefs from the army camping in the grounds. They worked like a precision unit, and it had only taken a day to teach them all of Nico's recipes. The head chef had complimented him on the menu. Nico had been thrilled.

He headed back to the cold pantry to check on how much stock there was. Shivering, he turned the light on and looked around. Everything looked in shipshape, and he was about to turn away when a heap of shiny bags caught his eye. What were they? There shouldn't be anything kept in a bag in here. He walked over and picked one up. Even stranger, it was an evidence bag. What was an evidence bag doing in here? Evidence of what? He reached into the bag and brought out an ear of corn.

ALEX STOOD on one side of the ballroom and looked around for Nico. Where had he gone? He looked over at Watkins, who nodded in the direction of the kitchen. Why wasn't Alex surprised? Nico spent an inordinate amount of time in the kitchen. He couldn't understand it. Daisy was an excellent cook who provided first-rate dishes. Surely she didn't need to be overseen that much? Then again, he knew how close Nico had become with Daisy, and he knew Nico always prepared his breakfast. Perhaps Daisy had taught him that. Perhaps he was still seeking her advice on house matters? Alex wanted to tell him that he didn't need to spend so much time on the house. He didn't want Nico to be a slave to it. He wanted his boy to pursue his own interests as well as pay his debts. There was no doubt in his mind that he was deeply in love with Nico. He had placed his faith in the Goddess and She Had Weaved Her Web and Told Their Story. He sent up his thanks to Her and decided to follow Nico. No one would miss them for a couple of minutes, and he was tired of talking to fools. Thank Goddess he'd invited the officers. Without that sanity he'd be broken. Socializing was proving a lot harder than war. He sent up more thanks for Nico. Would he have been able to do this without the boy? He didn't think so. He'd have kicked the lot out within half an hour of their arrival.

He was waylaid by Lunette, of all people. He'd managed to avoid the man most of the night.

"Your Grace," Lunette said, pretending surprise. "Why, how wonderful. I hoped we might be able to spend some time together tonight and it seems The Goddess Smiles On Us."

Alex was in no mood for High Speech. With a brusque "If you'll excuse me, Lunette," he made to continue on his way, but Lunette moved into his path.

"But surely, Your Grace, you can spare a fellow a minute or two? I was with my great friend Alphy, but he's gone to dance with my daughter. My Zinsa, you know. Well, of course you know. I must confide in Your Grace, just a little confidence between friends, you understand? I think we may be family soon. A happy announcement, I must say, though there can be no announcement at all whilst His Highness lies ill." Might be family?

Alex shuddered at the thought. Never, he promised himself. Even if Alphy did marry the girl. Nothing to do with Alex or Nico. And he wasn't letting Lunette anywhere near Nico. The man was a creep.

Lunette gave a fawning smile and continued. "I'm a proud papa, Your Grace. I cannot hide it. And I don't want Your Grace to worry. Alphonse may be losing his father, but I stand ready to fill the gap. Alphonse will be a son to me, I assure you." He paused, clearly expecting some sort of thanks. Alex stared at him and stayed silent. Did the fool really think he could take the place of the king in Alphy's life? Lunette hadn't finished, and ignoring Alex's stare, said, "Of course I'll be there to offer advice to the young king. He will find no one more loyal than the two of us, Your Grace. I'm sure you'll agree."

"Prince Alphonse will have all the support he needs from his brothers, Lunette. He needs nothing from us. Now if you'll excuse me." He gave a tight bow and walked around the man in his way.

He turned the corner into the kitchen corridor and walked straight into Nico, almost knocking him off his feet. He made a grab for the boy and managed to keep them both upright. "Thank you, Your Grace," gasped Nico as he regained his balance. "Now, come with me." He grabbed Alex by the wrist and pulled him down the corridor. Alex noticed he had an evidence bag clutched in his other hand. What was Nico doing with an evidence bag?

Nico tugged him into a small square room. Very basic, there wasn't even plaster on the walls. An old square stone table was positioned in the center. "What's this?" he asked. "I don't think I've ever been in here."

Nico placed the evidence bag on the stone table. "It's a scullery, but that's not important. I want you to look at this." He drew an ear of corn out of the bag.

Alex looked at it. He looked at Nico, who gestured to the corn impatiently. He looked at the corn again. "It's corn, babe. Not sure what I'm supposed to say here."

"There's something wrong with it, Alex," Nico said, gesturing again to the corn.

Alex picked it up. "Is it off?" he proffered, looking closely at the ear. "Not ripe yet?" He hesitated to give another guess.

"It's not natural, Alex. It isn't a natural plant."

"Well, of course it's natural. What else can it be? Have you been listening to Watkins, Nico? Has he been filling your head with conspiracy theories?" Alex thought his boy was better than that. He was almost disappointed.

"No, I haven't been listening to Watkins," replied Nico. "And he hasn't filled my *pretty little head* with anything. I've been listening to the plant, Alex, and this plant isn't talking."

Alex looked up when Nico started speaking, and he winced at the words "pretty" and "little." Was that really what he sounded like? Then the rest of what Nico had said hit him. Did he just say the plant wasn't talking? Was his boy ill? Had the ball proved too much for him?

"No, I'm not ill," shouted Nico. "For Goddess's sake, Alex, listen to me. This plant is not natural. This plant is an abomination. Do you understand me? An abomination." He took the plant off Alex and threw it on the table. He took Alex's hand. "You know that I have had a priest's training? You know that I was trained as a healer?" He waited for Alex's nod. "As part of the training for both those vocations, I learned how to listen to plants. Plants talk to me, Alex. They tell me what their properties are, what nutrients they provide, what vitamins. If they have healing powers, they tell me what they are. I can't explain to you how that happens. I don't have enough time. We need to talk about this menace, and it is a menace, Alex. The damage that this crop can do to our ecology is immense. We think we have food shortages now, wait until this plague takes root in our soils, wait until it's carried across the country by the wind."

Alex realized Nico was working his way into a temper and he needed to stop that. He took Nico by the shoulders. "Slow down, boy. Slow down. Now start again. You can talk to plants?"

"No, I *listen* to plants, but that's not important. What's important is this is an abomination."

"Nico." He spoke sharply, and Nico looked up at him. "I understand that it's important, babe, and I'm, well, I'm a bit taken aback that you listen to plants. I can't understand how the subject has never come up before. But Nico, we're in the middle of a ball. Is there anything that we can do about this now?"

"Do about this now?" Nico repeated in disbelief. "Well, of course there are things that I can do now. I can notify the Grand Seers, and they in turn will notify the priests. We need as much help as we can get. Forget the ball. This is an attack on our ecology. Don't you understand that? Our ecology! I need to go and meditate. Once I've comm'd the Grand Seers, that is."

Alex thought quickly. "Go and contact the Grand Seers. Set in motion whatever you have to. I'll go back to the ball and I'll meet you in there. Meditation is going to have to wait, babe."

TEN MINUTES later Alex found himself talking to a group of Elites who were discussing the spirituality of the tea ceremony. They appeared to think the shape of the tea bag was important. He wondered what Nico would think of that. He wondered where Nico was. How long did it take to contact the Grand Seers? He looked around the ballroom and was surprised to see Nico walking around the dance floor. Nico was supposed to come straight to him. He looked in the direction Nico was going and could see Grand Seer Edward sitting forward at one of the tables. Lunette appeared to be questioning him on something, and Grand Seer Edward was trying to wave him away. Nico reached the two men just as Grand Seer Edward slumped over in his chair. By the time Alex got to the group, Nico had the man stretched out on the floor and was laying him on his side. "What help do you need?" said Alex.

Lunette answered him. "Oh, I think we're fine, Alex. Nico is just checking him over. I think he's just had too much to drink. Don't you agree, Nico?"

Alex was incensed by the man's forwardness. Who did he think he was calling them by their first names? "I was speaking to His Highness," he said to the man curtly. "If you'd be so kind to move out of the way?"

He knelt down next to Nico. "Is he okay?"

Nico nodded. "He will be. He should wake up in a minute, and I'm going to move him to a guest room. I think he'll need fluids. Can you find Healer Vincent for me?" Alex nodded to Watkins, who had also joined them.

Grand Seer Edward started to wake up, and Nico spoke calmly to him until he was fully awake.

"I do apologize, Your Highness. I don't know what's come over me." Nico assured him there was no need to apologize, but the man continued to do so as Watkins and Healer Vincent helped him to his room. Nico went with them and Alex was left in the ballroom to see to their guests.

NICO ENSURED that Grand Seer Edward was comfortable, and made his way back to the ballroom. He needed to find Alex. Both he and Vincent were convinced the Grand Seer had been poisoned. Which meant there was a poisoner at the ball. Nico had his own ideas about that. Lunette was the first person to come to mind. But why would he try to poison Edward? Nico couldn't think of a single reason for the Grand Seer to be targeted. He'd got as far as the hallway when he met the man himself. Nico kept his face schooled.

Lunette gave one of his obsequious bows. "I wondered where you were, Nico," he said. "Alex was asking for you. I believe that he's out on the veranda looking for you."

"His Grace is looking for me?" Nico wondered why, but with a small bow in Lunette's direction, he made his way to the veranda at the side of the house.

He wasn't alone when he got there, as one of the servers was walking Ollie at the other end of the veranda. He looked around for Alex but couldn't see him anywhere. He stepped out farther and stood by one of the lamps lighting the area. Suddenly Oliver started to bark and ran for Nico, leaping up to push Nico over just as a shot exploded into the night air. Nico fell to the veranda with Oliver landing on top of him. Two guards from inside the ballroom rushed to his side, with one speaking hurriedly into his comms unit. Within seconds more guards had appeared, and Nico was surrounded. "Stay still, Your Highness," said one. "We need to see if you're hurt."

Nico sat up, pushing Oliver off him whilst still stroking the agitated animal. "I'm fine," he said. "What was that noise?" His question went unanswered as more guards arrived, spread out, and started to search the grounds.

There was another commotion, and Alex pushed his way through the guards, going to his knees beside Nico. He started to pat Nico's body whilst yelling for a healer. "Are you okay, babe? Tell me you're okay. Tell me you haven't been hit. Oh, Goddess, please don't be hit," he pleaded.

Nico took hold of his hands. "I'm fine, Alex. Really, I'm fine. There's nothing wrong with me," he assured him. "Let me stand up and you'll see that I'm fine." Alex pulled him close, slamming Nico against his chest. He held him fiercely, his breath in rapid gasps, and Nico's first instinct was to calm him down. He reached up to cup Alex's cheek, gently stroking the cheekbone with his thumb. "I'm all right, Alex. You don't have to worry. I'm all right."

Alex continued to hold him but his heart rate started to slow and his breathing calmed. After a few moments he looked down at Nico. "Let's get you inside, babe. You're not safe out here. What are you doing out here, anyway?"

"I was looking for you. Lunette said you were out here looking for me."

"What?" Alex helped Nico to stand. "Lunette told you that?"

Watkins appeared at their side. "No sign of anyone, Alex. We've searched the gardens and found nothing."

"Then they must still be inside." Alex was grim. "Surround the house, Watkins. No one in and no one out. And find Lunette. I want to talk to him."

"We can't keep the guests all night, Alex," reasoned Nico. "Surely you only need to see Lunette? And perhaps Haven. I was surprised to see him here."

"Haven? Do you mean that upstart from Tarn?"

"Yes, he was in the ballroom. I didn't think he was invited."

"Find Haven," Alex instructed Watkins. "Nico, we can't allow anyone to leave without questioning them. Someone tried to shoot you, for Goddess's sake. They all get questioned, and I don't care if it takes the rest of the night to do it."

"Well, I guess that will make the ball memorable," said Nico, knowing that there was no use in arguing. He wasn't going to change Alex's mind.

PART SIXTEEN

IT WAS a long time before the ballroom was cleared. The Elites didn't take kindly to being questioned, but Alex couldn't have cared less. Whilst they didn't announce that an attempt had been made on Nico's life, it was clear that something had happened. The gossip running through the Elites was that it was something to do with the Grand Seer being taken ill, and both Nico and Alex were happy to let that stand. Haven could not be found, and Alex was forced to the conclusion that he had gotten out before the lockdown commenced. Lunette, when questioned, said that Haven had told him that Alex was looking for Nico; he was simply passing the message along. Alex clearly didn't believe him but there was nothing he could do, especially with Alphy standing up for Lunette.

It was a somber party that met for breakfast the next day. "I want some coffee," announced Alex when he and Nico made their way to the long sitting room. Oliver came with them, since he hadn't left Nico's side since the night before. Nico decided Alex probably needed the coffee and made the order on his mini comm.

They were joined by Jael and Watkins, and once they were all settled with a drink, Alex took charge. "So what do we know?"

"We know that someone took a shot at Nico. We know that Haven was at the ball but he wasn't invited. We know that he is a big friend of Lunette. We know that Haven has disappeared. We *think* that Lunette had something to do with the shot, but we don't know if he took the shot himself. We can't prove that Lunette is lying. That's about the sum of it, lad," said Watkins.

"No, it isn't," interrupted Nico. "We know that the corn isn't natural. It's an abomination."

Jael and Watkins turned to him. "You mean the conspiracy theory is true?" demanded Watkins. At Nico's nod, he continued. "I told you, lad," he said to Alex. "I told you that conspiracy theories are worth listening to. Now perhaps you'll pay attention when I speak, lad."

"I always pay attention when you speak, old man," retorted Alex. "But yes, it would appear that particular conspiracy theory has some fact in it. But why would anyone want to produce corn that isn't natural? It doesn't make sense."

"Lunette is the one encouraging everyone to grow that corn. In fact, he's the head of the Corn Consortium here in the Sixth Land," said Jael thoughtfully. "It was a main topic of conversation last night. All the Elites are hurrying to get on the bandwagon. They're impressed with how much money the corn can make."

"How is it making money if it's not natural?" questioned Alex. "Where's it going to? Have we heard from the men?"

"Not yet, but I'm expecting news any day," Watkins said.

"In the meantime, I've sent the corn for analysis to Academia Hall. Perhaps they can tell us more," said Nico.

"So we know there's a direct link between Lunette and the corn, but it still doesn't explain why someone shot at Nico."

"Perhaps he knows that Nico would put a stop to it. With the power given to him as Royal Prince of the Goddess, it's within his remit to do so."

"And I fully intend to stop it," said Nico. "But I could do that through my duties as a priest. I don't need to be a Prince of the Goddess to do it. No, I think there's another reason. It might be something to do with the letter that I brought from the capital."

"What letter?" demanded Alex. "I don't know anything about a letter."

"It wasn't meant for you," replied Nico. "It was meant for the Grand Seers here. The Grand Seers in the capital sent it and told me not to tell anyone. So I didn't." He shrugged. "But Haven clearly knew I was delivering something because he tried to get it off me in Tarn. I just pretended not to know what he was talking about."

"And you're only just mentioning it now?" Alex shouted. "What the hell was in the letter?"

"Grand Seer business," Nico said haughtily, not amused at Alex's tone.

"Well it's my business now," retorted Alex. "And if it concerns you in any way, then it was always my business."

"I don't suppose you know what was in the letter?" Jael interjected.

Nico nodded. "Oh yes, I read it before handing it over. I thought that best in the circumstances."

"It wasn't Grand Seer business, then?" snapped Alex.

Nico gave him a cold look. "I could argue that Grand Seer business is my business, since I'm apparently head of the religion," Nico snapped back. Alex stopped glaring and had the grace to look shamefaced. Nico took pity on him.

"It was about my duties as a Royal Prince of the Goddess," he said. "In particular, what happens to the succession."

"Why?" asked Jael. "What happens to the succession?"

"I get to decide who is the new king."

NICO WORRIED about the signs of strain around Alex's eyes. After he'd made his announcement, the room had descended into chaos. He'd been forced to admit that he could, if he wished, take the role of king himself. Alex had stormed out of the room and into the garden at that point. Nico had let him go. Alex clearly needed to calm down. Now they were both in their bedroom and getting ready for bed. He looked at Alex and sighed. He didn't want his warrior to be tense and unsettled. It wasn't good for him. Unfortunately, Nico didn't think Alex would accept any healing or massage from him. Alex needed to talk, but Nico knew that it would be him who had to do the actual talking. He decided to take the bull on by the horns.

"You're angry because I didn't tell you about the man in Tarn," he said. Alex looked at him, waiting. "And because I didn't tell you about the letter for the Grand Seers," Nico said with a sigh.

"You should have told me," said Alex.

"You're not being fair," Nico retorted. "You're acting as if what we had *then* is the same as what we have *now* and it isn't. It's different."

Alex sat up, still staring at Nico, and waited. He really was very good at the long silence, thought Nico. Well. If he was going to be given the rope, he'd have to just make sure he didn't hang himself.

"It's different now, Alex. If the Grand Seers gave me an envelope now, you're the first and only person I would tell. It wasn't like that in the beginning. I didn't know you. All I knew was that we had great sex. And that I kind of liked you. You've always been very easy to get on with. But I didn't know you. I didn't know if I could trust you. It was Grand Seer business and none of yours. Don't you understand that?"

"You think it was none of my business that you might be king one day?"

"I have no intention of being king, so, yes, it was none of your business."

"You are pledged to me!"

"And I'm keeping my pledge. I'll always keep my pledge. Don't you know that?"

Alex went still. Nico went over to him. He put his arms around Alex's neck and laid his head on Alex's shoulder. Alex's arms went around him. Nico felt him relax. "I know I've kept things from you, but I never will again. You have my word as a Priest and Healer of the Goddess."

"Do I have your word as a lover?" Alex rumbled. "Do I have your word as my husband? Do I have your word as a man?"

Nico kissed him. Deep and loving, showing all the emotion that he felt for this man. All the love, all the desire, and all of the need, an ever hungry need that couldn't be satisfied. How could Alex think he'd ever give up on this?

"I need to protect you," Alex murmured between kisses. "I need to know that you're safe, that I'm keeping you safe. That you're always going to be here. I need to know that I'm not going to lose you. Can't lose you, can't ever let you go."

"I do need you to protect me, Alex," whispered Nico. "I know that I say I can protect myself, and I can, but there's a part of me that I can't protect and I need you to protect it for me. I need you to protect my heart, Alex. Can you do that?"

"I can do that." Alex kissed him again, his turn to show his emotion through the action. "I want more than a year and a day," he said when they finally separated.

Nico smiled. "So do I. A lot more."

"I love you," Alex said.

Nico nodded. "I know. I love you too."

Nico settled into his husband's arms as they snuggled in bed. There was so much to do. They had to discover what was going on with the corn. They had to challenge the Elites' belief that all the money should be theirs. They had so many problems in the Sixth Land, all of which would need resolving. He wasn't afraid, though. He was eager to face the challenges. With Alex by his side, he could accomplish all that and more. Before he fell asleep, he took some moments to thank the Goddess. She'd been right all along. The Gleaning had been his fate and look where his fate had taken him. With love and family, he was blessed.

KATIE HOWE is a compulsive daydreamer. When she's not daydreaming, she's reading. Romance has always been her genre ever since she read Daddy-Long-Legs when she was eleven. Since then she's had more favorite authors than she count and her 'instant buy' list far exceeds her budget.

Katie lives in Manchester, UK, and is fiercely proud of her city. She loves living in a multicultural environment and one that values equality. She's had a variety of jobs but only lasted two days in telesales. Happily married to a man who can still make her laugh after twenty-five years, Katie has brought up three children and gained a couple of degrees along the way. Unfortunately, English Language wasn't one of them. Katie writes escapism. She believes that everyone needs to escape, even if it's just for the length of a book.

Katie can be contacted at:
E-mail: katiehowe2015@gmail.com
Facebook: www.facebook.com/katie.howe.52035

Also from Dreamspinner Press

ALICIA NORDWELL

ADVERSE
EFFECTS

SAVING CAEORLEIA

www.dreamspinnerpress.com

Also from Dreamspinner Press

www.dreamspinnerpress.com

Stalked
Susanna Hays

Also from Dreamspinner Press

www.ingramcontent.com/pod-product-compliance
Lightning Source LLC
Chambersburg PA
CBHW060103260626
47160CB00005B/1782